A TRICKY TREAT

A MULBURY MYSTERY

JUNO HARVEY

Book cover by Melissa Williams Design

ISBN: 978-0-6456511-0-2 (ebook)

ISBN: 978-0-6456511-1-9 (paperback)

To Michelle

ONE

Rosemary Exeter crouched on the pavement under the veranda on Goldmarket Road to tie the flapping tablecloth more firmly to the leg of the trestle. Despite the glorious spring day with its aqua sky and mellow warmth, she wished she was inside The Preserved Mulbury and not serving at the tables set up outside. The breeze, mild though it was, threatened to pull the gingham from its fastenings, and Rosemary imagined the sticky mess of jam and pickles and puree if the tablecloth wrenched her wares to the ground.

'Having trouble, dear?' Mrs Lionel reached across from her table laden with green cleaning products to smooth the wrinkles from Rosemary's cloth.

'Yes.' Rosemary stood up. 'That's the third time I've fixed it. I should have insisted we kept our shops open as usual.'

'Oh, I don't think so.' Mrs Lionel smiled at a family who'd stopped at her stall. 'Having our tables set up like this gives Mulbury a real village gala feel.'

Mulbury was awash with tourists fossicking through the

various stalls of the Gala, laughing and chatting as they made their way along the shopfronts on Goldmarket Road to the artisans' marquees set up in Goldmarket Square. Mrs Lionel's green cleaning products were selling well, their fresh herbal scents pulling in tourists intent on spending money after being holed up throughout the bitter winter. It was a little too early in the season to have fresh pots of berry jam available, so Rosemary was relying on leftover marmalade, mint jelly and wholegrain mustards.

'Hello, Mum,' said a low voice in her ear. 'Why are you looking so grumpy?'

Rosemary turned to Honey Blossom and gave her a quick hug. 'Not grumpy,' Rosemary said. 'More *annoyed*. I prefer being inside my shop.'

Honey chuckled, rubbing her belly self-consciously. 'So would I, at the moment. Can I get in? I need to use your...'

Rosemary moved aside to allow her daughter to sidle past and open the shop door. The bell jangled frantically, making the ginger tabby who'd been sitting on the windowsill flatten her ears. 'Sorry, Sunny,' Rosemary heard as Honey shut the door.

'Isn't she beautiful?'

For a split second, Rosemary thought Ronnie was talking about the cat. It only took a glance at his besotted face as he stared after Honey to realise he meant his wife. 'Of course she is.'

'Oh, yes, I know. I mean, she's always beautiful, but carrying Tallulah makes her extra beautiful, if you know what I'm saying.'

Rosemary often thought she had no idea what Ronnie was saying, but she appreciated his unabashed love for Honey. Secretly, she thought Honey's late pregnancy was showing on her face, with blue shadows under her eyes and weariness in her walk. She turned back to Ronnie. 'Is there anything special you've come to see at the Gala?'

Ronnie swept his hand through the air at the stalls along the Road and in Goldmarket Square in front of them. 'Well, I really wanted to look at the old bottles the children dug up when they visited Roman and Jules, and I heard Gerry has a display of old photographs that he found in his cellar. And Franco makes his special hazelnut and chocolate croissants for Gala weekend. I can't resist those. Then there are those artisans in the Square I've never seen before...'

Rosemary let him talk, nodding occasionally as he pointed at each table and marquee in turn. His enthusiasm was infectious, though, and she found herself thinking about buying turmeric scones from Rakisha, an apron from Patti and even a decent coffee from Kelly (but only if Ronnie did the coffee buying for her). *Step foot in Kelly Flanagan's café? No way.*

'... don't you think?'

Rosemary blinked at Ronnie's question but was saved from trying to answer by the reappearance of Honey at the door. The bell jangled noisily as she closed it behind her. 'Thanks, Mum. That's better.' Honey smiled at Ronnie. 'Are you talking Mum's leg off again?'

'No, was I? I don't think so.' Ronnie's face mottled as patches of red appeared. 'I was only saying that Jasper has a good deal on his range of sword and planet science fantasy. You should check it out, Rosemary.'

'Actually, Mum, that's not a bad idea.'

'I don't read sword and planet-'

'Doesn't matter.' Honey gave her mother a little push. 'Go and see Jasper. We'll look after the stall. I bet you haven't had a chance to look around.'

'True.' Rosemary gave her daughter a pat on the cheek. 'I won't be long.'

'Take your time.' Honey pulled Ronnie in beside her, expelling Rosemary, and turned to an older woman holding up two jars of mint jelly.

Rosemary walked the few steps to Jasper's second-hand book table. Cleverly, he'd set up a portable bookshelf along his window frontage, allowing customers to browse freely while keeping the bargain books on the table close to him. He smiled broadly as Rosemary approached, and tucked his long, dark hair behind one ear. 'Rosemary.'

'Jasper,' she said, surveying his products. 'A few gaps there. Doing okay?'

'Better than an average Saturday, which is fabulous.' Jasper shifted his smile to a man who brandished a credit card in one hand and a dictionary of symbols in the other. 'Got time for a coffee?'

'*I* have.' Rosemary waved her hand at Honey and Ronnie. '*You* haven't. How about I get tea for us?'

'I could really do with a coffee.' Jasper handed the man back the dictionary in a brown paper bag stamped with The Read Mulbury's logo of an open book with Jasper's face peering over the top.

'I'll get them, Jasper, my friend,' Gerry Yale called from the stall next to The Read Mulbury. 'Patti's working so hard here, she's sending me to get the morning tea. I'll add your order to the list.'

'Thanks, Gerry,' Jasper said as the little man wandered over. 'Patti's display is amazing.'

Although the shops under the veranda on Goldmarket Road were about the same size, the display of upcycled clothing from Patricia's was so immense that it extended to the edge of Jasper's bookshelf on one side and around the corner on the other. Amongst the flurry of skirts and tops made from rejected curtains and tea towels, Patti Yale whirled and laughed, delighting her customers with her energetic bouncing. The skirt of her own tule-filled rocka-billy dress slapped against people and racks alike as she pulled examples of garments from their coat hangers to hold up against customers in the little crowd.

'Oh, yes, amazing,' said Gerry. 'She's going gang-busters, and I can barely keep up.'

Rosemary regarded him thoughtfully. Gerry could hardly keep up when Patti started her enterprise and had only three shirts to sell. At the rate Patricia's was growing, they were going to need a bigger shop and then Gerry would have to do some real work.

Gerry saw her looking at him and grinned. 'And you, Rosemary? A coffee? A cake of some kind?'

'Excuse me,' said a voice behind Gerry, making him scuttle sideways. 'Sorry. Couldn't get through.'

A middle-aged woman in a pale-yellow sundress held the grips for a wheelchair containing a thin, elderly woman whose neatly combed hair sat proudly on her head in a masterful bun. She looked straight ahead, a maroon purse clasped on her lap, with matching lipstick drawn heavily on narrow lips.

'I am so sorry,' said Gerry, bending slightly to address the older woman. 'I was too busy chatting to my friends to notice you.'

'You've noticed us now.' The older woman waved her hand impatiently. 'Now move. We need to get through.'

'We could stay here for a moment, Mrs King,' said the woman pushing the chair. 'We could look at the books.'

Mrs King glanced haughtily at Jasper's display table. 'Books? I don't consider these flippant things *books*. Where are the classics? I don't see any Henry James or Albert Camus or Hilary Mantel.'

'I do have them,' said Jasper politely. 'Over there on the bookshelf.' He pointed at the shelf near Patti's display.

'As if I could get in there without louts knocking the chair and being altogether rude.' Mrs King straightened her handbag in her lap. 'Janet, take me over the road. The sooner I get to see the historical photographs, the sooner we can leave this wretched place.'

'Yes, Mrs King. I thought it would help...'

'Well, it hasn't.' Mrs King banged the arm of her wheelchair with her bag. 'Move along.'

Janet gave a last longing look at the display books and pushed the wheelchair past Rosemary without acknowledging her, shopping bags swinging from the handles. Rosemary watched as they paused at Mrs Lionel's stall long enough for a purchase before Janet bumped the wheelchair awkwardly over the road to Goldmarket Square.

'Doesn't look like everyone considers a visit to Mulbury a treat,' said Jasper.

'A tricky treat, for sure. Some people never have a good time, even when they're having a good time.' Gerry sighed, then clapped his hands together. 'So, coffee and cake?'

'I'll come over with you,' said Rosemary. 'I can help you carry things back.'

'Splendid, Rosemary.' Gerry doffed an imaginary hat to Jasper. 'See you soon.'

They walked together over the road, and into the buzzing crowd in Goldmarket Square. Several groups gathered under the ancient Exceptional Tree to gaze up into its magnificent canopy. Others balanced their food items on the poles that supported the entangled barricade that protected bystanders from falling branches, and Rosemary saw their puzzled looks at the odd structure that weaved in and out of the tree's drip line like a maze with no entry.

Gerry disappeared into Kelly's Mullings of Mulbury while Rosemary strolled around the other stalls. Volunteers from Big Town had set up a historical display of items from the gold rush: sluicing pans, puddling wheels, and shovels. They chatted excitedly to anyone within earshot about Mulbury's former gold glory, skipping over, thought Rosemary, the terrible events that had also affected the town, such as the bushfires on Scarlet Tuesday.

Next to them hung Gerry's photographs, a grand presentation of the old town with its Victorian buildings and wide streets. She could see the photograph of the shops on Goldmarket Road as they had been in their heyday: the haberdashery that was now Patti and Gerry's shop, the printery that was Jasper's The Read Mulbury, the sweet shop that was hers, and the tinker's that was Mrs Lionel's The Green Mulbury. Next to the photographic display were stalls for handmade leather goods and items carved from wood, all managed by artists Rosemary only knew by their email request to exhibit.

Rosemary moved closer to scan the photographs and take in the old bank that was Roman and Jules' The Leftover Restaurant and the grand (now dilapidated) mayoral residence recently acquired by Robert Sparkling. She glanced around the crowd but Robert was not there, no doubt working on the start of many renovations. Just in case, she turned to see the garage where he operated during the week, but its door was firmly shut and the lights were off.

From the corner of her eye, she saw Gerry beckon from the doorway to Mullings, so she weaved her way through jugglers and face-painters to where he stood balancing a cup drink tray containing four coffees in one hand and a tray of slices in the other. She snatched the coffees from him just as they slanted heavily towards the ground. 'Thanks, Rosemary,' Gerry said in relief. 'I was doing so well but I lost my grip-'

A sudden strangled cry cut across the cheery noise of tourists. The crowd noise faded, then rose to high-pitched concern as several people leapt forward toward the historical display.

'Hold this.' Rosemary shoved the coffee sleeve back at Gerry before running to the centre of Goldmarket Square. She pushed her way through the gawping semi-circle of people surrounding the display to find the wheelchair containing Mrs King flipped on its back, with its occupant clutching her throat and making fish-like gasping noises. The wheelchair attendant, Janet, was trying to soothe Mrs King and make a phone call at the same time.

'Are you ringing emergency?' said Rosemary. 'Let me.'

'Thank you,' said Janet, kneeling stiffly. 'The chair tipped over. I knew I had too much weight on the back.'

Rosemary put a hand on the distraught woman's shoulder. 'I think this is more than an overturned wheelchair.'

'Oh.' Janet tugged at its handles. 'If I could just get her out of it.'

A tall, cinnamon-haired man thrust his way forward and eased the chair out from Mrs King, holding her legs carefully before lowering them down. 'Here,' he said, taking off his leather jacket and handing it to Janet. 'A pillow.'

As Janet lifted the woman's head tenderly to place the jacket underneath, Rosemary finished her call. 'Ambulance on its way.' She gave the man a brief smile. 'Thanks, Robert.'

'Any idea what happened?' he murmured.

Rosemary shook her head.

'She was just looking at the exhibits,' Janet said, her eyes still on her charge. 'I don't know-'

Mrs King's hand shot out and grabbed her carer's arm. 'Janet! There-' Her hand dropped heavily as she fell into unconsciousness.

TWO

The ambulance made quick time on its well-worn path from Big Town to Mulbury. The crowd scattered as the vehicle mounted the curb and drove up to where Mrs King lay breathing shallowly. They assessed her efficiently and lifted her on to a trolley.

'Oh,' said Janet, wringing her hands. 'Is she going to be alright?'

'Who are you then, love?' said one ambulance officer kindly.

'I'm Janet Spinney. I look after Mrs King. I do her house as well.'

'Well, Janet, Mrs King is in good hands. Why don't you follow us to the hospital?'

Rosemary wasn't the only one who had noticed the state Janet was in. Robert stepped forward and put his hand on her elbow. 'Ms Spinney, I can drive you, if you like. We'll take your car and someone can get me later.' He smiled. 'Or Rosemary could take you, if you'd prefer.'

'Please, call me Janet,' said Janet. 'That's kind of you.' She wrung her hands. 'I don't think I can drive, and I don't mind who drives me, but I do need to be with Mrs King.'

They watched the ambulance doors close and the vehicle rumble slowly across the Square and away before Robert turned to Rosemary. 'I'll drive Janet. It'll give me a break from tackling the ravens nesting in my chimney and in my walls and in every space they can squeeze.'

'That's the sort of problem you face when you disturb creatures who've taken over a building.'

He gave her a quick grin. 'Can you come and get me from the hospital?'

'No.' She shrugged at his puzzled look. 'I'll send Ronnie in my car. I'd better stay here in case I'm needed.' She indicated the Square, the crowd and the stalls.

'Yes, you're probably right.' Robert gave her a rueful smile. 'Gala committee members should hang around. Unfortunately.'

Rosemary eyed him as he led the shivering Janet away. He gave a last wave as they arrived at the woman's car, but Rosemary didn't wave back. Instead, she swooped up the jacket that lay on the ground, stroking it free of dirt, and put it over the back of the wheelchair. Some of the crowd watched her with interest as she pushed the chair over the road, but the majority were already strolling among the stalls sipping coffee as if nothing had happened. Only the group of leather artisans who'd been closest to the incident still looked shocked.

'Oh, Mum, is that lady alright?' said Honey as Rosemary appeared.

'I don't know.'

'Was she injured? Did she fall? Was it a heart attack?'

'Honey, I have no idea. I am not a nurse. Mrs Lionel would have had more of an idea.'

'Well, dear, I'm not a nurse anymore.' Mrs Lionel slipped out from behind her trestle table and studied the wheelchair. 'I can tell you, though, this chair is top of the range. Not that I'd expect a low-end product to be used by Mrs Caroline King.'

'You know her, Mrs Lionel?' Ronnie came to stand next to her. 'How come?'

'Ronnie, you must expand your knowledge of *grand people* if you're going to stay a private investigator.' Mrs Lionel gave Ronnie a little push to remind him she was joking. 'Mrs Caroline King is the matriarch of a pioneering cattle breeding family and owns a station roughly the size of this state.'

'Oh,' said Ronnie.

'I've never heard of her,' said Honey. 'Have you, Mum?'

'Vaguely.' Rosemary frowned at Mrs Lionel. 'There was something recently on the news about her. Something about who will inherit the cattle empire when she's gone.'

Mrs Lionel nodded. 'That's right. She inherited it from her husband, "Mad" Morgan King, they called him, and it's been in steady hands ever since. She rebranded it to suit herself. You might even recognise the logo if you saw it. Looks like a leaf.' Mrs Lionel drew a four-sided shape in the air. 'Caroline King has an excellent business head.'

'Who has an excellent business head? You must be talking about us.'

Rosemary turned to see the Hubbard sisters standing on the pavement. Hannah's short, tufty hair was held back by a cotton headband while Heather's hair, matched in its golden colour but not in length, flowed wildly down the younger woman's back. Holly stood a step or two behind her sisters, Hubbard hair in a sensible ponytail, and watched over the Square.

'An old lady collapsed in the Square, Hannah,' said Honey. 'You missed it.'

'Yeah, that'd be right. We were still working.' Hannah waved her hand back in the direction of the animal produce store across from The Green Mulbury. 'We've closed up a bit early because we changed the oaten hay delivery until Monday.' She strained to catch Holly's eye. 'I don't think Robert will mind.'

'He won't,' said Holly, joining her sisters. 'Our new boss doesn't mind anything we do.'

'That's lovely to hear, dear,' said Mrs Lionel as Heather rested her head on the older woman's shoulder and started twirling a grey curl around her finger. 'Heard anything from your father?'

'He made it to his Queensland haunt,' said Holly. 'He's going to use his share of the sale money to buy a shack up there.'

'A *studio*, Holly,' said Hannah. 'Artists have *studios*.'

'Don't get smart, Hannah.' Holly shifted to face Mrs Lionel, her back pointedly to her sister. 'Anyway, he's bought a new guitar and he'll have a place for him and his muse to write music, and he gave each of us a bit of money.'

'I'm glad to hear it.' Mrs Lionel stroked Heather's hair. 'How are you liking the new owner of Mulbury Feeds, Heather?'

Heather smiled slowly, lifting her head from the older woman's shoulder, her bright blue gaze settling on Rosemary. 'Robert is a sparkle,' she said solemnly.

'Don't get her started, Mrs Lionel,' said Hannah, shaking her head. 'Heather thinks Robert is the best thing since sliced bread. He's going to build her a new taxidermy room at the back of the produce shed.'

'Goodness,' said Mrs Lionel. 'That is very nice of him.'

'He's ridiculously nice,' said Holly. 'Any business idea we have, he's all for it.'

'The garden centre is going well?' asked Rosemary.

'Booming,' said Hannah. 'I cannot believe how many people get excited over mushroom compost.' She looked along the pavement and waved at Jasper. 'Selling much?'

'Not bad,' said Honey. 'I've had to restock your table, Mum.' She arched her back, then straightened with a sigh. 'I need to move around a bit now, though. Sometimes I feel this baby falls asleep right on my sciatic nerve. Are you okay to watch your stall?'

'Yes. Thanks.' Rosemary stooped to fold the wheelchair in two, placing the leather jacket on her table at the same time. 'Ronnie, do you mind taking my car to the hospital in Big Town and picking up Robert? I imagine they'll want this wheelchair, too.'

'No problems, Rosemary. Oh.' Ronnie smiled at Honey. 'If that's okay?'

'Of course it is.' Honey gave him a kiss on the cheek, then a little push. 'I'm going to see what Patti's up to. Coming with me, Heather?'

Heather skipped away happily to walk beside Honey as Ronnie pushed the chair to Rosemary's car. Mrs Lionel smiled after the blonde woman. 'And Heather's okay with your father gone?' she said to the remaining sisters.

'Yeah, she's good.' Hannah scratched under her headband, then flattened it against her scalp. 'She's happy enough helping us and stuffing her birds. Dad rings her every couple of days.'

'And us,' Holly said. 'He talks to us as well.'

'Yeah, but he's really keeping tabs on Heather.' Hannah sighed. 'I sort of wish she had other things to do away from the shed...'

Holly looked at her sister sharply. 'What do you mean, Han?'

'Don't get cranky at me, Holly. I only mean that Heather is perfectly fine if we keep running Mulbury Feeds, but if we stop, what does she do then?'

'Are you going to stop?' asked Rosemary. 'I thought you were working up to buying back the business.'

'Yes, that was the plan.' Hannah shrugged. 'We'll see.'

'We will always look Heather after,' said Holly fiercely. 'Always.'

'I know.' Hannah punched her sister's arm lightly. 'I don't worry about that. But it would be nice for her to have something else to do. You know? Get some life experience other than throwing hay bales around.'

'She's an amazing taxidermist.'

'Well, yeah, but that's not a skill that's readily transferable, is it?'

'It'll work out, dear,' said Mrs Lionel, patting Hannah's arm. 'Now, I need you to do something for me. Can you help me lift out more containers of liquid soap?' She flexed knobbly fingers. 'These hands aren't as strong as they used to be.'

'Sure can, Mrs Lionel.'

'I'm going exploring,' said Holly. 'See you later.'

'I'll catch up with you,' said Hannah, disappearing inside The Green Mulbury with Mrs Lionel.

Rosemary took her place behind her table and had a busy half an hour of serving customers in her and Mrs Lionel's store. Just as she was feeling it was definitely lunch time, Gerry hurried up to her, carrying a coffee and a paper bag.

'So sorry, Rosemary,' he said, panting. 'All that excitement in the Square and then Patti had a run on clientele just itching to be fitted and needed me. I've given Jasper his drink as well.' He handed her the cup. 'It'll be iced coffee now.'

'Right.' Rosemary took the proffered drink, feeling it cool under her fingers. She shook her head as Gerry offered her the bag. 'I'm getting lunch.'

'Have it for afterwards,' he said, putting the bag on the table. 'It's one of Kelly's finest. A raspberry slice.'

Rosemary put her finger on her lip to hide the curl that happened automatically whenever Kelly's raspberry slice was mentioned. She was on the verge of telling Gerry that Kelly used jam from The Preserved Mulbury, albeit without telling Rosemary, to make her *finest* when they were both distracted by the sight of a woman zigzagging across the road trailing a crocheted coat behind her. A car slowed down to let her by, although she seemed not to notice, and wandered past without acknowledgement.

'Ah,' said Gerry, 'is Rakisha alright?'

'Hard to tell,' said Rosemary. 'Although, even for Rakisha, she looks dishevelled.'

Mrs Lionel had noticed the woman as well. She walked to meet her just as Rakisha stumbled up the curb and caught the woman's hand. 'Careful there, dear.'

'Oh.' Rakisha halted on the pavement, blinking in Mrs Lionel's face. 'Oh. Mrs Lionel, darling. I didn't see you there.'

'I'm not sure you're seeing much at all, Rakisha.' The older woman tugged at Rakisha's hand to lead her over to a chair by the window of The Green Mulbury. 'Sit there for a moment and I'll get you a cup of tea.'

'Oh, thank you, darling Mrs Lionel.' Rakisha put a hand to her head, bangles catching in her flyaway grey ringlets. 'Not caffeinated tea, darling. Herbal. Something...'

'Soothing?' suggested Mrs Lionel. 'Camomile?'

'Yes, camomile. Perhaps with a dash of honey...' Rakisha's gaze wandered back to the Square.

'Honey. Certainly.' Mrs Lionel waggled her head at Rosemary. 'Have a chat with Rosemary, dear, while I get the tea.'

Rosemary left Gerry and went to stand next to Rakisha, lifting the bedraggled coat from where it had pooled on the ground and giving it a good shake to free it from the dirt. Rakisha's hand snaked out and grabbed it back. 'It's fine, thank you, darling.' She cuddled the coat to her chest.

'I haven't seen you wear that before,' said Rosemary, glancing inside The Green Mulbury to see Mrs Lionel walking back towards them with cups on a tray. 'Is it new?'

'New?' Rakisha held the garment out from her body, studying it as if she'd never seen it before. 'See the cosmic swirls of thread? The intricate pattern of the universe? The detail of heavenly bodies?'

'No,' said Rosemary. 'I see quite ordinary shell and puff stitch patterns.'

For the first time since sitting down, Rakisha's face lost its dreamy look. She glared at Rosemary. 'Well, darling, of course you can't see what I can see. I don't think you have it in you at all to notice anything cosmic.'

Rosemary said nothing.

Rakisha hugged the coat again. 'This was our mother's; the only reflection of her inner thoughts she ever made. She was...'

'Ditzy?' said Rosemary.

Rakisha eyed her. 'I was going to say *introspective*, darling.' She squeezed the coat harder. 'Anyway, this was our mother's. And *she's* not getting it.'

'Here we are,' said Mrs Lionel, the tray against her hip

as she pulled the shop door wider, letting the croaks of the electronic frog motion sensor fill the outside air.

Rakisha clutched her head. 'Mrs Lionel, darling. That frog...'

'I know. It disturbs your karma.' Mrs Lionel set the tray down on the corner of the trestle table. 'I'll duck back in to get the teapot.'

'Wait.' Rosemary reached out to touch her friend's arm. 'I have the answer to why Rakisha looks so...'

'Out of sorts?'

'Yes.' Rosemary crouched down to Rakisha. 'Who's not getting the coat, Rakisha?'

'*Her!*'

Mrs Lionel glanced at Rosemary in alarm. 'Who, dear? It's clearly someone who makes you feel very upset.'

Rakisha nodded her head vigorously, making her hair fling all over Rosemary as the beads in her long earrings rattled against each other. 'Yes, darling, yes! She does! She always has! And now she's coming here, to my place, to *my* Mulbury!'

'Rakisha, who?'

Rakisha flopped the coat into her lap and blinked up at Mrs Lionel with watery eyes. 'Silkie! My sister Silkie!'

THREE

The Mulbury Gala wrapped up at the end of the weekend without further mishaps involving unconscious old women or irate siblings. The mild weather had continued but, as the stallholders were packing up late on Sunday, a stiff wind started, playing havoc with marquees and produce alike. The shop owners along Goldmarket Road simply dumped their products back into their shops and scurried across the road to help those in the Square. 'I'll pack these up later,' shouted Gerry to Jasper as they tried to manhandle the notice boards of historic photographs into Patricia's.

'How about putting them in my bookshop for now?' Jasper yelled back over the sound of Patti's garment racks banging against the door where they'd been placed higgeldy piggeldy in the rush to get them inside.

'What a great idea!' Gerry started backwards to The Read Mulbury, his round torso all but hidden by the board.

Rosemary held the heavy door open as they carried the photographs inside and kept guard as they fetched the remaining two from the flapping marquee. It wasn't shop stealers she was guarding against; it was the mischievous wind which had picked up strongly and threatened to push over Jasper's piles of books he'd dumped to the side of the doorway. She watched as the artists and volunteers from Big Town dismantled the rest of the marquees in the Square, rolling them roughly and sliding them into their cars before leaving with cheery waves.

'Everything done over there?' asked Rosemary as the men came back for the third time.

'Mostly,' said Jasper, trying to blow hair away from his face as it whipped around his head. 'There are some boxes Mrs Lionel said the artists could pick up another time. Aren't we lucky that the wind didn't start until it was over?'

'Very lucky,' said Gerry, lowering the edge of the photo board down and wiping his forehead with the back of the hand. 'What an effort! Thanks for letting me put these here, Jasper, my mate. Oh, I could do with a drink now.'

'I can make tea,' said Rosemary.

'Thank you, but I think I'd better help Patti with her dresses. Not that we're expecting too many customers tomorrow with the Gala finishing, but we do need to have a clear doorway just in case.'

Jasper leaned on the door as Gerry left for Patricia's, finally getting it to click closed. Silence filled the bookstore as it locked the wind out.

'Well,' said Jasper, glancing at Rosemary with a hint of a blush starting on his neck. 'I could do with a cup of tea.'

'And a hairbrush.' Rosemary plucked a long strand of black hair from Jasper's face and threw it back in line over his shoulder.

'Look who's talking.' Jasper caught the end of Rosemary's long braid and dragged the hair tie from it. 'This was just about to come out.'

'Thank you,' said Rosemary, plucking it from his palm

and running her fingers through her long, silver-streaked dark hair. 'I'll plait it again later.'

'Oh.' Jasper hesitated with his hand out to stroke her hair again. 'I so rarely see it out of its constraints.' The blush had reached his face.

Rosemary took a step back to shake her head and let the hair fall about her shoulders. 'There's the reason. How could I make jams and jellies with this hanging all about the place?'

The look on Jasper's face did not seem at all concerned with the fate of hair in the preserves. Rosemary frowned. 'Jasper.'

'What? Oh, sorry.' Jasper ran his raised hand through his own hair, settling it down his back where it hung almost as lengthy as Rosemary's. 'You know...' He smiled sheepishly.

'Yes. Now. Tea?'

Jasper's disappointment was easier to ignore once Rosemary was busy with making tea in his little kitchen. She could hear him talking to his old dog Snowy, who spent most of his life upside down asleep on the couch, as Jasper shifted the notice boards from the shop to his living area. She took mugs of tea out into the dim interior of The Read Mulbury and helped him re-stack his shelves, listening to him chat about the sales he'd had, and trying not to think of why it seemed so difficult to be more than friends with the gentle Jasper Lu.

MONDAY WAS PREDICTABLY SLOW in tourist-dependent Mulbury, which suited most of its residents. Rosemary opened as usual but spent the morning leafing through Aunt Lilibeth's recipe book in the hope of inspiration. There were always surprises to be found in the well-loved old book, no matter how many times she went through it, and today was typical of that. A small recipe at the bottom of a back page caught her eye.

The door jangled and Mrs Lionel stepped in, pausing in the doorway to scuff a few leaves back outside. She made her way to the shop counter and regarded Rosemary closely. 'You're deep in thought,' she said.

'How do you know that?'

'You have that look in those hazel eyes of yours.'

'That look?'

'Yes.' Mrs Lionel leaned on the counter. 'Your business look.'

'I hope I'm not as transparent to everyone in Mulbury.'

'Oh no, dear, only a best friend could read Rosemary Exeter like a book.'

Rosemary narrowed her eyes at her best friend. 'That's reassuring. I think.' She turned the book to show Mrs Lionel the little recipe. 'I'm thinking of starting a new line of preserves using native ingredients.'

'Ah.' Mrs Lionel nodded thoughtfully. 'Then you need to talk to Roman.'

'Why?'

'His farmer friend, Justin.' Mrs Lionel tapped the book. 'He'll be able to help you with produce. He grows so many wonderful things on his farm.'

'That's good. I would like to source locally.'

'Of course. What about Honey's idea of making sweeties from your fruit? Candied quince, isn't that what she suggested? You could do those products as well.'

Rosemary's phone peeled the first few bars of a merry tune. 'Her ears must be burning. It's Honey.'

'Get it then, dear. It might be about the baby.'

Rosemary answered the phone on speaker. 'Honey. I'm here with Mrs Lionel.'

'Hello to both, then! How are you after the big weekend?'

'Glad it's over,' said Rosemary.

'It was delightful,' said Mrs Lionel. 'I'm storing some boxes for an artist to get later, so hopefully we get to know what they thought of it. I would like them back next year.'

Honey chuckled, the sound rich in Rosemary's ears. 'That would be good. You'd prefer to just have the shop open, Mum?'

'It wasn't only that. Organising Galas is a big job. Marquees, insurance, safety concerns about the Square-'

'At least you didn't have to worry about The Exceptional Tree dropping branches on anyone's head.'

'No. Rakisha's Entanglement barricade keeps people away from danger.' Rosemary rolled her eyes. 'Who would have thought?'

'How are you, dear?' said Mrs Lionel into the phone. 'Everything well?'

'Yes, I'm good. You know, sort of tired.' Scratching noises echoed through the phone as she shuffled on her seat. 'Although something's changed. I feel more pressure than anything else.'

'Tallulah's head is well and truly down. She's getting ready.'

'Yes, that's what the midwife said. I saw her this morning. She gave me the impression that everything was perfectly normal.'

'I'm pleased to hear that,' said Mrs Lionel. 'Won't be long now.'

'No. But Tallulah has to hang on for a little bit. I've got more cakes to make this week.'

'You aren't still working, Honey?'

'It's okay, Mrs Lionel. I've temporarily closed Honey Blossom's Academy of Dramatic Experiences. I'm sticking to cake creation for the time being. At least I can rest when I want, and the only one to hassle me is Cuddles. He does that by looking at me with his big brown eyes, begging for cake crumbs.'

'You can put him outside if he bothers you,' said Rosemary, picturing the Golden Retriever smiling at her.

'I do!' Honey laughed. 'Then he presses his nose up against the glass doors.'

'Where's Ronnie today?'

More shuffling noises. 'That's why I'm ringing you, Mum. Ronnie's gone to see Uncle Geoffrey at the police station. Geoffrey has another job for him.'

'That's lovely, Honey,' said Mrs Lionel. 'Geoffrey knows a good private investigator when he sees one.'

'Ronnie's got a reputation for decent work now. Although, this case is going to be slightly different. It's funded by the victim.'

'Isn't that usual for a PI?'

'Well, yes, but Uncle Geoffrey has been asked to keep a very close eye on things. He says the case is *political*.'

Mrs Lionel frowned. 'It involves politicians?'

'No. It involves Mrs Caroline King.'

'Ah.' Mrs Lionel nodded to herself. 'Very political then.'

'Why is that, Mrs Lionel?'

'Mrs King is a very wealthy woman. With wealth comes power. And she's sharp. She may look frail these days, but I wouldn't want to cross her.'

'Someone crossed her,' said Rosemary. 'Otherwise, she

wouldn't be in contact with the police. I'm guessing this means she didn't die after her ordeal.'

Mrs Lionel scowled at her friend. 'It would have been on the news if Mrs Caroline King had died. She's very fortunate that the ambulance responded so quickly.'

'I guess,' said Honey, moving again. 'We'll know more when Ronnie comes home.' More creaking noises.

Mrs Lionel glanced at Rosemary. 'Are you alright, dear?'

'Braxton Hicks contractions.' Honey gave a heavy sigh. 'You know, false ones. Easing off now.'

'Perhaps you'd better go and have a rest.'

'I'm fine, Mrs Lionel. I can't rest now. I've got frogs to make. Toads, actually.'

'Someone wanted their cake shaped like a toad?'

'An invasive cane toad, as well. Yuck.' Honey chuckled again. 'At least I don't have to worry about making the cakes pretty. Although I thought I'd put a smile on their faces and make them a shade more appetising than their usual colour.'

'I wouldn't eat a cane toad cake,' said Rosemary. 'Even if it was lime.'

'Fussy, Mum! Anyway, enough about me. What are you making now?'

'Nothing at the moment. I was just discussing a new recipe with Mrs Lionel.'

'Oh, let me guess! Apple relish? Quince chutney? Pumpkin jam?'

'No. And I don't have apples or quinces in my larder.'

'But you've got pumpkins. I can smell them.'

'You can smell pumpkin?'

'Pumpkin and ginger. A thick, spicy fragrance that reminds me of winter fires and hot toddies and playing board games on your dining room table.'

Rosemary shook her head at Mrs Lionel.

'Mum, you've added a hint of nutmeg. It's earthy. The steam is wafting up to the ceiling and heading towards the shop. You'll have customers banging on the door to get the first jars.'

'You're crazy, Honey Blossom.'

'I know. Bye, Mum. Bye, Mrs Lionel.'

'Bye bye, dear.'

'Love you, Mum.'

'Love you, too.'

Rosemary ended the call and slipped her phone in her pocket. 'I wonder why Mrs King has contacted the police?'

'No doubt Ronnie will tell us in good time.' Mrs Lionel straightened, stretching her legs one at a time. 'I'll see you tonight at Rakisha's.' She smiled suddenly. 'Bring an empty mind with you.'

'Why?'

'Rakisha's sister will be there.'

'And?'

'Didn't you know? Silkie is a *sensitive*.'

'What on earth is a sensitive?'

But Mrs Lionel just tapped her finger against her nose and left Rosemary standing at her shop counter with the ghost of yet-to-be-made pumpkin jam around her.

FOUR

Rosemary closed the shop right at five o'clock and headed back into her living quarters to do a little research. Sunny met her at the doorway between the shop and the house, staring at her mistress with vivid, green eyes. 'Did you know?' said Rosemary, stooping to run her hand along the cat's arched back. 'Your eyes and mine are very similar? They change colour according to the light.'

Sunny tipped her head obligingly away from the dimness of the shop's interior, making her eyes brighten to gold. *That's what makes us mysterious,* she seemed to say as she stalked back to her bed near the couch.

Rosemary shook her head. It wasn't like her to be awed by eye colour or wary of strangers, but the term 'sensitive' had lodged in her head like an irritating burr. Dinner at Rakisha's was at six-thirty, so she boiled the kettle and sat at the table with an afternoon brew to flick through the internet in search of information. She'd just read "sensitive people are highly responsive to external and internal stimuli" when a knock at the door broke her concentration. As she went back into the shop, she saw Ronnie's police officer, uncle Geoffrey, and a young constable through a gap in the blinds.

'Sorry to disturb you, Rosemary,' said Geoffrey, a broad smile on his strong face. 'I'm looking for Robert Sparkling. He's not at the garage.'

'No. He'll be at his house.'

'Which is…?'

'The old mayoral residence.'

'Ah, yes, that makes sense.'

'Why?'

'Oh, the Sparklings have a reputation for acquisition. He owns the garage and the mayoral residence?'

'And Mulbury Feeds.'

'Almost half the town.' Geoffrey shook his head. 'Some have it lucky. Anyway, thank you.'

'This is about Mrs Caroline King.'

Geoffrey studied Rosemary closely. 'I assume you know I can't say anything about an active case.'

'I thought it was a private investigation?'

The older man scratched his head. 'Well, yes, but it's…'

'Political.'

'A useful word in these circumstances. Thanks again. Come on, Christopher.' Geoffrey ushered the constable in front of him and began the trek to the mayoral residence.

Rosemary stepped through the jangling doorway to watch the police officers cross the road. They'd only gotten halfway when Geoffrey pointed suddenly, and the two men veered back to Mulbury Feeds where Robert and Holly stood in front of a pallet of potting mix. Geoffrey spoke to Robert and Holly stepped back, accidentally knocking the young constable who caught her as she tripped. Even from where Rosemary stood, she could see Holly's face redden.

'Spying on the neighbours?'

Mrs Lionel had come along the pavement and stood next to Rosemary, chuckling.

'Always.' Rosemary grinned at her friend.

'I saw Geoffrey pull up, and I guessed he's doing some scouting about what happened on Saturday. They'll be stepping carefully with anything to do with Mrs King.'

'She wields a lot of power.'

'In her own way.' Mrs Lionel held up a bundle of cloth. 'I've been to see Patti. I'm washing these swatches for her. She's so busy, poor love, that I feel I need to help.'

'She could afford to pay an assistant.'

'Yes, probably, but businesses take a while to get on their feet. She's well on her way, but I still feel she could do with a little support from others.' Mrs Lionel poked Rosemary gently in the arm. 'You could help her.'

'I don't sew.'

'Set up her computer system for her, like you did for Jasper when he was in hospital. That would be a real help.'

'Right.'

'Anyway, I'll put these in the machine and then it must be nearly time to go to Rakisha's.'

'I'm meeting Jasper for a walk first.'

'Well, pick me up when you finish. I'll be waiting.'

Rosemary just had time to see Mrs Lionel back into The Green Mulbury and notice her welcome to Percy before Jasper shut the door to The Read Mulbury and wandered down the pavement with his hands in his coat pocket. 'Ready?' he asked.

'Almost.'

Rosemary changed swiftly into her walking shoes and followed Jasper as he crossed the road and headed up the hill. Robert was gone from Mulbury Feeds, although Holly still stood out the front frowning at a clipboard as if she'd forgotten what she was doing. Rosemary caught up with Jasper. 'You're speedy today.'

'Am I?' He hooked his hair behind one ear. 'Sorry. Lost in thought.'

'Right.'

He glanced sideways at her. 'Want to know why?'

'You'll tell me if you want me to know.'

'But aren't you curious?'

'Jasper. Tell me or not. It's your business.'

He chewed his lip momentarily. 'I'm not sure it *is* my business. I mean, it is, but not directly.'

Rosemary said nothing.

'It's Helena. And Iris.'

'Your sisters.'

'Half-sisters.'

'Right. Has something happened?'

'Helena rang. She wants to meet up in the city. With Iris, thankfully, or I wouldn't go. Helena wants to talk.'

'Is that a good thing?'

'I'm never sure with Helena.'

'Right.'

He halted, staring straight ahead. 'Do you think I should go?'

'Of course.'

'But Helena is so...'

'Jasper.' Rosemary took his arm. 'I know you don't get on with your big sister-'

'Half-sister.'

'Whatever. But you're a strong, independent man in his mid-fifties.'

'I'll always be the little brother.'

She shook his arm. 'Yes, but you've got this. You are a man who won't be bullied anymore. Right?'

He smiled wanly and started walking again, keeping her hand on his arm by locking it to his side. 'Yes, I hear you, Rosemary. I need to go. You're right. It's only...'

'Yes, she'll probably bring up the family curse business, but you know what I think of that.'

Jasper was silent as they walked past the mayoral residence with its single light blazing in the back room, reminding Rosemary that she still had Robert Sparkling's jacket, then made it to the top of the hill. The setting sun threw long shadows around the cemetery, darkening the old headstones. They'd walked to the end of the low stone wall before Jasper spoke again. 'You think my family curse is nonsense.'

'You know I do.'

'It isn't. I've had it all my life. It's attached to me.' He put his free hand on his chest.

Rosemary tried not to let her sigh of exasperation show. Jasper had recently had some bad luck, getting sick for instance, but good luck followed it: getting better when so many didn't. Not that he saw it that way. He also blamed the curse for him finding a skeleton in his backyard even though it had been buried there fifty years ago. She was sure he spent too much time mulling over the many incidents in his past that could be attributed to a family curse. *Jasper is difficult to reason with,* thought Rosemary, but gave his arm a squeeze. 'It'll be okay, you know.'

He shrugged. 'Maybe.'

'Come on. We'll be late to Rakisha's and end up having to eat the dregs of a nut bar.'

'That might be preferable to what she's serving for mains.'

Rosemary chuckled as they walked down the hill and back to the shops under the veranda of Goldmarket Road, where Mrs Lionel was waiting with a cane basket on her arm.

'What is that?' asked Rosemary.

'I'm bringing dessert. Vegan apple crumble.'

'But isn't it Rakisha's turn to cook for us, Mrs Lionel?' said Jasper, puzzled.

'She's a bit flustered. I thought I'd help her out.'

Rosemary frowned. 'You are helping too many people out at the moment.'

'Oh, shoosh.' Mrs Lionel held out her basket. 'You carry it. That will help me.'

'I'll duck inside first to get Robert's jacket.'

Rosemary went inside, scooped up the jacket, and patted Sunny on her windowsill as she went. The cat refused to look at her. *Out again,* she seemed to say.

'You know I'll be back soon,' said Rosemary, running her hand along the cat's soft coat. She went back outside, took the basket from Mrs Lionel and led the way back over the road towards The Sweet Potato. Rakisha lived in the little flat above the shop, and it was usual for drifts of sandalwood incense to float from the top windows and waft into the Square. Tonight, though, the fragrance was some-what more pungent, and Rosemary's nose wrinkled.

'Unusual,' murmured Mrs Lionel, walking with her arm looped through Jasper's.

Rosemary gritted her teeth and knocked at the café door. It swung open at her touch, and the three of them made their way past a group of rattan chairs surrounding the one table in the shop to the stairs at the back. She could hear a woman talking, a long low flow of words that lilted like a song. *That's not Rakisha,* thought Rosemary. *It's too smooth.*

It wasn't Rakisha, although at first glance Rosemary

thought she'd been wrong. A woman stood in the middle of Rakisha's cotton-draped living room, holding a glass of deep ruby liquid out in front of her and appearing to address Roman, who stood rock still with his wife chuckling beside him. As Rosemary, Jasper and Mrs Lionel appeared, the other guests stopped staring at the woman and started gazing at them in such an expectant way that Rosemary narrowed her eyes.

'Hello, darlings,' said Rakisha dully, emerging from behind Roman, Jules and Robert. 'Welcome.'

'Rakisha,' said Mrs Lionel quietly. 'Are you alright? You sound...'

Rakisha flicked her long, unruly hair from her shoulders so it gathered in a cloud down her back. 'My sister,' she said, pointing to the woman with the ruby drink. 'Silkie.'

Silkie turned at the sound of her name, the hair that was just as long as Rakisha's but completely opposite in its dark sleekness, falling forward so it framed her face. Thinner than her sister's, it still bore a family resemblance, as did the array of layers arranged on her body. The difference, Rosemary noted, was that Silkie's attire was carefully constructed, whereas her sister's was careless.

'So,' said Silkie.

Silence fell as everyone waited for her to finish, but Silkie only moved her gaze from Rosemary to Mrs Lionel and then finally Jasper.

'Well,' said Mrs Lionel finally. 'Hello, Silkie. I'm-'

'Dorothea Lionel. Yes. With Rosemary Exeter.' Silkie pointed a long, gold-painted fingertip at Rosemary. 'And you. You're Jasper Lu.' She walked forward to place a light finger on Jasper's sternum. 'So sad. You are so very sad.'

Jasper's face paled.

'Right,' said Rosemary, stepping forward with the basket

held in front of her, making Silkie drop her touch. 'This is for you, Rakisha, from Mrs Lionel.'

'Oh.' Rakisha took the basket and, for a moment, the smile on her face was almost normal. Then her mouth drooped. 'Thank you, darling.' She turned and disappeared into the next room.

The silence fell again, broken first by Robert, who raised his glass of the same red liquid. 'Cheers, all.'

Those with glasses followed his action, and Jasper made a swift escape to a side table to pour the newcomers a drink. Rosemary walked to Robert, sidling past Jules, Roman and Kelly in the tight space. 'I brought your jacket,' she said, handing it over.

He folded it over his arm. 'Thanks. I've been looking for it. It's a bit of a family heirloom.' He used his glass to point at the crowd. 'Talking about family, this could be a fun night.'

Rosemary frowned. 'I didn't come here for fun.'

'You came to hear what the Detective Inspector was asking me.'

'No.'

'Really?'

Rosemary studied Robert's night-black eyes. He had a slight smile on his face, giving him the aura of someone highly entertained. 'No,' she said. 'Not my business.'

'Not mine, really, either.' He shrugged, sipping his drink and pulling a face. 'Cranberry and lemon. Rakisha says it cleanses the palette.'

'She's into cleansing all her bits and pieces.'

'I think she'd like to cleanse her sister right away.'

'Do you know why Silkie's here? I didn't even know Rakisha had a sister.'

'No idea, but Rakisha doesn't seem pleased.' He lowered his glass. 'I'm going to tell you, anyway.'

'Tell me what?'

'About what the police came to see me for.' Any amusement dropped from his face as he leaned closer to Rosemary's ear. 'They wanted to know whether Janet had said anything in the car about Mrs King.'

'Had she?'

'No, the poor thing seemed genuinely upset.'

'What's it got to do with Janet, anyway?'

'Maybe nothing, but maybe everything.' He lowered his voice. 'I suspect the police think that Mrs King's collapse was not only the result of her frail condition.'

'Someone hurt her?'

'Indirectly.' He leaned so close that Rosemary felt the warmth of his breath on her neck. 'They diagnosed Mrs King with Takotsubo cardiomyopathy.'

'Which is?'

His breath tickled her cheek. 'Broken heart syndrome.'

FIVE

Rosemary didn't have time to respond to Robert. A shriek came from the kitchen, and Roman hurried through the doorway, thrusting his glass at Robert as he went. The crowd left behind could hear him muttering. 'It's alright, Rakisha, it's alright. We'll fix it.' Rakisha responded with moans. Mrs Lionel went to help, but Jules caught her arm. 'Roman will do the trick,' she said to the older woman. 'I suspect it has something to do with dinner.'

The pungent smell that had infiltrated the air outside was now in the dining area, a sharp mix of charcoal and mushrooms. Jasper slunk over to the window facing Gold-market Square and heaved it open a few inches, which cooled the room but dissipated much of the unpleasant odour. Behind Rosemary, Hannah found a box of matches on a mantlepiece and lit a wedge of incense lying in a pottery dish. Kelly held her nose and hurried to stand by the window while Robert went to help Mrs Lionel with setting the table, a job that looked like it had been abandoned mid-way. Only Silkie stayed where she'd been before Jasper had darted away. She faced the action but did not join it.

A few minutes later, Roman appeared at the doorway, beaming. 'Dinner will be but a minute,' he said. 'Rakisha asks that you be seated.'

'Do you think it'll be safe to eat?' said Hannah, not so discreetly. 'I mean, it's risky enough at The Sweet Potato at the best of times.'

'Well,' said Kelly, sliding smoothly into the chair nearest the window, 'we don't come here for the food, not really.' She gazed shrewdly around the room until she came to Silkie. 'There's always something to be gained from getting a glimpse of Rakisha's inner chakra.'

'Kelly, dear,' said Mrs Lionel with a frown. 'Monday dinners are a social event and not a chance to make judgement calls on others.'

Kelly's short bob swayed heavily as she shook her head. 'You are too nice, Mrs Lionel. Now where's that Franco?'

'He rang me,' said Jasper. 'He had to dash to Big Town to buy flour and then got a flat tyre. He said to give his apologies.'

'That man,' said Jules, arranging her dress over her knees as she sat next to Kelly. 'He never makes it to Monday dinners.'

'Do you reckon he gets sick of food?' said Hannah, plonking herself next to Jules. 'He cooks all day and night, serves and sells it, prepares for the next day. He's on a food-making treadmill.'

'I don't think he works any harder than you,' said Robert, sitting at the head of the table next to the young woman. 'Or your sisters. Where are they, anyway?'

'They would have been here,' said Hannah, filling her glass from a chipped jug on the table. 'But Heather got caught up with a bird and Holly said she hadn't quite finished checking stock.' She shrugged. 'I understand not being able to move Heather until she's finished taxidermy-ing but Holly looked a bit out of sorts.'

Mrs Lionel gave Robert a reproachful look as she sat next to him. 'You aren't working those girls too hard, Robert Sparkling? They have very strong work ethics and some-times don't know when to stop.'

Robert held both his hands up. 'I swear, Mrs Lionel, I don't ask them to work after hours or do anything extra.'

'He'd have to pay us overtime if he did.' Hannah grinned. 'Maybe there is some advantage to not owning your own business.'

'I used to work in a call centre,' said Kelly. 'Had a horrible supervisor who refused to give us enough breaks. Give me my own business any day.'

As stories about tyrant bosses started around the table, Rosemary slipped into the chair next to Mrs Lionel's.

'I get my money's worth out of the Hubbard sisters ten times over,' said Robert quietly to Mrs Lionel with only Rosemary overhearing. 'I can't actually get them to slow down.'

'It's not in their nature, dear.'

'Aren't they working towards buying the business back?' said Rosemary. 'That was the original plan after Richard sold it to you.'

'They haven't mentioned it for a while,' said Robert, twisting his glass between his fingers. 'I'll be ready for when they do.'

'Did I glimpse Geoffrey going to see you today?' asked Mrs Lionel. 'I thought I recognised his unmarked vehicle.'

'Yes.' Robert shook his head. 'I couldn't help him.'

'Mrs Lionel will know about broken heart syndrome,' said Rosemary, her arm over the back of her friend's chair. 'She was a nurse.'

'Thank you, dear, but that doesn't mean I know every-thing.' Mrs Lionel looked curiously at Robert. 'Do you have a broken heart?'

Rosemary had never seen Robert's face become such an interesting shade of puce before. She hid her smile behind her glass. 'Mrs King has it. It's why she collapsed.'

'Mrs King has a broken heart?' Mrs Lionel looked over the table and out the window. 'She's such a tough woman. That's terribly sad.'

'I don't think it literally means a broken heart,' said Robert. 'I mean, you couldn't live with a real broken heart.'

'No, you couldn't.' Mrs Lionel brought her focus back to him. 'I've seen people die of a broken heart. Oh, not literally broken. But the amount of people I've seen that wither away to nothing after their husband or wife has died... it may not be scientific, but I know it to be true.'

'But Mrs King didn't die,' said Rosemary. 'What did you say the real name was, Robert? Some sort of cardiomyopathy?'

'Takotsubo cardiomyopathy.'

Mrs Lionel tapped the table gently as she thought. 'Now I have heard of that. Never quite understood how it manifests. Never known anyone with it... hmmm.'

'Is it bad?'

'Well, dear, it isn't good, but it's rarely fatal.' Mrs Lionel patted the pocket of her dress and found it empty. 'Do you have a pen, Robert? Perhaps a bit of paper as well?'

Robert reached into his jacket pocket and placed a fountain pen and a small notepad on the table. Mrs Lionel unscrewed the lid of the pen and made a few strokes. 'I've not seen one of those for a while,' she said, and started drawing earnestly.

'Bower Bird Blue?' asked Rosemary over Mrs Lionel's soft curls.

'Midnight Cloud,' said Robert.

'You know your inks,' said Mrs Lionel, sitting back. 'But do you know anatomy?'

Rosemary swivelled the notebook slightly to see what Mrs Lionel had drawn. 'That's a heart. With its four chambers.'

'That's right.' Mrs Lionel used the pen to mark each. 'Left and right atria; left and right ventricles. This is, roughly, the correct shape of each if they are in good health.' She drew over the top of one ventricle and used cross-hatching to fill it in. 'This, however, is what happens in Takotsubo cardiomyopathy. The chamber of the ventricle changes shape. It's how it gets its name.'

'From the shape of the ventricle?'

'Yes.' Mrs Lionel added a few more lines. 'It's called after a Japanese octopus trap, which is what it looks like. The patient experiences symptoms like that of a heart attack or angina, but this is a quite different condition. People generally recover after a few months.'

Rosemary studied the paper closely, then sat back. The table was quiet, with the rest of its occupants staring into the middle of the room. Frowning, Rosemary turned to see Silkie standing like an ethereal Elven queen, her arms outstretched and several thick silver bracelets catching the light from Rakisha's half-moon light shade. Tears were streaming down her face as she gazed at Mrs Lionel. 'I heard you,' Silkie said breathlessly. 'I heard about your broken heart.'

'Not mine, dear,' said Mrs Lionel evenly. 'Someone else's. I haven't had my heart broken for decades.'

Silkie blinked once or twice, whether to clear her eyes

or at Mrs Lionel's words, Rosemary found it hard to tell. 'Perhaps not you, wise Mulbury crone, but this table is full of broken hearts.' She put a hand shakily to her breast. 'I feel it. Here. In me. In my own aching chamber of hurt.'

Luckily, thought Rosemary later, Hannah's outright guffaw was covered by Roman walking into the room with an enormous pot of something steaming and announcing that dinner was served. Rakisha followed closely behind, clutching a basket of bread. She took one look at her weeping sister and charged at her. 'Silkie, darling,' she said, pushing the basket roughly towards Silkie's chamber of hurt, 'put this on the table. I'll bring out the yoghurt.'

Roman settled the pot on the table and lifted the lid, letting the rich fragrance of lime escape.

'Is it edible, Roman?' asked Hannah, looking doubtfully at the pot.

'It is, my lolly,' said Roman.

'Sweet, I assume he means,' said Jules to Hannah.

'I added a touch of citrus and a lot of coconut cream,' said Roman, stirring the dish with a large wooden ladle. 'Bowls, please.'

No one refused to eat, which, thought Rosemary, was more than could be said for the last time Rakisha made Monday dinner. Silkie was left holding the breadbasket until Jasper stood up and guided her into the end seat, tugging the bread from her and putting it next to the pot. She smiled at him as he offered his serviette to staunch her tears. Roman sat next to Rosemary, so she didn't hear what Silkie was saying, but Jasper's face went the bright crimson usually reserved for encounters with herself.

The vegetable curry was a success, with many people having second helpings, and Rakisha brightened, talking feverishly to Kelly, who was not even trying to listen. Jules leaned across the table to Robert. 'How are the renovations going? I remember what it was like when Roman and I did up our place. Luckily for us, we didn't have to live in it at the same time.'

Robert put down his fork. 'To tell you the truth, it's harder than I thought.'

'You could get in more trades people, dear,' said Mrs Lionel, wiping her bowl with a knob of bread.

'Yes, I could, but that's not the issue. It's more a planning problem.'

'Trouble with the council?' Kelly turned her back on Rakisha, who didn't notice and kept talking. 'Planning permits are notoriously tricky. I could help you.'

Rosemary swore Kelly batted her eyelashes.

'Thanks, Kelly, but that's not the problem either. It's just that the house is so big.'

'It *was* the mayoral residence,' said Roman. 'The mayor was a big man, in spirit and body, so I heard.'

'Precisely, Roman.' Robert stretched his hands out. 'The house is cavernous. No wonder they used it as a hospital during Scarlet Tuesday.'

From the corner of her eye, Rosemary saw Silkie stop with a fork halfway to her mouth.

'I don't know where to start.' Robert shrugged. 'I'm sorry. That sounded ridiculous.'

'Not at all,' said Kelly. 'Perhaps you'd like to brainstorm with others about it? I could come over and have a look. I have quite an interest in old buildings.'

Not that I've ever heard of, thought Rosemary, but said nothing as Kelly started on about floor plans and power points and cornices. She glanced over at Mrs Lionel to share a knowing look, but her friend was staring at her plate. Rosemary leaned closer. 'Are you alright?'

Mrs Lionel pushed her bowl away and turned to Rosemary. 'I think I know why Geoffrey's asking about the incident with Mrs King.'

'Because she demanded it?'

'Perhaps, with reason.' Mrs Lionel tugged the drawing of the two hearts out from under her bowl and pointed at the octopus pot shaped ventricle. 'Do you know what causes this to happen?'

'No.'

'Shock.' Mrs Lionel stared at Rosemary with blazing eyes. 'Sudden, harsh, emotional shock.'

'Like what?'

'A fierce argument. Intense fear. A sudden illness. The death of a spouse. The death of a *pet*.'

'Lucky that didn't happen to you.'

'My Percy is still around, even if I am the only one to see him.' Mrs Lionel shook her head. 'No, something happened to Mrs King that shocked her deeply.' She lifted the paper up and gave it a light shake. 'And that something must have happened at the Mulbury Gala.'

SIX

The rest of Monday dinner went by in its usual camaraderie style. Rakisha became increasingly vocal the more her sister sat quietly, but Silkie's apparent loss of voice did not fool Rosemary. She noted the sideways glances Silkie made at Jasper, who also noticed it and, if the shaking of his apple crumble spoon was a sign, it was affecting him. Silkie occasionally whispered to him, so quietly that it could have been mistaken as a low breeze sweeping the table.

When Rosemary announced it was time she left, Jasper leapt to his feet quickly, his chair tipping into a chime hanging dangerously low from the ceiling. There were a few minutes of frantic ting-ting-tinging as he grabbed the chair, then the chime, and ended up with his hair caught in the fishing line holding the clashing pieces of hollow metal. 'Ouch,' he said as Rosemary extracted him.

'Be more careful next time,' she said as they went down the stairs with Mrs Lionel.

He grunted. 'I didn't do it on purpose. I mean, who hangs a wind chime so low?'

'Rakisha,' said Mrs Lionel, opening the door for them. 'But I don't think that was what Rosemary meant.'

Jasper went through the door and turned to help Mrs Lionel down the one step into Goldmarket Square. 'What else did I do?'

'You sat next to Silkie, dear.'

'Worse,' said Rosemary, stopping for a moment to look into The Exceptional Tree. 'You sat Silkie next to you.'

'She's okay.' Jasper stood next to Rosemary and plunged his hands into his pockets. 'In a different kind of way.'

'She's not okay, not for you.'

'What are you saying?'

'Just what I said. A person like Silkie, with a tendency towards grand exclamations, can be really dangerous to-' Rosemary pointed suddenly. 'Look, a tawny frogmouth.'

'Where, dear?'

Rosemary waggled her finger at the upper branches of the Tree. 'See? It's on the-'

'Finish what you were going to say, Rosemary.'

Rosemary turned at Jasper's stiff voice. 'Third branch from the top.'

He shook his head, dark hair spilling over his shoulders like a cape. 'You know that's not what I meant. You were going to say how dangerous Silkie could be to a person like me, weren't you?'

'Was I?'

'Yes, you were!' He flicked his hair back. 'You don't have any faith in me at all, do you? You think I'm a superstitious man who believes in curses and fairy tales, and that I could be completely sucked in by someone who dares to pay a little bit of attention to my inner pain!'

'Jasper, dear,' said Mrs Lionel, sounding shocked. 'None of us think like that.'

'Oh, Rosemary does.' Jasper stepped back as Mrs Lionel went forward with an outstretched hand. 'She doesn't know what it's like to have bad luck dog you all your life. She thinks I'm stupid, only worthy of her pity and certainly not of any other emotion.'

Rosemary watched as he walked backwards. The light in the Square was coming mainly from the two streetlights on Goldmarket Road plus the small squares of Rakisha's living quarter windows. It threw Jasper's face into shadow, but she didn't need to see his face to know that it would be hard with fury. 'Jasper,' she started.

'No, Rosemary, no.' Jasper was now so far away his voice was thinning. 'Just leave me. Leave...' He turned abruptly and ran across the road to The Read Mulbury. Rosemary heard the heavy sigh of his door as it closed. The turned lock echoed into the Square.

'Goodness,' said Mrs Lionel, shrugging her jacket up a little. 'I hope Jasper's alright.'

Rosemary gave a brief shake of her head. They walked back to their residences without talking. Mrs Lionel patted her on the sleeve before they went their separate ways.

Inside, the house was cosy. Rosemary sank onto the sofa without either turning on the light or taking off her jacket. Sunny rose from her bed and jumped lightly into Rosemary's lap, padding her thighs before curling up contentedly. Rosemary didn't stir. Jasper's words rang in her head. *Only worthy of pity. Only pity...*

Lights flickered onto the back porch, cast by Mrs Lionel's dining room globes. Rosemary could hear the faint noises of Mrs Lionel's bedtime preparation through the dividing wall: murmurs to the ethereal Percy, the hiss of a kettle for the camomile tea the older woman took to bed each night, the thud of shoes shaken off. Finally, the light went out and Rosemary was in darkness again. No lights had come and gone from the other side where Jasper Lu's home joined her own.

ROSEMARY WOKE WITH A START. Magpies carolled in the early morning, but it was a kookaburra that had roused her, its deep-throated cackle right outside her window. She sat up, rubbing her neck, and shifted Sunny from where she still curled on her lap. The bird was on the railing outside, looking in at her with intense brown eyes. It opened its mouth again, sang its bushman's alarm, and flew off on heavy brown wings. She crossed the room and flung open her glass doors, but the bird had gone.

Outside, the sun tinged the world with peach as it started its ascent. The night on the couch had left Rosemary with a cricked neck, and she rubbed it harder as she walked to the railing and leaned over. To her far right, a light was on in the big tin shed of Mulbury Feeds, and next door, Mrs Lionel's kitchen light glowed warmly. She wandered over to the left, putting her elbows on the railing that separated her porch from Jasper Lu's. 'Jasper?' she called softly, but no one answered.

Rosemary went back inside and began preparations for the day. Tuesday was an average sale day, but usually busier than Mondays. There was a regular monthly busload of senior citizens from the city due, which meant making sure that there were a variety of condiments on display, including the gift packs of marmalade and pickles that were so popular. Rosemary ate a hurried piece of toast, then spread gift boxes, tissue paper and cards across the dining table and started putting them together. It didn't entirely relieve the despair she felt when she thought of Jasper yelling at her, but it filled the time until she could go next door and apologise... apologise for what, exactly?

'Probably being insensitive,' she said to Sunny.

The cat watched her from the windowsill before curling her tail around her body, its tip rising and falling gently. *And what's wrong with being insensitive?* she seemed to say.

Nothing, thought Rosemary as she tied a box with blue ribbon, *except that it's the opposite to being sensitive.* Or, as Mrs Lionel had said about Silkie, *a* sensitive.

At five minutes after opening time, she hung a "Back in 5 pickly minutes" sign on her door and went to The Read Mulbury. The interior was dark, and when she tried the door, it was locked. She pushed at it again to make sure.

'Oh, Jasper's gone out.'

Rosemary turned at the voice. Patti stood with arms loaded with garments, apparently on her way to hang them on the racks lining the street. 'Where's he gone?'

'He didn't say.' Patti shook her head so that her apricot-coloured hair bounced neatly on her shoulders. 'Only that he was off for the day with Silkie.'

'Silkie?'

'Yes. Showing her the sights, no doubt. He's such a lovely man. Gerry offered to sit in the bookshop, but Jasper didn't think it mattered today.'

'He said that?'

'Or something like it.' Patti leaned back into Patricia's. 'Gerry, sweetie, come and talk to Rosemary.'

'There's no need-'

But Gerry was there, puffing his way out of the shop with another load. 'Oh, hello, Rosemary. Sorry we didn't make it to dinner last night.' He held his arms up briefly. 'We had all this to do.'

'An order?'

'Oh, hundreds of orders!'

'Not hundreds, Gerry.' Patti finished hanging her load and dabbed a finger on her forehead. 'But lots. The video clips are out, you see, with my garments on the models.'

Rosemary's thoughts were with a certain bookseller who never left his business unattended unless he was sick, so it took a moment to realise Patti meant that the promotional video clips made by director Adelia Lochard and featuring Patti's creations were now public. 'You mean the dress for a male wrestler, a pair of stylish pants for a very short woman, and headgear for a vaudeville singer?'

'That's right! Oh, Gerry, Rosemary remembered!'

'Having a famous documentary maker wanting you to design clothes was pretty memorable.' *Especially,* thought Rosemary, *when Adelia Lochard had taken a liking to Jasper and followed him around.*

'Yes! And the work I've had from the moment they came out! Kelly and Jules are scouting op shops for me, and we've done several moonlight missions along the back roads of Big Town looking for abandoned garments waiting to be transformed into beautiful objects.'

'This is one we found, Rosemary.' Gerry's arms were now empty except for one skirt that resembled a bunch of rags tied together with an iridescent purple band. 'Well, actually, I found it.'

'Yes, you clever man. It was hanging out of the drain and I would have missed it.' Patti leaned forward to give her husband a kiss on the cheek. 'I was too busy looking in the trees.'

Rosemary nodded briefly. Why abandoned garments would hang in trees, and what the final thing was that they had found, were questions she found she had no desire to have answered. Instead, she raised a hand in farewell and turned back to The Preserved Mulbury, glancing once more into the bookshop as she went. Before she could enter the shop, her phone rang. 'Honey,' she said once she'd fished it out of her pocket.

'No, sorry, Rosemary. It's not her. It's me.'

'Ronnie. Why aren't you using your own phone?'

'Oh, well, it fell. Into the dishwasher.'

'And it broke?'

'Well, no, not broken exactly, but it got washed. In the dishwasher.'

'You didn't notice that it had fallen in.'

'No. I'd been looking for it all morning. It must have fallen out of my pocket when I was loading the breakfast plates.'

'So, you're using Honey's.'

'Only to call you. I wouldn't leave her without one, not when Tallulah's so close.'

'Honey is fine?'

'Honey is gorgeous.'

'Yes, Ronnie. But is she well?'

There was a scuffle as the phone scratched along something hard. 'Hi, Mum. Yes, I'm good. Putting the last whisker on a rat.'

'A cake rat.'

'Of course. What else would I be doing?'

Honey's chuckle echoed down the line as the phone scraped its way back to Ronnie. 'Rosemary?'

'Yes, Ronnie?'

'I need to come to Mulbury to try and work out Mrs King's movements on the day of the Gala. You see, she has-'

'Takotsubo cardiomyopathy.'

'Oh. Yes. You know? Well, anyway, she's recovering, but

she's quite fragile. Apparently, she's having trouble remembering what happened that day and she really wants to know.'

'She may never remember.'

'I think that's the issue. She's determined to find out, but she won't say *why* exactly.' Ronnie paused. 'I'm wondering whether she thinks she was set up to get such a fright she'd die of a heart attack and people would inherit her money.'

'Is that likely?'

'Well, she's a trillionaire or something. I suppose there would be people to benefit from her death.'

'She has family.'

'Yes, so maybe one of them wanted to see her off.'

'You'll need to check their financial situation as well as retracing Mrs King's steps. Or wheels, rather.'

'Yeah. I was hoping you might remember who was around that day better than me. I wasn't taking much notice.'

'Between Mrs Lionel and I, we would give you a good idea.'

'Oh, brilliant! Can I come and see you tomorrow? First thing.'

Rosemary thought of the kookaburra. 'I'll be up at dawn.'

'Oh. Well. I won't be that early.'

'Any time, Ronnie.'

'Great, thanks. See you then.'

The phone call ended without Rosemary saying goodbye or hearing Honey do the same. She jangled back into her shop and came face to face with a red-faced and raging Rakisha.

SEVEN

Rakisha wore the same crocheted coat she'd clutched at the Gala, although this time it covered what Rosemary could only deduce was Rakisha's sleeping attire. The white gown dragged along the floorboards as the woman paced the inside of The Preserved Mulbury, leaving a dancing trail of dust motes in her wake. Rosemary frowned. Really, it was so hard to keep dust out of these old buildings despite the amount of cleaning she did and the town's dry, bushy exterior did nothing to help.

'...only.'

Rosemary focused on Rakisha again. The woman had stopped directly under the skylight and stared at Rosemary as if waiting.

'I'm sorry, Rakisha. I momentarily had my thoughts elsewhere. Could you repeat what you'd just said?'

'Darling, I said that she must be told to go! She sits in the middle of *my* living room, meditating to *my* monological chants and lighting *my* hand-coated incense sticks. She's ruining my spiritual ease. Not to mention, darling, the amount she is stealing. But she will listen to her Akita only.'

'Akita.'

'Well, darling, that's what she calls it.' Rakisha gestured frantically at her chest, making her array of thin bangles clash and jangle. 'It's in here, the thing she says *advises* her. The voice in her soul. She calls it Akita after our mother.'

'Your mother's name was Akita.'

'No, darling, that's what she called her cat.' Rakisha shook her head and stamped her foot. 'You don't see, darling, how our family was when Mama was alive. She was the one. The only one.'

'Your mother was bossy.'

'Not bossy, darling, not bossy. *Connected*. Mama connected to the world and its tendrils and roots. She knew things, Mama darling did. Sometimes through Akita but also by listening to the whispers of the wind.'

If Rosemary hadn't been scrutinising Rakisha closely as she talked, it would have been easy to assume that the woman had lost her marbles or had been reading too many of Jasper's high fantasy trilogies. But Rakisha's face was as serious as it could get. *She's stating the facts as she knows it,* thought Rosemary, and felt an unusual wave of tenderness towards the upset woman.

'Rakisha,' she said, 'I don't understand what you're talking about. Perhaps I can help you work this out over a cup of herbal tea.'

Rakisha's arms dropped to her side and her head drooped, spilling a fluff of hair over her face. 'Oh, Rosemary, darling, thank you. I am not hydrated nearly enough to face this today.'

'Come on, then. Before any customers arrive.'

Rosemary herded Rakisha into her living area and gestured to the couch. As Rakisha sank thankfully into its cushions, she spotted Sunny. 'Of course, you have an Akita as well, Rosemary darling.'

'No.' Rosemary put the kettle on and rummaged in her cupboard for her citrus blossom and honey tea. 'I have a Sunny and she does me fine.'

Sunny rose from her bed, stretched, and stalked away to jump lightly onto the windowsill. She blinked at Rosemary. *I have you. Not the other way around.*

Rosemary chuckled as she brought the pot of tea to the coffee table and sat it in front of Rakisha. Now that the other woman was still, Rosemary could see that her face was lined and unhappy, completely different to the animated, painted features that were Rakisha's norm. 'I guessed you were talking about your sister when you said that she should go away.'

Rakisha nodded. 'Silkie, darling. She needs to go...'

Rosemary handed her a mug of sweet-smelling tea. 'Can't you just ask her to leave? It is your house she's staying in.'

'No, darling, I can't.' Rakisha hiccupped as she sipped her tea. 'She is my sister, and we are bound together. She is here and she will stay until her Akita tells her it is time to go.'

'Why is she here? I didn't even know you had a sister.'

Rakisha wriggled her shoulders. 'Sisters, darling, are complex. You don't have one?'

'No.' Rosemary thought of the Hubbard sisters and their intense support for one another. 'Surely sisters aren't always complex.'

'My mother's sister caused her pain. Now Silkie is here, mimicking Aunt Ruthie. It's a family thing, darling. I can't explain.'

Rosemary nodded, not really expecting to understand. 'You said Silkie was stealing from you?'

Rakisha nodded vigorously. 'Silkie steals, yes, constantly.'

Rosemary thought of Rakisha's house with its hand-spun rugs and badly made pottery mugs. 'Do you have much to take, Rakisha? I see you living a... simple life.'

'Yes, darling, simple, but rich. Oh, so rich.' Rakisha sipped noisily. 'My mind is full of the goodness of the earth and the depth of the universe.' She pointed her finger at Rosemary. 'That, darling, is what she steals.'

'The universe?'

Tea slopped down Rakisha's gown as she gestured. '*My* universe, darling! Mine! Silkie does not take material things, but she sucks souls. She uncovers secrets. She stirs the cerebral pot.'

As Rakisha took a long draught of her fortifying drink, Rosemary studied her drawn face. It certainly looked as if something had been taken from the woman in front of her. Without her usual zap, Rakisha looked unremarkable, an empty woman. Rosemary leaned across the couch and tapped Rakisha's leg. 'Well, my friend. You've got to take it all back.'

More tea slopped as Rakisha sat up. 'What do you mean, darling?'

'You say that Silkie is stealing from you? You go right in and take it back.'

'But, darling, it's not that easy...'

'Who said it was going to be easy? Nothing important is easy.'

Quiet fell as Rakisha swished the remains of her tea around her mug, frowning. She straightened once or twice, then fell back into a slouch as if the thoughts that had almost lodged in her head disappeared once more. Finally, she drank her dregs and set the mug down. 'I do hear you, Rosemary darling. I do hear what you say.' She stood, plucking at her gown and the crocheted coat until they both fell heavily about her shoulders. 'I am not brave like you.'

'Bravery comes from facing your fears, Rakisha.' Rosemary stood as well. 'You are a brave person or you wouldn't be in Mulbury today. One day you turned up here, and here you've stayed, making your living and giving back...' Rosemary floundered '...to the Earth.'

'Yes, darling, I know.' Rakisha folded her arms across her chest and tilted her head to one side. Her face, grey and worn when she had first sat down, had gained a tinge of pink and her eyes, usually the colour of rain clouds, had a hint of sunshine in them. She smiled at Rosemary, but it dropped from her face quickly. 'I've just realised why I am here, Rosemary, darling.'

'You need a pot of jam.'

'No, darling, no jam today.' Rakisha's hands went to her hair and unsuccessfully tried to push it away from her face. 'It was to warn you.'

'Right.'

'Yes!' Rakisha stepped away from the couch and waved her hands at the wall. 'About Silkie.'

Rosemary laughed. 'Is Silkie about to steal something from me, too?'

Rakisha shook her head, hair flouncing back over her face. She clawed at it. 'Not *about* to, Rosemary darling. She's already taken it.'

Rosemary automatically looked around the room, but everything was in its place.

Rakisha waved her hands again at the wall behind Rosemary's kitchen area and Rosemary felt a thread of cold steal into her blood. 'What are you trying to say?'

'Silkie,' said Rakisha, suddenly still, 'has taken your Jasper.'

MRS LIONEL WAS PRESSING Patti's cleaned swatches of leftover material when the bus full of senior citizens arrived. She'd set up the ironing board at the back of the shop so she could continue work while they browsed the shelves. A group of about ten ladies came in, making the electronic frog croak in one long continuous stream, and milled about, exclaiming over the handmade goods in the store. Mrs Lionel smiled at Percy as he came to the doorway from her living area wagging his tail, and then retreated in his usual shadowy fashion as a smartly dressed woman approached. 'Hello,' said Mrs Lionel, placing the iron in its holder. 'Can I help you?'

'I am not a regular visitor here,' said the woman in a high, nasal voice.

'Would you like an introduction to the town and its history?'

'No,' said the woman. 'Certainly not.'

Mrs Lionel eyed the woman. She was thin and straight, a bit like one of the older branches of The Exceptional Tree, particularly with the dullness of her skin. 'Perhaps I can assist you with some green cleaning products?'

'Whatever for?'

'To clean.' Mrs Lionel pulled her shoulders back. 'Greenly.'

'No. I don't clean. I have a girl to do that.'

'Well, perhaps you could purchase something for your girl.'

'I am not interested in your quaint little products.'

Inside the house, Mrs Lionel heard Percy growl. She waved a hand at him behind her back. 'Then it seems I cannot help you.' She picked up the iron again.

'I believe you can.' The thin woman stretched out a limp hand and Mrs Lionel put the iron back down and shook it briefly. 'My name is Miss Lianne O'Shannessy. I am a friend of Mrs Caroline King.'

'I am Mrs Dorothea Lionel and I am a friend of Ms Rosemary Exeter.'

Miss O'Shannessy regarded Mrs Lionel sternly for a moment, then laughed once, her face relaxing a little. 'You have spirit.'

'I am not a horse, Miss O'Shannessy.'

'No.' The thin woman folded her hands together. 'You are what my mother used to call a Dover.'

'And what did your mother mean by that?'

'You are someone as strong and straight and as imposing as the white cliffs.'

Mrs Lionel thought for a moment, then nodded. 'I'll take that.'

'Good. Now.' Miss O'Shannessy stepped closer. 'What can you tell me about the incident surrounding Mrs King on Saturday?'

'Nothing.'

Miss O'Shannessy shook her head impatiently. 'You must know something.'

'Even if Mrs King had signed a subpoena, I can't tell you anything. I didn't witness it.'

'But you were here, so the little man from the end shop tells me.'

'Gerry? Yes, we were all here. Mrs King came past, wheeled by her companion.'

'Janet Spinney.' Miss O'Shannessy nodded. 'I've read about her. And then what?'

'She bought soap from my stall.'

'Mrs King?'

'Janet Spinney. A quick purchase before Mrs King directed her across the road.'

'And then?'

'I'm afraid that's where my observation ended.'

Miss O'Shannessy glanced around the shop, but the other ladies bunched together sniffing herbal oils. 'Did Mrs King seem emotional at all?'

'She did not appear to be enjoying her outing.'

Miss O'Shannessy nodded slowly. 'Nothing else? Sad? Angry? Fearful?'

'I don't know Mrs King apart from the occasional media story, so I'm not the person to ask about her personal state.'

Miss O'Shannessy pursed her lips and stepped back, pulling the thin strap of her handbag higher on her shoulder. 'I see.'

'I'm very sorry I wasn't much assistance,' said Mrs Lionel, trying to keep her voice light.

'Well. Thank you.' Miss O'Shannessy turned abruptly. 'Good day.'

Mrs Lionel watched the woman exit and turned her attention to the cheerful crowd of fragrant oil buyers. *Well, Miss O'Shannessy,* she thought as she packed bottles into paper bags, *you asked the wrong Mulburian your nosey questions.*

EIGHT

Rosemary slept little again. Jasper came home late, his front door sighing open after midnight. She listened as he took Snowy out and then went back inside. Silence fell. She lay in her bed, stiff as a dead pharaoh, glad at least that there had been no signs of Silkie in his house. It was a relief when the kookaburra once more heralded the new day.

She spent the first part of the morning sorting out stock in the cellar, trying not to listen for Jasper's movements next door, then waited impatiently for Ronnie. She was at the point of ringing him to establish what time he was arriving when a white station wagon decorated with a large bee pulled up outside The Preserved Mulbury. Ronnie stepped out, his pale, red hair catching in the wind so it stood up in multiple directions. He looked pleased with himself, even more so when he saw Rosemary at the door of the shop. 'What do you think?' he called across the bonnet of the car.

Rosemary came over and studied the car. It was a new-ish model with purple seat covers and a tennis ball on the back seat. 'You have a new car.'

'Well, yes. We had to get one for when Tallulah arrives.

Honey doesn't want her in the old bomb. But what do you think of that?' He walked around to her side and pointed at the bee.

Rosemary crouched to see it better. It was a native bee, blue and black striped, surrounded by writing. *Honey B*, the letter 'o' shaped into tiny cupcakes. 'Right.'

Ronnie's cheerful face subsided. 'You don't like it? It's a surprise for Honey. That's why I was so late getting here.'

'No. I like it.'

'But you don't sound like you like it.'

Rosemary sighed and stood up. 'I like it, Ronnie. Particularly the Australian bee. What I am concerned about is that Honey has started a cake creation business without considering how much work it is when you have a baby to look after.'

'Oh. Do you think it will be too much for her?'

'Nothing is too much for Honey. She's very capable. She will have to judge how many cakes she can do in one week based on how Tallulah is.'

'But I'll help.' Ronnie brushed his unruly hair away from his face. 'I will help her in whatever way I can.'

Rosemary reached out to put a hand on her son-in-law's shoulder. 'I know you will, Ronnie. I trust in that.'

Colour rushed to Ronnie's cheeks in that mottled way it did, leaving his face looking like a topography map.

'But you aren't here only to show me your car.'

'No. No, no.' Ronnie held up his satchel. 'I have work to do.'

'Come in, then. I'll tell you what I know.'

Ronnie went to the jangling door first and held it open for Rosemary before heading for the dining room table. He stooped carefully to stroke Sunny's striped back, opened his satchel, and pulled out his laptop. 'Tea?' asked Rosemary.

'Yes, please. I can read to you what I know while you're making it.' Ronnie paused. 'Sorry. Unless you would like a hand to make it?'

'I'm perfectly capable of making you a pot of tea and perhaps even putting jam on scones while listening to you tell me what's going on.'

'Oh. Okay. Scones? Oh, that would be great. I haven't had much to eat today.'

Rosemary smiled to herself as she uncovered the batch of scones she'd made earlier and set about heaping them with quince jelly. 'First, tell me why you have this investigation and not the police. Besides the excuse that everyone is using, that it's political.'

'Well, yes, the trouble is that it *is* political.' Ronnie leaned back in his chair and stared wide-eyed at Rosemary. 'Mrs King is a great supporter of the police department, apparently. She pays for the local police ball each year in honour of her late husband. They don't want to upset her, only they couldn't help but upset her in this case.'

Rosemary placed a large mug of tea and four buttered-and-jammed scones in front of Ronnie. 'You'll have to explain.'

'Well.' Ronnie consulted his laptop, his hand closing on a scone at the same time. 'Mrs King came to the Mulbury Gala on Saturday and collapsed in front of the historical display. The ambulance took her to the hospital where they investigated the cause and came up with stress cardiomyopathy, a condition triggered by, well, stress.'

'It's also known as Takotsubo cardiomyopathy.'

'Yeah, a condition mainly confined to older women and mimicking the symptoms of angina and other heart conditions.' Ronnie crammed the scone into his mouth. 'Lulily no' atal.'

'Usually not fatal.' Rosemary sat down next to him. 'Mrs Lionel explained.'

Ronnie swallowed. 'So, Mrs King rings up Uncle Geoffrey and demands that he investigate the people responsible for the Gala.'

'Why?'

'Well, then it gets interesting. Uncle Geoffrey couldn't get her to say why, and with nothing to go on, he can't take on the case.'

'Mrs King believes someone who organised the Gala caused her cardiomyopathy? That doesn't make sense.'

'She won't say anything more. Even to me when she hired me.'

'You spoke to Mrs King?'

'No. I wasn't allowed. I spoke to Janet.'

'Her carer? Was it Janet who wouldn't let you speak directly to Mrs King?'

'Janet said it was on orders from Mrs King's family. They think she's been through enough for the moment.'

Rosemary picked up her tea and took a few sips. From the little she'd heard about Mrs King, it seemed unlikely that the family matriarch would let anyone speak for her. 'What family has Mrs King got?'

Ronnie scrolled through his notes, giving him time to eat another scone. 'Twin sons and a daughter, all with partners, and some with children.' He frowned. 'None live anywhere near Mrs King or even the cattle station, which has a property manager. Mrs King has three residences, and she spends her summer in the south on a small property close to Mulbury, and her winter in the north near the coast, and any other time on the station.'

'And her family?'

'The sons are in Europe and the daughter is in Western Australia.'

'Are you saying that none of them are involved in the cattle empire?'

'One son is an actor; the other is an art historian. The daughter is a vet.' Ronnie flicked to another page. 'A small animal veterinarian. There are four granddaughters, too.'

'And yet they stop you, Private Investigator Edwards, from talking to the claimant.'

Ronnie shrugged and relieved the plate of another scone. 'That's what Janet said. The family wants to protect her, I guess, especially when they can't be with her. Still, I thought I'd do what I could on my own before trying again. After all, she is paying me a wage.'

'You're full time on the case.'

'No, I have other jobs as well.' Ronnie blushed again, high points of red on his cheeks matching the colour of the quince jelly. 'And I explained I needed a few hours here and there to help Honey. The cakes, you see. Mrs King was still prepared to employ me. I think Uncle Geoffrey must have made a recommendation.' His face hit scarlet.

'Lucky you.'

'You bet.' He brushed his fingers free of crumbs and started a new page on his document. 'Can you tell me what you saw, Rosemary? That would be a good starting point.'

Rosemary thought back to Saturday and how she'd gone with Gerry to get coffee. 'There were a lot of visitors in the Square.'

'But you saw Mrs King.'

'Yes. Janet had wheeled her across the road and they'd gone to look at the photographic display.'

'Mrs King was lying on her back.'

'The wheelchair was heavily laden so it wouldn't have taken much to overbalance if Mrs King jerked backwards.'

Ronnie sighed. 'She was lucky she didn't split her head open. Do you remember anything else?'

'There were artisan ware stalls, an old gold mining equipment stall, and several photo boards.'

'Photos? Maybe she saw something that shocked her?' Ronnie leaned closer, although they were the only two humans in the room. 'You know, on the photo boards...'

'There was nothing *shocking* on the boards, Ronnie. Not in the sense you mean. The photos, though, could have contained a shock to Mrs King. You could check them. They're in Jasper's shop.' At the thought of Jasper, Rosemary felt a tug in her chest. She kept her face steady.

'Oh, good, I will. What about the people looking after the display?'

'Mrs Lionel kept a record of who was in charge of each stall.'

'Awesome. I'll go and see her first. Jasper's shop is closed.'

'Again?'

Ronnie blinked. 'He's shut up shop before, though?'

'Only when he was sick.'

'It's okay, I'll catch him another time.' Ronnie stood, sliding his chair across the floorboards and making Sunny's ears flatten with the noise. 'I'll see Mrs Lionel. Is it okay to leave my things here?'

'Of course.'

Ronnie picked up a notebook, nodded, and left for The Green Mulbury. As he jangled out the door, the roar of a bus filled the shop momentarily, and Rosemary glimpsed the shadow of it carrying tourists away. She sat on, but no noises came through the wall from Jasper's side.

It was about six o'clock that evening, and Ronnie had long left with his list of stallholders, before the scrape of a key and the low sigh from a heavy door being pushed open told her that Jasper had arrived home. Rosemary was in the shop area, rearranging jars and dusting shelves that hadn't needed rearranging or dusting. She let him have ten minutes to himself, then headed out.

The front door to The Read Mulbury was unlocked. She pushed it open a little. 'Jasper?'

A light laugh echoed from the kitchen. Rosemary hesitated, then let herself into the shop. *Don't do this,* she warned herself, then ignored her advice completely and headed for Jasper's living quarters. Snowy's dark, snoring form was on the couch.

'Jasper?' she said again from its doorway.

Snowy grunted. The laughter stopped. Jasper appeared, hooking hair behind one ear. A smile warmed his face. He saw Rosemary, and the smile faded. 'Rosemary.'

'Sorry to let myself in. I just wanted to see that you were alright.'

He looked at her blankly.

'You've been away two days in a row.' The words sounded lame among the warmth of his lounge room, and she felt a slight blush on her cheeks.

'I'm alright.'

She studied him. Despite his unusually emotionless face, he did seem alright. His posture was straight and his cheeks were ruddy. Compared to how he was when he was recovering from his pneumonia or how he went when he discussed the rotten curse or, indeed, how he was when he was worried about Snowy, he looked positively glowing.

'Jasper?' said a voice behind him. A woman came into view, a slight, blonde-headed woman with a curious look in her enormous indigo-coloured eyes. Rosemary immediately thought of Miss Middleton, Jasper's favourite fictional heroine. 'Oh, hello.'

Jasper made a movement as if to shoo the woman back into the room.

'Okay, I get it.' She moved out of sight.

'Right,' said Rosemary.

'Yes,' said Jasper.

Rosemary turned without another word and headed back to The Preserved Mulbury, where Sunny was waiting with an alert, knowing expression. 'Not a word, Sunny,' said Rosemary, slamming a pot on the stove. 'Not a word.'

Sunny's tail tip rose and fell silently. *I never do say anything,* it implied.

NINE

Hannah Hubbard loaded the wheelbarrow with three pallets and made her way carefully across the road and up the hill to the mayoral residence. 'Not that it is that anymore,' she said to Heather, who skipped beside her.

'What, Han Han Hanny?' said Heather, shaking her head so that her long curls settled down her back.

Hannah grunted as she pushed up the last metre and turned into Robert Sparkling's new abode. 'This house needs a new name besides what we've been calling it for years.'

'I'll ask the ravens,' said Heather, whirling down the path to the front door. 'They've been here forever.'

'You do that.' Hannah let the wheelbarrow down with a thunk. 'This what you want, boss?'

The door had opened at Heather's first knock and Robert peered down at the sisters. 'That's great, Hannah,' he said, brushing his hair with his hand and making clouds of plaster dust float like a halo around his head. 'Don't call me boss, though. That reminds me of my father. We all called him boss instead of dad.'

'Why?' asked Hannah, coming to join him as he went back inside.

'It suited him.' Robert did a cutting motion with his hand as if he didn't want to talk about it anymore.

'Oh look,' said Heather, as they entered the huge central room of the building. 'Snow!'

The room was draped with painters' sheets and thick with settled dust. Hannah's feet left prints on the floor as she traipsed over to stand in the middle to look up at the plaster rose in the ceiling's centre. It stretched out to almost halfway across, a mass of flowers and gum leaves and what looked like blobs of stiff, opaque porridge. Robert came to stand with her, arms crossed, gazing up as well.

'What is that?' Hannah pointed at the mysterious blobs.

'I think they're meant to be gold nuggets.' Robert let his gaze drop to Heather, who danced around the room, creating puffs of white around her.

'That mayor was obsessed.' Hannah turned to Heather. 'Stop that now. This isn't snow and you're making everything go cloudy.'

Heather laughed and danced right out of the room into the rear of the building.

'Yes, obsessed and a bit too grand for my liking.' Robert smiled after Heather, then lifted his arms to show the size of the room. 'This was meant to be a ballroom, but by the time he'd built it, no one wanted to dance.'

'Except Heather.'

'If she'd been around back then, she could have had the entire room to herself.' Robert rubbed more dust from his hair. 'What am I going to do with a room this size?'

'Indoor tennis? No, badminton? No, wait.' Hannah poked her finger in Robert's arm. 'A theatre room for Mulburians!'

'The acoustics are terrible because of the ceiling.' Robert shrugged. 'Too high. Or the room is too big. I'd have to put carpet on the walls.'

'Yuk,' said Hannah. 'Oh well, maybe you can just stick your armchair in the middle and pretend you're the king or something.'

'I think I'll settle for an armchair in a room that's slightly smaller. This building has sixteen bedrooms, two kitchens and one bathroom.'

'Awkward.'

'I'm turning them into eight bedrooms, one kitchen and three bathrooms.'

'Better.'

He sighed. 'For one person.'

'You never know,' said Hannah, grinning. 'Your family might grow.'

A shout from the back made them turn as one and run. Heather was in the first kitchen, another vast room, this one with a long wooden table running down the centre and a disused fireplace at one end. She stood on the table with her arms wrapped around herself. 'What is it, Heather?' said Robert. 'Don't tell me you're scared of mice?'

'Heather scared of mice? No way.' Hannah stretched her hand out to her sister. 'What's going on, Heather?'

Heather stood still, head slightly cocked to one side. Shock drained from her face and was replaced by a broad smile. 'Look, Hannah.' She let one arm go and pointed along the table. 'See?'

'No. See what?' Hannah clambered up beside her sister and followed the line of her finger. 'I can see the table, the wall. Oh, and Robert's biscuit barrel.'

Heather shook her head impatiently. 'No, there!'

Hannah closed one eye and used Heather's straightened arm like a set of sights. 'Nope. Nothing there but those biscuits.'

Heather shook her head impatiently and lowered her arm. She refused the offer of help to get off the table and sat down cross-legged. 'She'll be alright,' said Hannah at Robert's concerned face. 'I'm only ever worried about Heather when she stops talking...' Her voice softened and disappeared.

To his credit, Robert let it go, walking back to the ballroom after sliding the biscuit barrel within reach of Heather, and Hannah didn't have to tell him about those terrible times when Heather slipped into her own world and left everyone else behind. She patted her sister's knee. 'Yell if you want me,' she said, as Heather absent-mindedly opened the barrel and pulled out several biscuits.

Back in the ballroom, Robert was once again gazing at the ceiling.

'What do you want the pallets for?' said Hannah.

'I thought I'd make boxes out of them.' He sighed. 'The more I delve into each room, the more things I find that I can't bear to throw out. I've kept everything, right down to lumps of wood and metal. I thought that if I could store them for another day, I'd be able to sort through them sensibly.'

'Okay. Where do you want me to take the pallets, then?'

'Dump them out of the wheelbarrow where they are and I'll sort them later.'

Hannah nodded, moving her gaze from the room with its achingly empty space to the broad staircase next to the kitchen door. 'This house has been here all my life, boarded up and mysterious. We used to call it the Castle until we found out what actual castles look like.'

'Would you like a tour?'

'Would I? Oh yeah!'

'Come on, then.'

Robert led the way to the stairs. They wound up in a tighter spiral than Hannah thought they would, as if the mayor wanted to keep his upstairs rooms a secret. At the top of the landing, a wide corridor stretched out in front of them, ending in a window that overlooked the town.

'More rooms here,' said Robert, pointing to each as they walked toward the window. 'Eight of them, four on each side, with the bathroom behind the stairs.'

Hannah peered into each room as they went, noting their drab walls and dusty floors. 'But where do you-'

They reached the end of the corridor. While Hannah had thought the window had been the only destination, she now saw that the corridor opened to a wide, airy space with two more windows—one on either side—letting sunlight flood in to light up the enormous bed at one end and a white couch with matching armchairs at the other. The room had been finished with paint of the palest blue, and the plaster rose overhead was elegantly pointed with mauve flowers and not a sign of any lumpy plaster nuggets.

'Oh. Wow!'

'Thanks,' said Robert. 'I think it's come up well.'

Hannah chuckled. 'So, you own one of the biggest homes in a two-hundred-kilometre radius and you choose to live in a space hardly bigger than our shed's office?'

Robert thought for a moment. 'Yes.'

'And when you do up the rest? What then?'

Robert shrugged and indicated the rooms behind them. 'I'll knock down some walls and double the room size up here. One will be an office; one will be a spare bedroom. I'll make one into a library snug, full of books and comfortable armchairs. The last one will do as a new bathroom.'

'You're going to keep your bed in here?'

'Yes. I like the light coming in.'

'And it's okay to just pull down walls wherever you want to.'

'Only if it's structurally sound and, luckily for me, only the façade of the building has any historical worth. Architecturally, anyhow, because the mayor didn't know his Georgian from his Victorian. The history of the place is much more worthy.'

'What do you mean?'

'Well, the mayor finished it in 1906, which was the year-'

'-the gold rush finished here.'

'Yes, no more gold to be found, not when you had to dig for it by hand. The town began to die, so the mayor's ideas of opulence and grandeur were too late. He lived here, but not happily.'

Hannah looked around. 'Didn't he die in here?'

'Lots of people died at home back then. He died downstairs in the front room from tuberculosis, followed tragically by the rest of the family. Apparently, the mother died in another room, and her six children in each of the others.'

'Erk,' said Hannah. 'Who would want to live in it then?'

'Exactly. It stayed in the extended family for decades, but nobody related to the mayor wanted to live here. They let it out to various people, apparently, then they sold it in the 1950s to Mr Panifax, who owned the sweet shop. He lived upstairs like I do and kept the bottom rooms locked up. Then the bushfires came. Mr Panifax was an old, old man by then and, in turn for a bit of care for himself, he let the bottom of the building be turned into a makeshift hospital and refuge centre for those affected by the fires. Once that crisis was over, they shifted him to an old folks' home and he died soon after. The place was boarded up until I came along. I bought it from a Panifax who'd inherited it somewhere along the line.' Robert sighed again. 'I guess they thought it would cost too much to get it liveable again.'

Hannah cast a sideways look at him. She knew money was no object to Robert Sparkling, but the state the house was in shocked her. 'You sure you want to do this?'

Robert smiled at her. 'You think I'm crazy, don't you?'

'Yeah, I do.' She waved her arms at the dilapidated rooms they'd walked past. 'They're wrecked! You could buy a really nice house in Big Town or the city or just about anywhere and you choose this?'

He hesitated. 'Well, I think you've got me there.'

'What do you mean?'

'You're right. This is a *choice*.' He grinned at her. 'I already have a really nice house in the city, but I lease it. I like Mulbury. It suits me.'

Hannah shook her head. 'You're confirming to me how mad you really are.'

'Does it worry you that you have a crazy boss?'

'No. You couldn't be worse than Holly when she gets going.'

Robert laughed and led Hannah down the corridor to the stairs. The handrail was cool under Hannah's fingers, and its smoothness was comforting, as if she could feel how steady and strong it had been for the occupants of the house over many years. As they descended, she let her other hand brush the walls and, although they were cobwebby and streaked with shredded wallpaper, it was easy to imagine the attraction of such a solid building.

Robert halted suddenly, jolting Hannah out of her reverie. 'Who's that?'

The soft sound of voices drifted up the stairs. They

crept down the rest of the way until Hannah recognised one. 'It's Heather.'

'Who is she with?'

'Holly, maybe?'

But when they entered the kitchen, Heather seemed alone, still roosted on the table.

'Heather,' said Hannah slowly. 'Who were you talking to?'

As Heather turned to her sister, Silkie popped up from where she'd been crouching on the floor. She stretched her arms up and put her head back before saying loudly, 'I feel you! I feel you, lost souls and unhappy wretches!'

TEN

Rosemary hadn't seen Rakisha since she'd left The Preserved Mulbury on Tuesday in a whirl of coloured crochet, clutching a pot of lemon balm jelly. Across the road, The Sweet Potato's lights were on and tourists wandered in. They usually came out swiftly again, as if the inside of the lit shop and its dull brown contents were too much. Rosemary was washing the exterior of her windows with Mrs Lionel's sweet-smelling glass cleaner, half an eye on The Read Mulbury, when first Silkie, then Rakisha, burst out of the cafe, making a family eating ice-cream cones in the Square jump so quickly the youngest member lost her vanilla. Over the howls of the little girl, Rosemary heard Silkie shriek, 'My Akita tells me!'

'You're a fraud, Silkie!' Rakisha screamed back. 'You don't have an Akita. Only Mama did! You twist words for your use. You've come back here as a hoodwinker and...'

But whatever else Silkie was disappeared with the sisters as they hurled around the corner of The Sweet Potato.

'Good heavens,' Mrs Lionel said as she stepped out of

her croaking door. 'I can hear Rakisha screaming from inside.'

'Yes. So can half the town.'

'Well, they make quite a sight.'

The family in the Square had turned to watch the pair as they went, apparently hypnotised by the flowing layers of purple, yellow and blue billowing behind them topped, in Rakisha's case, by a cloud of long, wispy grey ringlets, and in Silkie's, a sheath of smooth darkness. They'd also caught the attention of a new arrival, a young man who'd stepped from a blue sedan dressed in a neat white shirt and grey trousers. He shook his head at the retreating sisters and walked hesitatingly over to Mulbury Feeds.

'Doesn't look like he's buying dog food,' remarked Mrs Lionel, watching him disappear into the produce shed.

Rosemary frowned. The young man looked familiar, but his identity escaped her.

'You've been very quiet, dear.'

Mrs Lionel's calm voice took Rosemary's attention away from the young man. When she looked at her friend, she saw a depth of concern that took her by surprise. 'I'm usually quiet.'

'Busy, yes. Quiet, no.' Mrs Lionel stepped from her doorway and walked past Rosemary to the corner of The Read Mulbury. 'I don't hear you chatting with Jasper.'

'Do you normally?'

'Oh, yes, dear. Through my wall or from the back porch. Your voices form the background of my life, especially in the evenings.'

'Jasper was away.'

'But now he's back.'

Rosemary hesitated. 'He has a friend with him.'

'Oh?' When Rosemary said nothing, Mrs Lionel went

to peer in the window of The Read Mulbury. 'Do you mean the blonde woman sitting on one of Jasper's reading chairs?'

It took much restraint for Rosemary not to move. 'I've only seen her once. She is blonde.'

'Well, who is she?'

'They did not introduce me.'

'Did you introduce yourself?'

'No.'

'Well, then.'

'I wasn't welcome to introduce myself.'

Mrs Lionel came back to her friend. 'Peevishness doesn't suit you, dear.' She put a hand on Rosemary's arm. 'Go in now and make her acquaintance.'

Rosemary was saved from doing anything by the reappearance of Rakisha in The Square, looking around wildly. She spotted Mrs Lionel and Rosemary and waved frantically. 'Darling, darling, over here!'

'Which darling do you think she means?' asked Rosemary.

Mrs Lionel shook her head. 'We both fit the bill. Come on.'

They hurried across the road, but Rakisha turned and fled before them, back in the direction she'd come from.

'Goodness,' said Mrs Lionel, puffing slightly. 'That woman can run when she has to.'

Rosemary slowed to keep pace with her friend, but kept her eyes on Rakisha. The running woman turned into Robert Sparkling's home and disappeared inside.

'Maybe Robert's having a party.' Rosemary gestured behind them. 'Here come more guests.'

Holly Hubbard was sprinting up the hill, her hair coming loose from its ponytail, followed closely by the young man in the neat outfit. She paused as she reached

Mrs Lionel and held up her phone. 'It's Heather. Hannah called me.'

'Is she hurt? What's happened?'

Holly shook her head and bolted past. 'No, she's perfectly happy. That's just it...' She turned as well and entered the old building.

Mrs Lionel slowed and put her hand to her chest, panting more rapidly now. The young man who'd been pursuing Holly drew level with her and stopped. 'Are you alright, ma'am?'

Mrs Lionel nodded and waved his attention away. 'Yes. Yes. Too fast...'

'I'll see that everything is okay.' The young man nodded to Rosemary and took off after Holly.

Mrs Lionel took a deep breath in and let it out through pursed lips. 'Righto, I'm better now. But who on earth is that fellow?'

Rosemary looped her arm through Mrs Lionel's. 'I recognise him now. He was with Geoffrey when they came to talk to Robert about Mrs King's incident. A constable called Christopher.'

'The police?' Mrs Lionel hurried forward, towing Rosemary with her. 'What do they want with Heather?'

They mounted the steps to the front door and let themselves in. 'I don't think it's Heather that man is after,' said Rosemary as they went down the hall and entered the ballroom.

Mrs Lionel turned to her, but the bellowing from the next room drowned out any further queries.

'Silkie darling, this is... well, it's... absurd, darling. Just absurd!'

Rosemary and Mrs Lionel entered the kitchen to find Heather sitting on the long wooden table that took up its centre, Hannah underneath the table searching for some-thing, Robert leaning back against the old stove with his arms crossed, Holly and the young man bent over watching Hannah, and Rakisha shrieking at her sister, who stood with her arms held away from her body, palms up, underneath the window.

'There is no absurdity,' said Silkie, eyes closed. 'There is only the *feeling*.'

'Anything we can do to help?' said Rosemary mildly.

'Yes, darling, yes.' Rakisha stormed over to Rosemary and whispered loudly, 'She steals, darling. Now it's darling Heather.'

Heather sat serenely, cross-legged and smiling.

'She doesn't look stolen,' said Rosemary.

Rakisha shook herself irritably. 'Not her physical pres-ence, darling. Silkie is after her...' She thumped her chest twice.

'Nope,' said Hannah, crawling out from under the table and standing up. 'There is nothing in this room but us humans.' She started as she saw the others. 'Bit of a crowd now.'

'You rang me, Han,' said Holly, pulling the last of her hair from its ponytail. 'I was worried about Heather.'

'Holly Hol Hol,' said Heather, pointing down the length of the table. 'See?'

'*That's* what I'm talking about.' Hannah ran her hand through her short hair. 'Now she's seeing things.'

'Not seeing *things*,' said Silkie, pausing dramatically and surveying the room. 'She sees *them*.'

'Who?' said Holly. 'Us?'

'Not the living.' Silkie swept her hand, still palm up, in a wide half-circle. 'The others.'

'Oh, crumbs,' said Hannah. 'You think Heather can see ghosts.'

'A crude term,' said Silkie. She let her hand settle on her chest. 'Akita says lost souls.'

'She's lying,' hissed Rakisha, her face a dangerous shade of purple. 'We were talking about the Sparky house, how it was a hospital for the injured of Scarlet Tuesday. She knows people died in here, darlings. Her Akita did not tell her anything! I told her.' She staggered sideways.

The young man caught her before she fell. 'You'd better sit down,' he said, steering Rakisha to a chair. 'You don't look well.'

'Who *are* you?' asked Hannah, staring at the young man with her hands on her hips.

'Hannah,' said Holly, frowning. 'This is... well, I don't know.' She blushed.

'Christopher,' said Rosemary.

Christopher looked up and smiled. 'Only the boss calls me that. I'm Toffee.' He grinned sheepishly, making him seem much younger. 'Well, that's my nickname. It came from my little sister.'

'Great,' said Hannah without smiling. 'Hello, Toffee. What are you doing here?'

Toffee's complexion was a shade deeper than Holly's, but his blush was just as prominent. 'I was...'

'At the shed,' finished Holly. 'When you rang.'

Hannah narrowed her eyes, but Heather laughed, catching everyone's attention. 'See?' she said again.

'No, Heather, we can't.' Hannah tugged at her sister's arm. 'Come down off there and we'll go home. Haven't you got a bird to stuff?'

Heather slid gracefully from the table and smiled at Hannah. 'Wattle bird. Poor thing.'

'Yeah, well, you'll make him beautiful again.' She jerked her head at Holly. 'Coming?'

Holly nodded and followed her sisters from the kitchen. Toffee checked Rakisha.

'We'll look after her, dear,' said Mrs Lionel, placing the back of her hand on Rakisha's forehead. 'We're good at that. Thank you.'

Toffee nodded and strode after the Hubbards.

'Enlighten us, Robert,' said Rosemary. 'What have you got going on here?'

Robert pushed himself away from the bench. 'I'm just a fellow trying to renovate his house.'

'Right.'

He grinned. 'It seems quite a few people have a strong interest in what I'm doing.'

Rakisha fanned herself with the edge of her shawl. 'It's a *home*, darling. Not a house. *House* is so cold.'

'That's correct.' Robert squatted next to her chair. 'I don't have any earth-friendly coffee, but would you like an organic hot chocolate? You'd feel better afterwards.'

Rakisha clutched at his hand, tangling the shawl around them both. 'Thank you, darling. Thank you. I'm normally quite fine, you know. It's just...' She tugged her hand free and shook it at her sister.

'Silkie,' said Mrs Lionel. 'Would you like some tea?'

Silkie turned her head slowly to gaze at Mrs Lionel. 'Tea? I thought this man said chocolate.'

'Tea,' said Mrs Lionel firmly. 'At my place. Robert can entertain Rakisha here. At his place.'

Silkie regarded the older woman haughtily, making Rosemary stir. 'Great idea, Mrs Lionel,' Rosemary said. 'Let's go.'

Robert turned his back on Silkie to prepare Rakisha's

drink, leaving Silkie standing alone and looking, Rosemary thought, quite ridiculous in her coloured layers against the old, rendered wall of the regal house. Perhaps Silkie felt it as well, for she studied Rosemary for a moment before walking sedately to the doorway and out into the ballroom where Mrs Lionel was waiting.

'Thanks,' said Rosemary to Robert, who lifted his head to smile at her but said nothing.

Mrs Lionel had completely recovered from the race up the hill and walked so briskly back to The Green Mulbury that Silkie had to lift her skirts and hurry to keep up. Rosemary kept a pace behind, sensing that Mrs Lionel was on a mission and that Silkie was its target. When they got to the shop, Mrs Lionel opened the croaking door and ushered Silkie inside. 'Not you, Rosemary,' she said over the incessant croaking of the electronic frog. 'I'll let you know how I get on.'

Rosemary tapped the side of her nose. 'Good luck.'

'Oh no,' said Mrs Lionel. 'Luck has nothing to do with it when *my* Akita gets going.' She smiled and disappeared inside.

Rosemary chuckled and turned to head back to The Preserved Mulbury. The heavy door of The Read Mulbury heaved open as she reached her shop, and the little blonde woman came out, laughing uproariously, with Jasper in her wake. He spotted Rosemary, as did the woman, who gave Jasper a little shove in her direction.

For a moment, Rosemary thought he was coming towards her. He swayed but didn't move. There was a look on his face that she'd never seen before, a mixture of hurt and sadness. She waited, but he stayed where he was, chewing his lip and stiffening against the escalating number of pokes in the back he received from the blonde woman.

Finally, he straightened, turned, and went back into the shop, leaving the blonde woman by herself on the pavement. She took a step towards Rosemary, but Jasper's arm shot out of the doorway and caught hers, pulling her back.

Over the noise of the blonde woman's protest, Rosemary entered The Preserved Mulbury. Sunshine angled through the skylight, picking out the rich colours of the jellies that in turn reflected on the wooden shelves they sat on. The floorboards were warm and inviting, and Sunny curled on her side in the middle of the floor. But Rosemary felt a chill run through her and adjusted her jacket so that it snuggled into her neck. She frowned. Whatever was going on with Jasper had to stop, and if he wouldn't talk to her, there was another way to get to him.

'Feel like entertaining, Sunny?' she said as she stooped to stroke the cat's ears.

Sunny rolled over and stretched. *No,* she seemed to say, *but when has that ever stopped you?*

ELEVEN

Thursday night passed too quietly, even for Rosemary Exeter. She could hear the murmur of Mrs Lionel talking to Silkie well into the evening on one side of the dividing wall, and the occasional muffled laugh from Jasper's side. The shops under the veranda on Goldmarket Road were joined by a double brick wall at the front, but at the back, where living quarters had been added on here and there over the decades, the walls were single brick with plaster, much less soundproof. The familiar noises of her neighbours hardly bothered Rosemary normally, but they seemed irritatingly obscure that night, and she went to bed feeling prickly.

Mrs Lionel knocked on the door early on Friday morning. Rosemary let her in, a piece of toast in one hand. 'Lovely,' said the older woman, plucking breakfast from Rosemary and taking a bite even as she walked through to the kitchen. 'I'm very hungry.'

'Clearly.' Rosemary followed. 'Would you like some more?'

'Clearly.' Mrs Lionel smiled as she settled at the dining table. 'Silkie ate me out of house and home last night. She said that when her Akita was activated, she became ravenous.'

'You talked to her about her Akita?'

'Among other things. I was trying to get to the bottom of why she's in Mulbury.'

'To see her sister?'

'Not obviously.'

'Well, then?'

Mrs Lionel waited until a pot of tea and more toast were on the table. She helped herself to a slice, spreading it thickly with jumbleberry jam. 'Silkie hasn't seen her sister for five years, since their mother died. Not, she says, because she didn't want to see Rakisha but because her calling was elsewhere.'

'Right.'

'Silkie's calling took her to Europe, then Scandinavia, then Asia.'

'She's been around.'

'She was looking for fellow *sensitives*.'

Rosemary took the last toast slice and added honey from Justin's farm. 'That's what you said she is.'

'Well, that's because that's what Silkie tells her sister. Rakisha lets me know bits and pieces of her life, often spontaneously. She blurts things out and I think she sometimes regrets it.'

'Did she regret telling you Silkie was a sensitive?'

'Hard to know. She certainly didn't want to talk much about it, only I think she found me...'

'Kind, no doubt. She told the right person.'

'Perhaps.' Mrs Lionel sighed and took up her teacup. 'I don't judge. The older I get, the more I realise the things I know nothing about. Who am I to say that Silkie *isn't* a sensitive?'

'Rakisha doesn't believe her.'

Mrs Lionel set her cup down gently. 'It may not be a matter of believing. It could be envy.'

Rosemary sat back. 'Rakisha is jealous of her sister?'

'Well, dear, people are often jealous of their siblings. We always think they received preferential treatment from our parents, or they were gifted with the more intelligent genes, or had the lucky breaks in life. It's quite a natural thing.'

'I wouldn't know.'

'No. You'll have to take my word for it.'

Rosemary leaned forward, her elbows on the table. 'I cannot imagine you being envious of anyone.'

'Ah.' Mrs Lionel's blue eyes were bright. 'I am only human, after all.'

'What else did Silkie say?'

'She travelled the world to grow her abilities, to make herself *more* sensitive, as it were.'

'She thinks she's some sort of seer.'

'Well, not a *seer* exactly, but a reader of souls. It's her Akita.'

'Rakisha definitely believes Silkie doesn't have an Akita.'

'That seems to be the case. Apparently, their mother was a very astute woman and could read people as if she held one of Jasper's books. The mother always talked about listening to Akita.'

'Akita the cat.'

'Yes. The cat. Apparently, the cat was an excellent judge of character.'

They both turned to look at Sunny, who sat on her windowsill, a majestic orange figure, her tail wrapped neatly around her body. 'I can understand,' said Rosemary.

'I thought you would.' Mrs Lionel sipped her tea. 'Oh, lovely. I feel much better now I have something in my stomach.'

'Did she say anything else?'

'Silkie said lots of things, especially about her travels. She met with extraordinary people, so it seems, but perhaps none so wonderful as her mother.'

'It sounds like her travels were a reaction to her mother's death.'

Mrs Lionel nodded. 'I think so, too. And now she's back and has come to see Rakisha.' The older woman frowned suddenly. 'Apart from visiting her sister for pure family reasons, she seems to have another motive.'

'What motive?'

'Well, you see, I couldn't work that out.'

They sat in silence for a moment. Rosemary watched Sunny as the ginger tabby's eyes closed and she tucked her head into her chest. Even asleep, Sunny's presence was welcome: companionly and solid. It was hard to imagine life without her and, frankly, Rosemary didn't want to. She pushed her plate away and folded her hands together on the table. 'What happened to Akita?'

'Akita?'

'Yes. If the mother had Akita when Silkie and Rakisha were girls, surely she'd be long dead.'

'Oh, yes.'

'But Rakisha talks of her mother's cat as if it had been her mother's confidante for ever.'

'It probably had. Cats can live for a long time. I had a friend whose cat was twenty-four before it died. Rakisha possibly only meant her mother talked to it during the time it was alive.'

'I know someone who talks to their beloved pet even though he's been dead for quite some time.'

Mrs Lionel automatically looked at the floor, as if Percy was lying under the table. She caught Rosemary's smile. 'Some of us are lucky to have a friend forever, even in a delicate form.'

'Silkie said nothing to you about that last night?'

'About seeing Percy?' Mrs Lionel shook her head. 'She didn't notice him, although he was right there, keeping guard.'

'Not much of a sensitive, is she?'

'Who are we to know, Rosemary? Maybe she isn't sensitive to dogs.'

Rosemary leaned back again, stretching her hands over her head and sighing. 'It is certainly a world I know nothing about.' She let her arms drop. 'Changing the subject, but I thought I'd have a get together tomorrow evening.'

'A get together.' Mrs Lionel's eyes narrowed. 'What for?'

Rosemary stood and busied herself with removing the plates from the table. 'Well...' She glanced at the calendar hanging on the kitchen wall. 'It's the vernal equinox.'

'I see. Have you ever celebrated the spring equinox before?'

'No. No, I haven't.' Rosemary came back to the table to pick up the jam. 'I thought I might from this year forward.'

'I see,' said Mrs Lionel again, plainly not seeing. 'We're having our normal Monday dinner in a few days.'

'Monday is not the equinox.'

'No.' Mrs Lionel stood to take her teacup to the sink. 'But you could wait to check on Jasper's friend on Monday.'

Rosemary gave the jam jar lid an extra twist. 'Who said anything about Jasper's friend?'

'No one, dear. That's the point. Why don't you go into the shop and talk to Jasper?'

'I tried.'

'You tried *once*, I believe.'

'*You* could go in and ask who she is.'

Mrs Lionel took the teapot and placed it on the kitchen bench. 'I could, but I'm not going to. This is your mission.'

'It's not a mission.'

'It's becoming one.' Mrs Lionel's face softened, and she put a gentle hand on Rosemary's arm. 'I'm not sure what's happened between you two, but I see that it's worrying you.'

'I'm not worried.'

'Alright.' Mrs Lionel removed her hand. 'Agitated, then. Doesn't matter what I call it. You don't like Jasper not being the friend he always is.'

'I can cope.'

'No, you can't.'

Rosemary scowled. '*You* make me agitated.'

Mrs Lionel grinned. 'Excellent, because that's my role. *Agitator.*' She put her hands in her cardigan pockets and immediately pulled them out again. 'Oh, I almost forgot. I brought this in to show you.' She held out a torn-out news-paper page.

Rosemary took the aged paper. 'What is it?'

'Something I kept from years ago. If you turn it over, there's a recipe for apricot pie on the back, so I think that's why I had it. But look at the front.'

Rosemary tipped the page toward the light streaming in through the window in order to better see. A blurred black-and-white picture of a woman dressed in a smart tweed suit sat next to the text. 'That's Mrs King.'

'Yes. The recently widowed Mrs King, so I imagine that the newspaper was from about fifty years ago.'

'Her husband dies and the papers write it up?'

'Mad Morgan King was a very well-known cattle breeder and quite an aristocrat. Everyone called him King, as if he was.'

Rosemary scanned the article. 'He died of snakebite.'

'Yes, nasty. They think a brown snake bit him while he was checking the fences, but he kept working instead of coming straight back home. Or maybe he had no way of contacting anyone.' Mrs Lionel shrugged sadly. 'Very limited ways of communication back then. He was an older man and had smoked all his life. By the time they found him, he was in great respiratory distress and died before the flying doctor could get to him.'

'That left Mrs King with three little children.'

'And a cattle empire. Everyone expected her to sell up and move back to the city whence she came.'

'She didn't.'

'No. Mrs Caroline King never did what was expected, at least not in the time that I've known about her.'

'Good on her.'

'Oh, yes, dear. She is one to look up to. Such a shame her body has given out on her like it has. No doubt old injuries catching up on her, although she's slightly younger than me by a year or two. She's worked very hard in her time, mustering and feeding out and fencing. I found it hard enough working with my dairy cows and I had an entire team of farm hands. She would have had them as well, but it was worth her while to keep on top of things. People try to dupe women in traditionally men's business, or they certainly did back then.'

'You were never duped.'

'I didn't have to run my own farm. My husband had a good business head.'

Rosemary thought of Alasdair and tried instantly to forget him and his failed shoe-making business. 'Lucky you.' She handed the article back, but Mrs Lionel put it on the table.

'Keep it for Ronnie. A bit of background for him.' She turned to go, rubbing her hip and making Rosemary think that perhaps her friend was carrying one or two old injuries as well. 'Will I bring my chicken and leek pies?'

'Pies?'

'For your evening soiree, dear. Remember the equinox?' Mrs Lionel chuckled and left the shop without waiting for an answer.

TWELVE

The vernal equinox it may have been, but nothing about Saturday was remotely spring-like. Rosemary shivered as she stood at the window looking out onto Goldmarket Square. Rain belted the gravel and made the pointed gum leaves of The Exceptional Tree droop heavily. No one was out and about, not even Rakisha, who often wandered around in the rain to drench herself in nature's moisturiser, or so she had explained to Rosemary one wet winter day. Lights blazed in Mullings of Mulbury as Kelly served a group of miserable tourists who'd been caught out. Rosemary saw their radiant smiles as Kelly delivered hot drinks and sweet slices. 'Using my jam,' she muttered.

Sunny jumped up on the window ledge beside her, stepping elegantly over the display of dried herbs from The Green Mulbury and gingham picnic napkins from Patricia's. The shops under the veranda often exhibited each other's products, usually themed. Some of Jasper's second-hand garden books completed the look, with one on botanic gardens nestling artfully among the napkins.

A car pulled up outside The Preserved Mulbury,

splashing water onto the pavement from the flowing gutter. For a moment, Rosemary didn't recognise it, then the blue striped bee caught her attention. She pulled her jangling door open and held it so that Honey and Ronnie could run straight in.

'Oh, it's really warm in here,' said Honey, peeling off her coat straight away.

'It's comfortable,' said Rosemary, giving her daughter a hug.

'For you, maybe.' Honey smoothed her top over her belly and gave it a rueful pat. 'I'm always too hot these days.'

'It's because you're cooking a baby,' said Ronnie, shaking the water from his hair in a movement that reminded Rosemary of Cuddles, the Golden Retriever.

'Ha ha.' Honey headed for Rosemary's living area. 'I'm putting the kettle on. We've had an eventful morning.'

Rosemary raised an eyebrow in her son-in-law's direction, but Ronnie only shrugged. 'I dropped a cake.' His face burned. 'A unicorn landed on its head. Luckily, Honey had a spare hippo.' He smiled suddenly. 'Honestly, Rosemary, she is so clever! Can you imagine turning a hippo into a horned horse in less than twenty minutes?'

'No, I can't,' said Rosemary, but immediately understood Honey's beeline for a pot of tea.

'I can't stay,' said Ronnie, hitching his satchel up on his shoulder. 'I'm going to look at the photo boards at Jasper's. You know, I'm still on the case.'

'I know.' Rosemary hesitated, but grabbed Ronnie's arm as he was leaving. 'Can you remind Jasper about this evening? He hasn't replied to my text.'

'Yeah, of course. I bet he's been too busy.' Ronnie waved and left for The Read Mulbury.

Rosemary frowned. *Too busy, my-*

'Mum,' said Honey from the kitchen. 'What on earth are these?'

Rosemary entered her living quarters, where a slow fire warmed the room. 'They're Rakisha's nut drops.'

Honey poked at the heap of dull grey biscuits. 'Okay, what's a nut drop?'

'I'm not sure exactly, but Rakisha said they were excellent for your skin.'

'Do you eat them or spread them on your face?'

'Both?'

Honey sat down heavily and breathed out through pursed lips, rubbing her belly as she did. Rosemary watched in some concern until Honey's face softened. 'Braxton Hicks contractions?'

'Yep.' Honey shifted around in her chair. 'It's like having your insides squeezed. A warning about what's to happen, I guess.'

Rosemary said nothing but prepared the teapot and put it on the table in front of her daughter.

'Only six days to go, Mum.'

'If Tallulah's on time.'

'Yeah, so roughly six days to go.' Honey took Rosemary's hand. 'Do you think I'll be alright? As a mother, I mean?'

Rosemary sat down next to her. 'Yes, I do.'

'I'll do the best I can, even if it's not perfect.'

'And that's how I know you'll be okay. People who expect to be perfect mothers are severely disappointed.'

'Thanks, Mum.' Honey sipped her tea. 'Ahhhh. Better already.'

The shop door opened, its bell jangling furiously. Rosemary stood, giving Honey's hand a last squeeze before letting it go, and found Ronnie in the centre of the shop carrying a large photo board. 'Sorry, Rosemary,' he panted, spying her over the top of his luggage. 'Jasper said they'd be better in here.'

'Take them right through. I'll get one.'

'It's okay. Jasper's coming.'

Rosemary turned quickly. Another photo board worked its way into the shop, Jasper's head clearly visible over the top. He kept his gaze on the end of the board to stop it ramming a shelf and only saw Rosemary as he put it down to rest. 'Hello, Jasper,' she said.

He opened his mouth to say something but closed it before words came out. Strands of hair had worked their way over his face, but she saw how it blazed an uncomfortable crimson. His gaze flickered across her, through to Ronnie re-emerging from the living area, and back to Rosemary.

'Hey, thanks, Jasper,' said Ronnie, easing the board from the taller man. 'Only one more?'

Jasper nodded.

'I'll get it,' said Rosemary.

'No.'

It felt to Rosemary that, in the few days since she'd heard his voice, she'd forgotten the gentle timbre of it, the way its tone settled comfortably on her ears. She paused, waiting for more, but he just shook his head. 'I can lift it,' she said.

He put his hand up. 'No,' he said again, and this time she heard a hint of regret staining its pitch. She watched as he jangled out the door and battled the briskness of the day back to the bookshop.

Ronnie came into the shop, whistling as he went, and followed Jasper's footsteps. It was no surprise to Rosemary that it was Ronnie who carried the third and last board in by himself. She closed the door behind him. Outside, rain sprayed the windows deep under the veranda, making her view blur.

Back inside, Ronnie had set the boards along the back of the couch, forming a wall of photographs. Honey stood with her arm around her husband, contemplating the pictures. 'These are the ones found in Gerry's cellar?' she asked as Rosemary joined them. 'The ones he reckoned were saved from the Scarlet Tuesday fires?'

'Yes,' said Rosemary. 'A valuable find.'

'But what would they have to do with Mrs King?' said Ronnie. 'Why would they cause her to almost have a heart attack?'

'Cardiomyopathy is not a heart attack, dear.'

Rosemary swivelled to see Mrs Lionel standing in the entrance, her gaze glued to the photographs. 'You crept in.'

'Luckily I didn't steal your till.' Mrs Lionel stepped closer. 'I know how to keep your bell from jangling too loudly, Rosemary Exeter.'

'I wish I knew how to quieten your frog without unplugging him.'

'He's an excellent alarm.' Mrs Lionel tapped a photograph with a gnarly finger. 'There are our shops as they used to be.'

'Mrs Lionel,' said Ronnie. 'You know stuff. Is there anything here that would shock Mrs King?'

Mrs Lionel glanced at Ronnie and went back to looking steadily at each photo. 'Well, even if I know stuff...' she gave him a quick smile '... I'm not sure I know stuff enough about Mrs King. But let me see.' She touched each photograph. 'Gerry put these up, didn't he? They're quite random. There are pictures of the past year's Gala next to photographs of mine shafts. It makes it hard to see what's going on.'

'We could sort them,' said Honey. 'You could help us put them into rough decades, Mrs Lionel.'

'Yes, I could start now and then take them home to finish.' Mrs Lionel turned to Honey. 'I'm sorry, dear. How rude of me not to say hello or ask you how you're getting on. The photographs took me back.'

'That's okay, Mrs Lionel.' Honey rubbed her belly again. 'I'm as good as I can be at this stage. A little tireder, plenty of false contractions, lots of indigestion.'

'All quite normal, then.'

'So they say.' Honey approached the nearest board and pulled the tack from a photo. 'How about I pull them off and you put them in an order?'

'How about I get the bottom ones and you get the top ones?' said Rosemary.

'Ronnie can do the bottom ones.' Honey grinned at her mother. 'Haven't you got a party to prepare for?'

'The vernal equinox party,' said Mrs Lionel solemnly, not looking at her friend.

'Oh,' said Ronnie as he crouched at Honey's feet to unpin the lower photographs. 'I forgot to tell you Jasper said he was coming along tonight.'

Rosemary went to the kitchen feeling ridiculously lighter. In between serving one customer, making lunch for her extended family, and arranging nut drops and other more delicious nibbles onto platters, she allowed herself the fantasy of Jasper walking in with his normal smile and starting a conversation about Regency romances or old dogs or anything, really. Anything that meant he was talking to her again.

Mulbury continued to defy the day by becoming more wintery by the hour. The odd tourist that drove in slowed but kept going through the town and out the other side, perhaps hoping that it would be better weather in the next little town. Mrs Lionel shut The Green Mulbury mid-afternoon, clearly happy to be in Rosemary's warm living room sorting photographs. Honey went to have a rest and re-entered the room an hour later, looking much revitalised. Ronnie helped Rosemary shift furniture so that people could stand and mingle or sit and chat as they wanted. Sunny watched the action from her windowsill until Rosemary fed her a chicken dinner. After eating, the cat stalked purposefully away and disappeared into Rosemary's bedroom. *Don't expect me to entertain your friends,* she seemed to say as her upright tail went around the corner.

Robert was the first guest to arrive, Heather in tow. She chatted brightly to him as he came into the room, her blonde cascade of hair catching the glow of the fire and creating a light corona around her head. She spotted Mrs Lionel and left Robert, winding her arm through the older woman's and resting her head on Mrs Lionel's shoulder. Rosemary noted the hug Mrs Lionel gave her young friend, and the smile that lit her face.

'Heather is very fond of Mrs Lionel,' said Robert, taking the glass Rosemary offered. 'Although, I know no one who *isn't* fond of Mrs Lionel.'

'She's been like a grandmother to those girls since their mother died,' said Rosemary.

'Yes.' Robert dipped his head closer to Rosemary's ear. 'Has Heather... well, has she shown any signs of... does she talk...'

'Spit it out, Sparkling,' said Rosemary. 'Does she talk to her stuffed birds? Does she talk to live animals? Does she talk to the clouds?'

'Does she talk to *ghosts*?'

Rosemary sipped her drink thoughtfully. 'Heather is, on

the whole, a really happy person. In fact, since her sisters stopped fighting with their father, I haven't seen her so content in quite a while. I can't tell you whether she talks to ghosts, but I imagine that, if it was possible, then it would be Heather who could do it.'

'I see.' Robert drank noisily, then lowered his cup to watch something over Rosemary's shoulder. 'This should be interesting,' he said, pointing at the door.

Silkie swept into the room dressed in a deep purple velvet gown. She raised her hands at the small crowd and smiled benevolently. 'It is time,' she said. 'It will reveal all.'

THIRTEEN

It would have been a most dramatic entrance, but Rakisha appeared behind Silkie and shoved her in the back. 'Get out of the way, darling,' Rakisha said. 'This is heavy enough without you being in the way.'

Ronnie hurried over to rescue Rakisha, who was struggling to carry a wooden box into the room. He took it from her and carried it into the centre of the room where Silkie was tugging at the sleeves of her gown, trying to rearrange herself. A section of her long, dark hair had flown over to the other side of her head, giving her appearance a slightly lopsided look.

Amid the chaos, Jasper slipped into the room alone. Rosemary tried to catch his eye, but he seemed transfixed by the sight of Rakisha bending over, her layers of satin and crochet and cotton slipping around her middle, to open the box. 'This is why I brought it, darlings,' said Rakisha, tugging at the lid. 'It's stuck, sealed by the passing of time, and Mama's wish that her daughters could live in harmony.' She threw a jagged look at Silkie.

'I can help you,' said Robert, pulling a putty knife from

his pocket and running it under the edge. 'That should-' He took an involuntary step back as the lid flipped open, letting the stench of naphthalene burst out and filter through the room.

'Here it is, darlings,' said Rakisha, straightening so quickly she knocked into Ronnie. 'Mother's Akita.'

Rosemary flinched, imagining a taxidermized cat. Although she could tolerate, and even admire, Heather Hubbard's beautifully preserved birds, a cat was out of the question. It wasn't an animal, though. Instead, Rakisha held a leather-bound book.

'That is not Akita.' Silkie snatched at the book, but Rakisha was quicker and held it out of reach. 'That's...'

'Oh, yes, Silkie darling. Mother's journal.'

Silkie ran her hand through her hair to straighten it, resuming the appearance of a figure from another realm. 'The words of my mother will reveal...' she turned her gaze to Robert '... the gift.'

Everyone else looked at Robert, too, even Patti and Gerry as they joined the party. Patti's eyes were wide, but whether at the sight of the two grand dames in the middle of Rosemary's living room or at the dishevelled state of Gerry, Rosemary couldn't tell.

'Goodness, Gerry,' said Mrs Lionel, noticing Gerry and moving away from Heather. 'What on earth has happened?'

'I'll get you a chair,' said Jasper, lifting one away from the wall and putting his hand on Gerry's shoulder to steer him into it.

'He's alright,' said Patti, her hands flapping. 'I asked him and he says he's alright. He just wouldn't stop when I told him, and then he remembered we were coming here, and he dashed away when I said it wouldn't matter if we were late.' She appealed to Rosemary. 'Would it, Rosemary?'

'Not at all.'

'And you wouldn't be offended if we couldn't have come at all, would you, Rosemary?'

'No. Jules and Roman are busy with the restaurant, Kelly's gone to see her mother, and Franco is baking. It's not a compulsory party.'

'See, Gerry?' Patti bounced nervously. 'You could have stayed home and rested.'

Mrs Lionel pulled a chair up to sit next to the silent Gerry, whose glazed stare was still on Robert. 'Now, what's this, Gerald Yale? You should have listened to your wife. You look terrible.'

Gerry slowly looked to Mrs Lionel. 'Tired,' he mumbled.

'Do you have pain anywhere?'

'No.'

'What's he been doing, Patti?' said Mrs Lionel sharply.

'We're so busy.' Patti wrung her hands. 'We've been up nearly all night. Gerry's packed boxes and shifted them to the cellar because there's no room in the shop. I bought extra racks and they hardly fit. The kitchen table is covered with buttons and the bedroom floor with woollen jumpers and the spare bedroom is, well, not spare at all.' She let out a sob. 'And Gerry isn't as young as he was and look! I've nearly killed him.'

'Has he eaten today?'

Patti shook her head. 'No, he hasn't. He made me sand-wiches, but he said he was too busy-'

'Rosemary,' said Mrs Lionel. 'Get a fruit juice for Gerry and something decent to eat.' She waved her hand dismis-sively at the plate of nut drops.

'I have a leftover casserole in the fridge.'

'Yes. A plate of that.'

The room was quiet as Rosemary heated casserole while Mrs Lionel made Gerry sip orange juice. Some colour came back into his face, and the daze faded from his eyes. By the time he'd eaten half the bowl of casserole, he looked almost like the jolly Gerry that Rosemary had always known. 'Sorry,' he said, when he could take in the semi-circle of faces around him. 'I think I was a little over-stretched.' He gave a little chuckle.

Tension left the air, and guests started chatting among themselves again. Heather joined Rakisha at the box and, one by one, objects appeared and were stacked on the floor until a pile of material, feathers and jars of stones built up. Rosemary noted how Rakisha kept the journal tucked in her lap as she sat cross-legged on the floor next to Heather. Silkie crouched down, peering closely at everything that came out but not holding out her hand to take anything.

'Gerry,' said Mrs Lionel quietly, 'you really must do something about the business. It's getting away from you.'

'I know.' Gerry glanced at Patti, but Robert had taken her aside to make her eat something as well.

'You need an assistant,' Rosemary said, taking Gerry's empty bowl and replacing it with a plate of chocolate slice. 'You make enough money.'

'Well, we do now. For the first time, Patricia's is running at a decent profit.' Gerry gazed at his wife. 'She's so clever.'

'She won't be so clever if she has to look after you.'

'Rosemary...' said Mrs Lionel.

'It's true. No point in having a bespoke garment creation service if the bespoke part has to be put on a shelf to tend to Gerry's breakdowns.'

'Ruthlessly said, as always.' Gerry munched on the chocolate slice for a moment. 'I don't think we could hire just anyone, though, could we? They'd need to understand

Patti's genius and let her run with it. We can't have anyone bossy or grumpy. It'll be hard to find someone to suit.'

'Not as hard as you think,' said Rosemary, removing his empty plate.

'You have someone in mind for us?'

'You need to find that person yourself, Gerry.'

Gerry's face was more alert than Rosemary had seen it for some time. 'But you know someone! That means I probably know someone as well. Oh, I'll talk to Patti and we'll think about it. Thank you, Rosemary.'

Rosemary took his plate to the kitchen, shaking her head. A movement in the shadow of the open pantry door startled her. 'Jasper,' she said. 'What are you doing?'

'Waiting for you.'

For a brief second, Rosemary thought it was all over, that Jasper was his usual self with that barely disguised desire to be more than friends. Then he folded his arms and stared at her without a trace of warmth.

'I need to ask you a favour.'

'Right.' Rosemary put Gerry's plate into the dishwasher and stood straight. 'Ask away.'

'I'm going to the city on Monday.' He paused, but she said nothing. 'The shop will be shut, but I'm getting an order delivered that I couldn't change.' His eyes brightened. 'It's a box of Sanderson fantasies, special editions with hand-drawn maps. They were selling at auction...' He stopped, blinked, and seemed to remember who he was talking to. 'Well, anyway, they're very precious and I don't want them left on the doorstep. Can I give the delivery people your number?'

'Your visitor has gone?'

'Yes. I... She left this morning.'

Rosemary waited, but his lips were tight. 'Give them my number.'

He nodded for so long, his long hair fell forward over his shoulders and he dropped his clenched arms to scoop it back. 'I don't know what time I'll be back.'

'I'll put the box in your shop. I have a key.'

'Okay. Well, perhaps you could also let Snowy out? I usually take him with me if I go to Big Town, but the city is too far.'

'Of course. Anything else?'

'No, that's enough.'

It was enough in many ways. The conversation had left him looking exhausted, and he slunk backwards, hitting the pantry door, and walked out into the crowd, rubbing his shoulder.

Rosemary stayed where she was until Jasper was embedded in a conversation with Ronnie and then went around the room offering to refill glasses. Hannah appeared and made a beeline for a platter of food, her short hair ruffled and untidy. Rosemary handed her a full glass.

'Thanks, Rosemary.' She drank half of it in one go.

'Busy day.'

'I'll say.' Hannah shoved a whole mini leek and chicken pie in her mouth and held a finger up until she'd swallowed. 'You wouldn't guess how well the gardening side of things is going! Robert's going to buy a forklift for us. We've been doing internet searches on them.'

'Is that where Holly is now?'

Hannah scowled and took two more pies from the platter. 'No. She said she wanted to stay home tonight. She's been really weird.'

Rosemary thought of Hannah's older sister. Holly was

the sensible one of the trio of sisters, level-headed and seri-ous. 'Has she been alright since your father left?'

'Yeah, she's fine. I think, like me, she was happy to have him out of the way. Don't get me wrong. We love him. He's just better with his muse and his guitar sitting under a palm tree strumming to the fish. You know.'

Rosemary didn't feel like she knew such an existence at all, but she could imagine Richard Hubbard on a beach doing just as Hannah said. 'Do you think Holly has regrets about staying on in the business?'

'I don't know that, either.' Hannah drank the rest of her drink and held her glass out for Rosemary to refill. 'She works just as hard as she always has. Harder, in fact. She burrows down in the office and comes into the house right at dinnertime. And then there's the trips to Big Town.'

'The supermarket is in Big Town.'

'Well, yeah, we all have to go there on a fairly regular basis, but she's driven there twice already this week. Petrol, you know? It's costly.'

'That's not what's worrying you.'

Hannah paused in her attempt to put two more pies into her mouth at once. 'How do you...?' Her voice dropped to a whisper. 'You're right. I'm afraid she's going to leave us. She once said she would if Dad didn't sell us the business, and he didn't. Maybe she'll move away from Mulbury.'

Rosemary waited until Hannah had chewed thought-fully on her pies and swallowed them. 'Maybe she will.'

'That's not what I wanted you to say.'

'I know. But, Hannah, lives change. Sometimes suddenly.'

Hannah stared at her. 'Like yours did.'

'Like mine when Alasdair went. Like Mrs Lionel when

Mr Lionel died. Like Rakisha's when Mulbury was the end of the line for her.'

'You're saying that I need to go with the flow?'

'I'm not saying that at all because I know how hard it is. But understand this, Hannah Hubbard: you will always have the love of your family and that's what matters.'

Hannah's eyes, the colour of an autumn sky as were her sisters', welled suddenly, but she blinked the moisture away. 'Yes,' she said. 'I know.'

'Good.' Rosemary patted the younger woman firmly on the back. 'Now go and see what Rakisha is doing with Heather.'

Mrs Lionel wandered over to where Rosemary stood watching the two pairs of sisters crouching on the floor among the items from the box. 'What do you think she's up to?' Mrs Lionel said.

'Which one?'

'Rakisha.'

Rosemary frowned. 'I thought you'd say Silkie.'

'Well, her, as well. But why did Rakisha bring her mother's things to this party?'

'Honouring the equinox?'

'Honouring something else, I would think. Look how she's hiding that journal.'

Rakisha had wrapped the journal in her skirts. 'Not hiding,' said Rosemary. 'More like protecting. Silkie wants it badly.'

'Yes.'

As if she'd overheard the two women talking, Silkie snatched at the journal, pulling at Rakisha's various layers as she did. There was a scuffle, a blur of fabric, and then Silkie was on her feet with the journal held above her head.

'Give that back,' hissed Rakisha, scrambling up.

'No. It isn't yours.'

'It isn't yours either, darling.' Rakisha jumped to grab the journal, but Silkie's height kept it out of reach.

'Then neither of us can lay claim.'

'Which means both of us can.'

The sisters glared at each other.

Rosemary glanced around the room. It had quietened again. *More entertainment within these four walls than we've had since Jasper uncovered the skeleton in his backyard,* she thought.

'I've an idea, dear,' said Mrs Lionel, coming over to stand in between the sisters. 'I could keep the journal safe. I'm neutral territory. You can have it back once you work out a civil solution.'

Rakisha continued to stare at Silkie. 'Darling Mrs Lionel is right, Silkie. She could hold it for the moment.'

'But it should be tonight that all is revealed,' said Silkie, her arms sagging a little with the prolonged weight of the journal.

'Rubbish, darling. It's just that you think you need an audience to hear what's in that journal.'

Silkie's voice dropped dangerously. 'We both know what's in that journal.'

'You've already read it?' asked Mrs Lionel.

Rakisha shook her head. 'No, darling. That's just it. We haven't.'

Silkie's trembling arms lowered further. In a flick, Mrs Lionel had the journal and hugged it to her chest. 'There,' she said. 'I'll mind it for the evening and you can both come for morning tea tomorrow and look at the book together.'

For a moment, Rosemary thought that Silkie might harm Mrs Lionel, such was the darkness that crossed her face. She stepped forward. 'Steady.'

Silkie leaned back and rolled her shoulders. 'Alright then, green cleaning woman. Tomorrow.' She stalked from the room.

'Yes, darling. Tomorrow.' Rakisha gathered the various items from the box, dropped them in, and closed the lid. As she carried it away, Rosemary glimpsed determination on her face. It was one thing to face Rakisha at her happiest, but completely another when she was on a mission.

'I feel for Rakisha,' said Rosemary to Mrs Lionel, who was tucking the journal into her handbag.

'No need.' Mrs Lionel zipped her bag shut. 'It's Silkie who's in trouble.'

'You've read that journal?'

'No. But I can guess what's in it.' And that was all Mrs Lionel would say for the rest of the night.

FOURTEEN

It had been a lovely and unexpectedly lively evening, but it ended without Rosemary having further conversation with Jasper. His behaviour, she thought, was like a waterfowl: coming forward to eat and chat, and then slinking back into the shadows of the room. *He was wary,* she thought. *Of me?*

Sunny regarded her mistress balefully as Rosemary went around the room the next morning, picking up stray glasses and plumping the couch cushions. *Something's got your goat,* she seemed to say.

'I'm fine,' said Rosemary, whacking a cushion harder than necessary.

Sunny's tail twitched, and she stroked her whiskers with a delicate paw.

The morning was bright once again, but the temperature remained cool. Rosemary had customers the moment she opened, from a packed car of old friends who split to head into all the shops under the veranda at the same time. She held the door open to let two women in. 'Hello,' she said.

One woman went straight to the chutney shelf and

started picking off jars. The other stopped just inside and eyed Rosemary. She clutched a large but expensive bag, holding it to her chest as if either wanting to keep it close or was on the verge of showing Rosemary something. The woman cleared her throat. 'I have been next door to see that other woman.'

Rosemary frowned. 'Mrs Lionel?'

'Yes. I believe she's told me her name. Spirited woman.'

'That's one way to describe her.'

'Hmph. Anyway, she's busy.'

Rosemary folded her arms. 'Right.'

'You may be able to help me.'

Rosemary waited.

The woman tapped her fingers on her bag. 'I am Miss O'Shannessy.'

'I am Rosemary Exeter.'

'Ah. That other woman mentioned you the last time I saw her.'

'Right.'

'Yes. Now. Can you help me?'

'If you tell me what it is you need help with, I can try.'

'Hmph.' Miss O'Shannessy lowered her bag and unclipped the top. 'I am hoping you could tell me about this photograph.'

Rosemary took what the woman held out and studied it. Two young women looked back at her, their shoulders touching. The tiny picture had clearly been cut from another bigger one, as there were fuzzy parts of others standing next to them. The women looked grim. The one on the left had a twist of long hair over her shoulder, while the second's hair was shoulder length and styled into an uneven bob. It must have been cold. They wore thick coats, the first with it buttoned to the neck and the second with it open, displaying a heavy necklace that disappeared into the vee. A brick building was behind them with the edge of a solid door showing. 'I don't know these women.'

'I didn't expect you to, but can you recognise where they were standing?'

'No.'

'Oh.' Miss O'Shannessy leaned over Rosemary, standing so close that a waft of classic perfume tickled Rosemary's nose. 'Anything strike you?'

'They look sad.'

'Yes.' Miss O'Shannessy tugged the photo back and slipped her reading glasses on. 'And you're sure you don't recognise where they were? It's somewhere in Mulbury.'

'If I had the whole photograph, I might.'

'This is the only section I have.' The older woman sighed.

'Is there a reason you wanted to know about the photograph?'

'I'm having trouble remembering where it was taken.'

'Is it you?'

'Yes.' Miss O'Shannessy tapped the young woman on the left. 'That's me.'

'Perhaps the other person in the photo could tell you.'

'I've lost touch with her.' Miss O'Shannessy tucked the picture into her bag again. 'That's my problem these days. Losing touch, in many ways.' She clipped her bag shut. 'Thank you for trying.'

Rosemary went back to her counter to serve the other woman, who was in raptures about some jars of pickled olives. Miss O'Shannessy stood at the window, staring out at Goldmarket Square, her handbag to her chest again as if it was a living thing. She startled when her friend rushed up to her chatting loudly about kalamatas, and they went out the door together. Miss O'Shannessy indicated the Square, and they crossed the road.

There wasn't a chance to catch up with Mrs Lionel until the women from the car had settled themselves in the sunshine outside Franco's Patisserie to eat pies. Rosemary ducked out of The Preserved Mulbury into The Green Mulbury, shutting the door quickly to silence the frog. The shop was empty. 'Are you there?' she called.

'Hang on.'

Mrs Lionel appeared a moment later, struggling with a crate. Rosemary hurried to take it off her just before it slipped to the floor. 'Got it.'

'Good timing, dear.' Mrs Lionel nursed her hands. 'I couldn't hold it.'

'You shouldn't even be trying.'

'Perhaps.' Mrs Lionel spread her gnarly red fingers out. 'I keep hoping they'll strengthen up, but they only get weaker.'

'Ronnie can help you with the heavy things, as can I.'

'I know. You're both very kind. It's just...' Mrs Lionel clenched her fists and pumped them up and down. 'It's very frustrating! All I want to do is carry a silly crate.'

Rosemary tucked the crate onto one hip and used her free hand to pat her friend's shoulder. 'I can see you're frustrated. But if it was one of us, you'd be saying the same thing that I'm saying to you. Do what you can safely and let others carry the weight for you.'

Mrs Lionel frowned. 'I do wish you weren't so sensible sometimes, Rosemary Exeter.'

'I learned it from the best. Now.' Rosemary shifted the crate to both hands. 'Where is this going?'

As they worked together to restock laundry liquid, Rosemary told Mrs Lionel the story of Miss O'Shannessy's photograph. 'I wonder what she was really wanting,' the older woman said.

'I don't think she knew.'

'She told me she was a friend of Mrs King's.'

'She didn't mention Mrs King.' Rosemary put the last bottle in place and picked up the empty crate. 'Where will this go?'

'I can take it.'

'Yes, but I have it. Where will it go?'

Mrs Lionel grunted but led Rosemary into her living quarters and indicated the laundry. 'In there. And you might as well have a cuppa now you're here.'

Rosemary smiled, disposed of the crate, and sat at the little table where the photographs from the picture boards were stacked neatly in piles. 'Got these sorted?'

'As best as I can,' said Mrs Lionel over the singing of the kettle. 'It's very rough. Interesting, though.' She carried a tray of cups to the table, ignoring Rosemary's hasty attempt to help. 'I know we've looked through these before, but Robert wasn't here when Gerry discovered them. I've found a few of the mayoral residence that he might like to see to help with his renovations.'

'He'll like that.' Rosemary carefully dragged a pile toward her. 'Where are they?'

'Scattered throughout the decades, so they're in different stacks.'

'Anything useful for Ronnie?'

'Nothing obvious.' Mrs Lionel carried the teapot over, then sat with a sigh. 'But then it wouldn't be obvious, would it? Otherwise, Mrs King wouldn't be asking for an investigation.'

Rosemary swirled the pot absently. 'I'm not sure why she wants one.'

'Something shocked her badly.'

'Yes. I'm suspecting that she knows more than she's letting on but wants to see what Ronnie comes up with. It's like he's been given a puzzle with several pieces missing.'

'Well, dear, that's where you come in.'

'Meaning?'

'You are an excellent jigsaw dissectologist. And a bit of an enigmatologist. This puzzle will suit you well.'

'Thanks for the confidence.'

'You're welcome.' Mrs Lionel held her cup out. 'Are you going to continue to swirl or will you finally get around to pouring something?'

Rosemary still had the sweet tang of bergamot about her when she returned to her shop. There were enough customers to keep her occupied, but in between the browsing and the buying, she did more internet searching on Mrs Caroline King. There was hardly any mention of her life before marrying the cattle magnate except for where and when she was born, and the school she went to, brief though that was. After Mr King's untimely death, the media coverage of the family increased with Mrs King named business owner of the year for several years running. Her wealth was remarkable, but she remained taciturn in articles, and only discussed livestock and the weather. They were topics of immense importance to a cattle station owner but not to the average city-dwelling Australian. There was one cover story in an elegant fashion magazine, featuring Mrs King wearing a smart jacket emblazoned with her own four-arched leafy logo, while the rest were reserved for journals such as *Cattle Weekly*.

Late in the day, as Rosemary pulled the blinds down over her windows before settling in with Sunny for the evening, Holly Hubbard walked past. She was moving slowly; her phone glued to her ear. Although she had a slight smile on her face, her arm was tight across her body. She turned and saw Rosemary watching, and gave her a nod, walking faster so that she disappeared from view. Rosemary went back inside, stopping to pick Sunny up. 'What will happen to the Hubbard sisters if Holly leaves?' she murmured to the cat.

Sunny tucked her head under Rosemary's chin and purred. *What you said,* she seemed to say. *Nothing stays the same.*

FIFTEEN

Rosemary was still in bed when she heard the door to The Read Mulbury close. It was the heaviest door along the veranda, cut out of local hardwood decades ago, and had a distinctive thud as it locked. She waited and could just make out the gentle roar of Jasper's old Rover as he pulled away from the kerb. She stayed still until any sound of him completely disappeared, then slid reluctantly from her warm bed and padded to the kitchen.

Sleep had not come easily, and when it arrived, she'd had an old dream. Alasdair rarely entered her thoughts these days unless she was reminded of his defection, but he'd been there in her dream. He was in his workshop with a shoe on the bench and had put it down and walked away. This time, though, the shoe had not been blood-red but a dark tan, the same shade as Jasper's loafers.

And Robert Sparkling's boots.

The man himself walked into the shop right at lunchtime and caught Rosemary scoffing a very large slice of quiche. In the pause that followed while she tried not to choke, she noticed his feet clad in well-made leather work boots.

'Are you alright?' Robert asked, as she waved her hand at him.

She swallowed. 'Yes. All good. Now…?'

'Sorry to disturb you…' Robert said with a grin that suggested he wasn't at all. 'But did you have a key to Jasper's shop?'

'Yes. Why?'

'Well, I took a delivery of silicon sealer this morning and the truck driver left something for Jasper by mistake.'

'They were meant to ring me.' Rosemary dabbed her finger at her lips, checking for crumbs. 'Jasper asked them to.'

'Oh, sorry. The driver had the box in the house before he realised the problem, so I said that I'd deliver it. I didn't realise Jasper was away.'

'He's in the city for the day.'

'Okay, how come?'

'If he wanted you to know, I'm sure he would have said.'

Robert's face warmed slightly, giving his cheeks a healthy glow. 'Sorry.'

Rosemary shrugged. 'He asked me to look out for this box. It has precious fantasies in it.'

Robert's eyebrows shot up. 'Oh?'

'*Novels*. Fantasy *novels*.'

'Got it.' Robert turned away, but she saw his grin. 'I've left the box outside. Can we put it in his shop now? Don't want any precious fantasies to go missing.'

He held the door open for her and Rosemary walked through without looking at him. She'd already been in The Read Mulbury once that day to shift Snowy from his couch and coax him outside for a moment, but it had been a hurried visit as a group of loud croquet players had stopped at her shop on their way to a special tournament. As she opened the door this time, she was suddenly conscious of the musky darkness of the unlit room and the peace that lived among the books.

'Where do you think I should put it?' Robert asked quietly, as if he, too, found The Read Mulbury slightly reverential.

'On the table in the lounge room.'

Rosemary led the way. Snowy thumped his tail at them as they entered, and she ran her hand down his grey-speckled back. He sighed happily as he pushed himself up to sitting, then flopped down from the couch to the floor. 'I'll take him outside,' she said.

'Okay. I'll wait for you.'

Snowy took his time limping down the stairs and out into Jasper's neglected backyard. Gardening was not something Jasper was remotely interested in, much to Mrs Lionel's disgust. Rosemary waited while Snowy did a bit of exploring in the spring grass, then helped him back up the steps inside. 'Sorry,' she said to Robert, who leaned against the porch railing to watch. 'He takes his time.'

'As he should. He's an old boy.'

'Yes. Old and spoiled.'

Robert nodded. 'Oh, to be old and spoiled. Or just spoiled, actually.'

'And you aren't?'

He eyed her thoughtfully. 'No, I'm rich. It's not the same thing.'

It was the first time that Robert Sparkling had admitted to his wealth in front of her. Anyone realised who knew the town, but he was very low key about it. 'What are you saying?'

He smiled, dipping his head. 'Nothing, really. A bit of self-pity.'

'You're lonely.'

He raised his head. 'Aren't you? I mean...' He gestured behind him. 'There are a lot of single people in this town.'

'Doesn't mean that they're lonely.'

'Alone. Lonely. Sometimes it's the same thing.'

'And sometimes it isn't.'

'You're a cool one, Rosemary Exeter.'

'Is that a bad thing?'

'I don't know.' He smiled. 'It's how you are, so I guess it can't be.'

'You've only been in Mulbury for a short time,' she said, putting her hand briefly on his. 'You won't find it lonely after a while.'

'I'll take your word for that.'

She turned back to the house, avoiding his gaze, but stopped. 'Rich people stick together, don't they?'

'Pardon?'

'The Sparklings. Your family. Did they have anything to do with the Kings?'

'The cattle Kings?' Robert frowned. 'I don't remember them, but I was a shy lad, as you know. I often went and hid when we had visitors to the house.'

'Where did you hide?'

'Oh. You know. Here and there.'

'This was when you lived in March?'

'Yes. Where *you* lived. And Alasdair.' He watched her anxiously.

She shook her head. 'Yes. We did. I know there are few hiding spots in March.'

'There are if you need them.'

'Which I didn't.'

'Lucky you.'

'Your father might have known the Kings.'

'It's possible.'

She waited.

'You want me to ask?'

'Yes.'

'Why?'

'Background information. It never hurts.'

'Well, sorry, but I can't. My father and I aren't...'

'Compatible?'

'Speaking.'

She shrugged. 'Don't do it, then. I don't want to cause you any distress.'

He said nothing as they entered the house. Rosemary saw the old dog settled on the couch and walked back into the shop. Robert was behind her, but his footsteps stopped.

'Found a book?' she asked as she looked back at him.

He had his hand on one shelf but wasn't studying its contents. Instead, he had fixed his gaze on her.

'What is it?'

'The library,' he said.

'The library?'

'I hid in the library at school.'

'When visitors came to the house, you went back to school to hide?'

'No. Not for that. At lunchtimes. Books were my haven. All those stories to escape into.'

'You needed to escape?'

'Clearly, you didn't.' He wiped a hand across his forehead. 'The things that come at you out of the blue.'

'Are you alright?'

He slapped his hands to his side. 'Yep, all good. Will we go?'

Rosemary said nothing, but as she locked The Read Mulbury up, Robert standing a little away from her, she glimpsed his sad face. She tapped his arm. 'Mrs Lionel has something for you.'

'Oh? Soap?'

'No, although she would be more than pleased to give you some.' Rosemary walked toward her shop. 'She's been sorting the photographs Gerry had on display for the Gala and she found some of your house.'

'Really? That's great! They'll help with the renovation.'

'That's what Mrs Lionel thought.'

'I'll go and see her now.' He smiled. 'If she's not having lunch.'

Rosemary nodded and turned into The Preserved Mulbury while Robert went on to The Green Mulbury. The frog croaked gleefully until he closed the door.

Rosemary spent time straightening produce and thinking about what Robert had said at Jasper's. She would never have guessed he was lonely. Perhaps, if he'd hidden in the library as much as he said he had, he'd always been lonely? Robert was so busy with the garage during the day and the house renovations at night and on the weekends that she'd supposed he had no time to feel much at all. Part of her wondered why, if he knew loneliness was going to be an issue in moving to a small town, he had moved here at all.

The noise of the jangling door cut her musings short. Patti almost fell in, the weight in the box she carried tipping her forward as she stepped up. Rosemary caught the box and together they slid it onto the floor.

'Oh, I'm so sorry, Rosemary!' Patti stood up and checked her hair, smoothing a strand back into her shoulder length wave. 'I was heading for Jasper's, but then I remembered he was in the city today and besides, I think we've filled him up. Then I thought maybe Rosemary will help? Please?'

'Help with what?'

'Storage.' Patti stooped and patted the box. 'We're spilling out all over the place. Gerry keeps tripping over orders that I've lined up in the kitchen. Jasper's cellar is so full he can hardly get to his books. I'm hoping, really hoping, that I could put a few things here with you?'

'For how long?'

'Oh.' Patti tapped a long pink painted nail on her lips. 'Well, the orders I've done will be picked up by the end of the week, but then I've got those others that'll soon be finished. They'll go in the kitchen. Then I have a delivery of old ballroom dresses that were destined for the tip until Gerry spotted them on the back of a truck, so they'll have to go somewhere in the spare bedroom. Which means this box-' she kicked the one in front of her '-and the three others like it have no home for the foreseeable future.' She chewed her lip. 'I can't say, Rosemary, but probably for a while.'

'What's in them?'

'Undergarments. Not used! Perfectly new, but packets that have been opened in shops and can't be resold.'

'You have three boxes of undergarments.'

'Three boxes of *new* undergarments. I do have some ancient whalebone corsets that are well worn, but they're in a box in the pantry.' Patti swayed backward and forward on her ballet flats. 'Please, Rosemary. Can you help?'

Rosemary took in Patti's nervous face and the way her fingers were twisting together. 'I'll store this box for you.'

'Oh, thank you! And the others?'

'No.'

Patti's mouth dropped open, revealing perfectly aligned white teeth.

'Let me say that differently. Not yet.'

'Not yet? When?'

'Patti, when Gerry was here on Saturday night, he was exhausted. You agreed you could take on an assistant, but I haven't heard that you've advertised.' Rosemary waited.

'Well, no, not yet. It's been so busy and the netball team from Big Town are coming for fittings-'

'Precisely. That's why you need an assistant. For both your sakes. You look almost as tired as Gerry.'

Patti touched her face lightly. 'No, I don't.'

'No, you don't, because you're very clever with your makeup. However, I think you are.'

Patti's shoulders dropped. 'I am tired, Rosemary, but I can't be, can I? Patricia's is growing and it's just how I hoped it would be.' She put her hands to her mouth. 'Oh, I can't stop! I can't let it go under!'

'You need an assistant.' It was Rosemary's turn to kick the box. 'I'll take the other two boxes after you and I write an advertisement for your assistant and put it up on the job seeking sites.'

'You'd do that?'

'Of course.' Rosemary glanced at the clock on the wall above the olives. 'We'll do it tonight at dinner. It's at Roman and Jules's place. They won't mind if we put our heads together for a while.'

Patti stopped rocking. Her hands were still on her mouth and two fat tears rolled down her cheeks to join them. 'Thank you,' she whispered.

Rosemary opened the door and ushered her out with a gentle hand on her arm. 'It's fine, Patti. Really. Once you have more time to think, I'll show you how to operate a better financial software system.'

'Really?'

'That's what friends are for.'

Patti hiccupped once, dabbed her face with the back of her hand, and nodded vigorously. 'If there's anything I can do for you...'

Before Rosemary could dismiss the idea, Jasper's Rover came around the corner and pulled up outside The Read Mulbury. He got out, nodded curtly at the pair outside Rosemary's shop, and unlocked his door.

Rosemary let Patti's arm go. 'Thanks. But what I need to do is something no one else can help with.'

SIXTEEN

Rakisha pulled the curtains across the windows of The Sweet Potato and stayed for a moment, looking at The Exceptional Tree through the gap the curtains made. The sun was low, making the ancient gumtree cast long shadows that almost reached the café. Rakisha wished they would. It would be like a blessing, a benevolent touch of an old friend, one that understood the intricacies of life and the interplay of emotions-

'Rakisha, what time is this gathering tonight?'

Rakisha didn't need to turn to her sister to know that she stood halfway down the stairs, one hand firmly on the banister and the other on her hip. She would be dressed, too, in a towelling dressing gown with layers of thin coloured cotton underneath.

'Well?'

'Silkie, darling, dinner at the lovely Roman and Jules's residence is six-thirty, but you don't have to-'

'Will that woman give our journal back?'

'Mrs Lionel, darling. That's her name.'

'Well, will she?'

'Of course, darling. She would have given it back to us yesterday but...' Rakisha waved her hand around, finally facing her sister, who stood exactly as predicted.

'You were sick. Yes. I know. Your retching kept me up all night again.'

Rakisha placed a hand gently on her stomach. Saturday had been a horrendous night lying on the floor of the bathroom. It was punishment, she knew, for eating those delicious pies at Rosemary Exeter's. Chicken pies, for nature's sake! What had she been thinking, to devour the flesh of an animal without even thanking it for its life?

'And don't think it was the chicken that upset you. I saw you eat the cream-filled eclairs from that man you have not introduced me to.'

'Franco, darling? He's always too busy, but he often sends food.'

'Cream, Rakisha. Mama always said you were lactose intolerant.'

Rakisha rubbed her stomach. 'Yes, Mama always said.'

'Hmph.' Silkie pulled the cord of her dressing gown more tightly around her waist. 'Mama said a lot of things you took no notice of.'

'Oh, no, darling. I always noticed Mama.'

'No, you didn't. You didn't hear what she said about me.'

Rakisha tiptoed across the dusty floorboards of the café and stood at the base of the stairs. 'I heard Mama say quite a bit about you.'

'But not the things that mattered.' Silkie flounced around and headed up the stairs. 'Let's get there earlier than the others. We'll be waiting for that woman when she arrives.'

Rakisha dragged herself after Silkie. The last thing she

felt like was dinner with the other Mulburians, not because she didn't crave their company and not because it would be difficult to enjoy Roman's dinner, but because Silkie would no doubt force the centre of attention on herself. Frankly, she was sick of it but what could be done? She sighed, wishing for the thousandth time that Silkie had kept her chakra well away.

———

JULES OPENED the door to Rosemary and Mrs Lionel dressed in a typically elegant fawn linen dress. She smiled warmly. 'How lovely to see you both! Please, come in.'

Rosemary took Mrs Lionel's coat and hung it next to hers on the vast rack running down the hallway.

'So, where's Jasper?' said Jules as she led them into the dining area. 'He usually comes with you.'

'He's been away today,' said Mrs Lionel, smiling at Patti as she spotted the beaming woman. 'Perhaps he's too tired.'

'He hasn't rung to say he *isn't* coming.' Jules glanced at Rosemary. 'Have you heard from him?'

'No.'

Jules touched her shoulder. 'Okay. Sorry to bring it up.'

Rosemary said nothing as she went to the table and sat next to Gerry. Clearly, Jasper's coolness toward her had been noticed by others. She felt a prickly feeling down her back at the thought.

'Rosemary,' said Gerry, offering her water. 'Patti said you'd help us with our hunt for an assistant.'

'Yes.'

'That is really magnanimous of you.'

'Not magnanimous. I'm being realistic.' She studied him. Gerry's face was pale, and he had crescent moon shaped puffiness under his eyes. 'If you don't get help with that business, you won't be around to enjoy it.'

'Oh, well, no, I don't...'

She waited until he stopped blustering.

'Thank you, anyway.' Gerry sipped his water.

'What sort of person do you think would suit Patricia's?'

Gerry leaned forward. 'A little clone of Patti would be nice. Someone creative and imaginative. You know.'

'You want someone who will work hard, Gerry, not float around on the clouds.'

'Oh, that, too. Someone creative and imaginative and with their feet on the ground.' He lifted his glass. 'And who can lift heavy boxes.'

'That narrows it down.'

'Too much, do you think?'

Rosemary didn't reply, but pulled a piece of paper from her jacket pocket. 'Here's the list of things I thought would be useful. Customer service, experience with certain computer software, flexibility in work hours. Also, someone who doesn't want the limelight.'

'That's correct, Rosemary! We can't usurp Patti.'

'What's this, sweetie? You can't what?'

Gerry smiled up at his wife as she came to stand next to his shoulder. 'Rosemary is helping us with our hunt for an assistant.'

'I do appreciate that, Rosemary.' Patti chewed her lip. 'I know it's important, but there are so many other things to do...'

'I'll type it up and get some feedback from you. Then, if you want, I'll put it online. That'll save you time.'

'Oh.' Patti seemed lost for words. 'Gerry, isn't she...? I mean, thank you, Rosemary.'

'How will we repay you, Rosemary?' Gerry sat up suddenly and bit his lip. 'Oh. Maybe...'

'Gerry...' Patti put a hand on her husband's arm. 'We'll pay you back, Rosemary,' she said, looking at Gerry. 'You'll see.'

Rosemary frowned, but the doorbell rang, a deep chime that echoed around the room like Big Ben and cut short further talk. Jules went to it, and there was a flurry of activity as Silkie swept into the room with Rakisha behind. 'You are already gathered,' said Silkie, casting a scowl around the room. She turned to her sister. 'You said we were early.'

'I thought we were, darling.' Rakisha raised her wrist and tapped at a small watch. 'It's just past six-thirty.'

'Your watch,' said Roman, entering the room wearing a stiff white apron and carrying a wooden spoon. 'It is slow.'

Rakisha tapped the glass again as if in doing so, the little hands would jump to the correct time. 'Is it? I'm so sorry, darling. I hoped I haven't spoiled your meal.'

Roman grinned through his enormous moustache. 'No. It will be perfect. Won't you be seated?'

Rakisha almost ran to the table and thumped herself down in the seat next to Mrs Lionel. Silkie wafted on as if she hadn't heard Roman, and placed herself in the seat next to Rosemary, carefully arranging her layers as she did. A whiff of sage accompanied her. She leaned forward, elbows on the table, so that she faced Mrs Lionel. 'You have our mother's journal.'

'Yes, dear.' Mrs Lionel smiled. 'Would you like it back?'

'Of course, as it is ours.'

'Oh, I'm only minding it until you come to fetch it.'

'You don't have it with you?'

'Oh, no, dear.'

'You will bring it to us tomorrow?'

'I don't think so. You are coming for that morning tea we missed, aren't you?'

Silkie glared at Rakisha, then at Mrs Lionel. 'I came yesterday to see you, and again today.'

'But Rakisha didn't. You see, I'm minding the journal until *both* of you can come and fetch it.'

'I am so sorry, Mrs Lionel, darling,' said Rakisha, her hand on her belly again. 'I've been terribly unwell.'

'Perfectly understandable.' Mrs Lionel folded her hands and placed them on the table. 'I'll keep the journal safe until you both come and get it.'

'We are both here now.'

'But I don't have it with me.'

Silkie leaned so far forward her hair fell into a small dish of butter Jules had placed near a basket of bread. 'I don't need my sister with me to get something of my mother's.'

'Perhaps not,' said Mrs Lionel firmly. 'But, as a mother, I would like to see my children co-operate and I suspect if you have this journal, you won't share.'

'We aren't children!'

'You are someone's children. Therefore, you always will be children to me.' Mrs Lionel turned pointedly to Patti and started a conversation about ribbons.

Silkie slumped in her chair before grabbing her wine glass and taking a gulp.

'You seem very keen on getting that journal.'

Silkie turned to stare at Rosemary. 'It's only natural.'

'You think your mother wrote something in there important.'

'I know she did.'

'What would she have written that she hadn't told you directly?'

Silkie glared at Rosemary. The lines on her face were very clear now that she was close, and Rosemary calculated they were about the same age, with Rakisha then a few years younger. 'You have a nerve,' said Silkie.

'Yes.'

Silkie took another drink, then turned to Rosemary, stroking her hair so that it fell straight and dark over her shoulders. 'Our mother,' she said, 'was a difficult woman to understand. The journal will enlighten us. Mother spoke mainly with her Akita.'

'The cat.'

'The cat was just a medium through which she spoke. When the cat died, Mama still channelled her.'

'Right.'

Silkie sniffed. 'I don't expect someone like you to understand.' She put one long nail on the table and tapped it sharply. 'You clearly don't understand the curse of Jasper Lu.'

Rosemary stiffened. 'Jasper doesn't have a curse.'

Silkie tapped her nail again. 'That's what *he* said that *you* said.'

'I suppose you told him otherwise.'

Silkie raised her finger so that its sharp nail looked like a scorpion's tail. 'Of course. I understand curses. I *feel* them. It's part of being a sensitive.' Her hand went to her chest.

Rosemary leaned forward a little, irritation rising in her throat. 'If you're a sensitive, why is it you want to know what's in your mother's journal? Can't you *feel* what's in it?'

Silkie blinked at Rosemary and slowly lowered her hand. 'I waste my time talking to you.'

'I wish you wouldn't waste Jasper's time.'

Silkie smiled slowly. 'Ah, I see. You don't want me speaking to your Jasper.'

'He's not my Jasper.'

'No. Chances of that fade by the day, Rosemary Exeter.' Now Silkie leaned forward, so close Rosemary could smell the sage of her fragrant oil. 'You need to play along or watch it disappear.'

'I'm not playing with Jasper.'

Silkie stood as Roman entered the room, bearing a steaming pot of curry. 'Well, then. If you don't play, you lose. Simple as that.' She walked to a vacant chair at the other end of the table and sat.

Rosemary lost the hum of appreciation as Roman lifted the lid to the pot. Instead, she focused on the doorbell that was dinging in the distance. Jules led Jasper to the table, but he veered away from the empty chair next to Rosemary and went to sit next to Silkie. As the dark-haired woman gave Rosemary a cold smile, Rosemary dipped her head. If she wanted to keep Jasper a friend, how much would she have to compromise?

SEVENTEEN

Ronnie tugged his laptop closer to the table edge just as another cake landed dangerously close to his screen. He rearranged the papers balanced on his lap. The little house they'd rented a few years ago was perfect for back then when Honey had a job as a drama teacher and he was an accountant, but now that they both worked from home, it was crowded. Cuddles whined from under Ronnie's chair, and he bent to pat the golden head, knocking the table as he did.

'Ronnie! Careful. That fairy nearly fell off.'

'Sorry,' said Ronnie, giving the icing fairy a nudge to make her stand straight. 'This one's a beauty.'

'That one was a lot of work.' Honey pulled a chair out and sat down heavily, her hand on her abdomen. 'Leaning over the bench is getting very hard.'

'You could sit on a stool to do the decorations.'

'I try.' Honey shifted uncomfortably. 'It's hard with things like that.' She waved at the fairies dancing around the top of the cake. 'I need to see it from above.'

'This is the last one you're doing, right?'

'I'd finally caught up.' She ran her chestnut ponytail through her hand and swung it back over her shoulder. 'But then Karen Evans rang. She practically begged me for a volcano.'

'You're making her a volcano cake?'

'Well, I thought I would.' Honey folded both hands over her belly. 'It'll be easy, except that she wants it to erupt without spewing so much froth that it spoils the cake.'

'She wants an erupting volcano cake?'

'Don't sound so stunned, Ronnie. It can be done. I've just got to think it through. Oof.' Honey rubbed her side. 'I don't know what Tallulah's up to, but I don't think she has room.'

'Which is why you shouldn't be making erupting cakes.' Ronnie held up his bits of paper. 'I can support us.'

'Yes, I know, Ronnie. I just don't want to lose customers, especially when they make special requests.' She stood again and went to the sliding glass doors that opened onto their meagre backyard. 'Did I tell you I had a phone call from the city yesterday? This woman wanted twenty miniature softballs. She'd heard about my tennis ball cupcakes.'

'Did you say yes?'

'I turned her down, explaining...' Honey waved at her torso. 'But she booked me for later.'

'Honey,' said Ronnie, pushing his chair back carefully and going to give his wife a hug. 'You are extraordinary, but maybe you're taking on too much. I mean, you don't know how Tallulah and you will be in two months' time.'

'It's only twenty little cakes, Ronnie.' Honey stepped back irritably. 'I'll be able to do it.'

'Okay.' Ronnie took her hands. 'I shouldn't doubt you.'

'It's fine. You're only looking out for me.' Honey glanced

at the table. 'I bet you'll be happy to get more workspace back.'

'I can work from the couch if I have to.'

Honey raised their entwined hands and kissed the back of his. 'You are a lovely man.'

'And you are the most beautiful woman I've ever seen.'

She smiled. 'Well, aren't we lucky?'

'Oh yeah.'

'Anyway, enough of the lovey dovey business.' She snatched the papers from him. 'How are you going with this?'

Ronnie tried not to show his disappointment with stopping the lovey dovey business. Sometimes, he felt he would burst with the degree of love he had for Honey Blossom. She chose me, he often chanted to himself. *Me!* He grinned now, making Honey smile.

'Ronnie, enough! Tell me what you're doing.'

'What? Oh. Well.' He tapped the papers. 'This is all about Mrs Caroline King's past.'

'What about her past?'

Ronnie took his work back. 'She was born in the city, grew up in the struggling west, met and married Mr King while working as a jillaroo up north, had three children early into their marriage, but was Morgan King's confidante and advisor. Tragically, she was widowed when she was only thirty-two but took on the running of the station, very competently, by all accounts. She rebranded the business and made it her own. As far as I can work out, she may not have been liked by all, but reports say she had integrity and grit.'

'Sounds straightforward.'

Ronnie frowned. 'It does, doesn't it?'

Honey went back to her chair and sat. 'You sound a bit worried. Like it shouldn't be straightforward.'

'No one's life is straightforward, not really. And there are gaps, especially before she was married. And I don't get why Mrs King wanted to know who was at the Gala the day she collapsed.' Ronnie pulled out the chair next to Honey and sat as well. 'I've given her the list of volunteers and stall-holders and she said it wasn't enough. There's no way, though, that I could get a list of visitors. They came and went as they pleased.'

'What does it matter?'

'It matters to Mrs King. Something gave her such a shock her heart was affected.'

'I thought you said it was one of the photos she saw.'

'That would make sense, wouldn't it? She was in front of them at the time. I sent her photos of the photos, but she dismissed them. They weren't what she was after, she said. Nothing I've given her seems to satisfy.'

Honey leaned over to take her husband's hand. 'How can you tell? You've never actually spoken to her directly.'

'That's right. She wants everything to go through Janet Spinney, so that's who I call or email.'

'Maybe Janet's the key, then.'

'What do you mean?'

'She was there. She also acts as the liaison between you and Mrs King.' Honey let Ronnie's hand go and rubbed her side. 'What does she think of Mrs King?'

'I don't know.'

'You've never asked?'

'No, should I?'

'Of course, Ronnie! You might be working for Mrs King, but that doesn't stop you asking innocent questions of her carer.'

'Innocent questions? They won't be, really, not if I'm digging for information.'

'Ronnie, your kind face will never betray the fact that your questions *aren't* innocent. It's one of the many things you have going for you as a private investigator.'

Ronnie felt his cheeks warm. 'Thanks, Honey.'

'Yes, okay,' Honey said as he reached over to kiss her. 'Go and do it now.'

Honey left for the bedroom, leaving Ronnie to dig his phone out and dial Janet's number. It rang for a long time, and as he was about to kill the call, a timid voice answered.

'Hello, Miss Spinney,' said Ronnie. 'It's-'

'Mr Edwards. I know because I can see your number come up. Mrs King is asleep and doesn't want to be disturbed.'

'That's okay, because she never wants to talk to me. I was ringing to talk to you.'

'Me?'

Through the phone, Ronnie heard footsteps, then a door creaking closed. 'Yes, if that's alright. I was checking my notes and thought that I'd run them past you.'

'I don't think I'm going to be much help.'

'Oh, you never know. How about I read out what I've got and you can tell me if I've missed anything?'

'Well, alright then.'

Ronnie read through the history of Mrs King's life pretty much as he'd told Honey. Janet didn't make a sound until he got to the end. A brief, quiet sigh told him she was still listening.

'Does all that sound correct, Miss Spinney?'

'Please call me Janet. Everyone does.' The woman sighed. 'You are correct, Mr Edwards.'

'I'm just Ronnie, if you like. Is there anything I've missed?'

'Everything you've said is correct.'

Ronnie pushed his paper along the table and sat back in his chair. 'The trouble is, that information is really what everyone knows about Mrs King. I got it from searching the internet. Mrs King's life is repeatedly referred to in newspaper articles and magazines. They all say the same thing.'

Janet was silent.

'Is it true, do you think?'

'Is what true?'

'Everything I've just said.'

'It must be, mustn't it?' Janet was on the move again, her footsteps echoing on a hard floor. 'It was in the papers and on the internet.'

'Well, yeah, there's no reason to think it isn't true, but it's all very mundane. I thought Mrs King's life would have been more exciting. Is there anything exciting that you could tell me?'

'Only those times she fell off her horse or was in the crop duster accident.'

'Yeah, I read about those.'

'Then you know all you need to know.'

'Oh, I doubt that. You've known her for a very long time.'

'I have been in Mrs King's employ since she was married.'

'What's she like as a boss?'

'She's a fine boss.'

'What does that mean?'

'It means that she's like any other boss. She expects people to do their job well and without complaining.'

'Like you do.'

'Like I do.'

'Does she reward you? I mean, she's a wealthy woman. Does she give you bonuses or gifts or anything?'

Janet chuckled. 'Mrs King doesn't do that sort of thing. She always says she pays fairly and that should be enough. Which it is because she *does* pay fairly. She appreciates people who work hard and gets rid of people who don't.'

Ronnie gripped the phone harder. 'She's got rid of people?'

'Oh, yes, lots of people. If they don't meet her expectations, they're out.'

'So, there could be people out there holding grudges against her?'

'Maybe. But if you don't work hard, you shouldn't keep your job, should you?'

'Probably not. Can you remember anyone who might have been particularly angry about being fired?'

'A couple.'

'Who, Janet?'

'I'm not giving you their names.'

'Why not?'

'It's none of your business.'

'Well, it could be. You see, something that day gave Mrs King a real fright. Maybe it was the sight of one of those people? Maybe they'd threatened her before?'

'No one's threatened Mrs King.'

'Are you sure? She's a wealthy woman. She may have been on the end of threats before. You know, *pay up now or we'll tell the world your secrets.*'

It wasn't a good thug accent, but Janet gasped and the phone went dead. Ronnie called back straight away, and the ring went on even longer than before Janet answered, sounding worse than ever. 'I'm sorry, Janet. I didn't mean to scare you.'

'It's alright. I'm alright.'

'I scared you.'

'Only a bit.'

'I scared you because you've heard a voice like that before.'

There was a long silence. Ronnie strained to hear any sound through the phone, but there was nothing.

'Janet?'

'I'm okay.'

Ronnie kept his voice quiet. 'I'm right, aren't I?'

'No, not really.'

'Oh. Can you explain what you mean?'

'No, Ronnie. It is not my story to tell.'

'Will Mrs King say more, then? I'm really stuck as to what to do next.'

'Mrs King will speak when she's ready. I can't do anything about it.'

'Because it's not your story to tell.'

'That's what I said.'

'You could ask whether she would tell me more. I don't need to know everything, but I do need something, otherwise it's not much use me continuing. Please. Would you ask whether I can speak to Mrs King directly?'

'She's frail.'

'I know. But I won't take up much time.'

There was quiet again, although this time Ronnie could hear a light shuffling, as if someone was stirring on a sofa. *Mrs King?*

When Janet spoke again, it was clear and crisp, with no trace of the fear that had touched her last words. 'I'll get back to you, Ronnie.'

'Thank you. That's great.'

'But...' The voice dropped again to a stealthy whisper. 'Don't hold your breath.' The line went dead.

Ronnie tucked his phone back into his pocket. Honey hummed in the bedroom and Cuddles sighed as he slept on the kitchen floor. If Mrs King hadn't been threatened, then why was Janet so upset at his thug voice?

It was halfway through dinner before the penny dropped. Ronnie dropped his knife and fork and grinned at his bewildered wife. 'I've got it, Honey.'

'I hope it's not catching.'

'What? No, I mean, I think I've got what's holding Mrs King back.' Ronnie reached across to grab Honey's hand. 'She's got a secret she doesn't want anyone else to know.'

EIGHTEEN

Mrs Lionel opened the blinds on her shop window right at ten o'clock to find Rakisha and Silkie waiting on the pavement under the veranda. Rakisha was twisting her hands together but her sister stood calmly, her gaze directed over Rakisha's head to the corner of the street where no doubt Patti and Gerry were busy wheeling dress racks out for display. Rakisha was the first to see Mrs Lionel and gave a frantic wave. 'We're here, darling,' she shouted through the glass. 'Here for Mama's journal.'

Mrs Lionel opened the door, triggering the morning croaking of her frog, and stood back to let the sisters in. It was quite cool outside, the sort of dull day that doesn't invite tourists to tour, so Mrs Lionel was quite content to lead the others through the door into her living area. Percy pricked his ears up from his spot near her chair and she shook her head briefly at him so that he settled again. 'Tea?' she said, turning to check.

Silkie eyed her thoughtfully. 'Peppermint, please,' she said before turning to look at Percy's spot. The way her gazed brushed past him, though, was a blessing.

'And you, Rakisha?'

'Oh, darling, do you have any valerian?'

'I do. I have every sort of tea you can imagine, although I mainly drink the more ordinary type.'

Rakisha nodded vigorously and went to stand at the glass door leading to the porch. Outside, the wind was moody, sweeping the occasional leaf across the decking before going sullen again. Mrs Lionel watched Rakisha and her trembling hands. *This is not an easy visit,* she thought.

'The journal?' Silkie asked as Mrs Lionel carried a tea tray carefully to the table.

'I'll fetch it now. Please, take a seat and help yourself to the lavender biscuits.'

Despite having the journal for several days, Mrs Lionel had not opened it, resisting the temptation by wrapping the notebook in an elaborate knot of linen tea towels. She brought it to the table and sat down to unpick the package slowly, her fingers aching with the effort. Silkie's fingers crept along the table, but Mrs Lionel slid the book away and kept at it until the material fell away, revealing the battered journal within.

It wasn't a special book, rather one covered by cheap and peeling leather over pages that had yellowed with age. It smelled musty, too, a little like some of the books Jasper received in good-willed donations and had to air for many days before displaying. There were traces of long-gone silverfish as well in the hollows of the edges. 'Well, here it is. Shall I read it?'

'No!' said Silkie. 'I will read it.' She smiled smugly and reached out.

'No, darling, give it to me,' said Rakisha. 'It was in mother's things and I've kept them for many years.'

Mrs Lionel held the book up. 'You see, this is where

trouble starts. Neither one of you should really have it first over the other.'

'I should,' said Silkie. 'She's had it for years and didn't bother to even look at it. My turn now.'

'But darling, you *told* me not to look through the box until you arrived. I've kept it for oh-so-long. It's my turn first.'

'Why don't you sit together and read it?' Mrs Lionel stood up and gestured Silkie to move next to Rakisha. 'Then you'll both find out at the same time what's in it.'

'That does sound fair, Silkie,' said Rakisha. 'We can read Mama's words together.'

Silkie sat still for a moment, then moved ungraciously across to Mrs Lionel's abandoned chair. Mrs Lionel slid the book between them and opened it to the first page.

Silence fell. From where she stood, Mrs Lionel couldn't see the words on the page, although she made out the small section at the top that was probably a date and a block of curly cursive that sat underneath. The sisters' heads were together, grey curls from Rakisha clinging to Silkie's black strands. From the top, they looked so dissimilar that it would have been an easy thing to say that they weren't related at all, but as they turned the pages together, their heads tipped as one to the same angle and their free hands clenched in identical fists.

Mrs Lionel felt the air of intimacy and moved back into the shop, carrying her tea with her. There were still no customers, but the shop was light and fresh, with the fragrance of rose strong from a newly made batch of pot-pourri. She sat herself at the counter, making notes about what to make for the new season, and didn't notice the sisters until they were once again in front of her.

Rakisha had the journal under her arm. 'Thank you, darling. We're going now.'

Mrs Lionel looked from one to the other. 'Everything alright, is it?'

'No,' said Silkie tightly.

'All was revealed then?'

'Yes.' Rakisha smiled, but there was no warmth in it. 'We have to go away now and absorb…' She gestured to the book.

'Well, dears, have a lovely day of it.'

Silkie stalked out, letting the door close on her sister and making the frog croak maniacally. Rakisha heaved it open again and trotted after her sister.

Before the door closed, Rosemary slipped in, carrying an empty plastic bottle.

'Refill, dear?'

'Yes, please. Laundry wash, thank you.' Rosemary handed the bottle to her friend, who turned to the large pumping containers in the room's corner. 'Did you give them the journal?'

'Yes, they have it.'

'Any idea what was in it they were so excited about?'

'No idea whatsoever.'

Rosemary accepted the full bottle. 'None?'

Mrs Lionel smiled at the disbelief on her friend's face. 'None. I did not read a word, not in the time I had it nor over their shoulders.'

'Was I suggesting that you had?'

'Yes. It's in your eyes.'

'Surely not.'

'Surely is. I suspect you would have read it if the journal had been at your place.'

'We'll never know because it wasn't.'

Mrs Lionel grinned. 'No, it wasn't.'

Rosemary spun the bottle in her hand. 'You are annoyingly virtuous at times.'

'I know.'

Rosemary turned to go.

'Wait, dear.'

'What is it?'

'Have you talked to Jasper since he returned from the city?'

'Yes. I told him they delivered the box.'

'Is that all?'

'Was there meant to be more?'

Mrs Lionel sat back on her stool and put her folded arms on the counter. 'Rosemary, dear, of course there was meant to be more. What is this ridiculous thing that's between you and Jasper? You're the best of friends.'

For a moment, she thought Rosemary was going to shrug and continue her way back to The Preserved Mulbury. Something more subtle, though, sent a slight shiver through Rosemary's shoulders. 'I hurt his feelings,' she said softly.

'Ah. You were a bit hard on him.'

Rosemary put the bottle on the counter and swept the hair tie from her braid, raking the long mass with her fingers as she spoke. 'It's that curse he thinks is his. For an intelligent man, he makes no sense. Curses aren't real.'

'Jasper thinks they are.'

'You and I know they aren't.'

'Do we?'

Rosemary didn't answer, instead twisting her dark hair into a tighter plait that exposed the long streak of silver running from her right temple. 'You don't believe in curses. You're a medical woman.'

'I may not believe in curses, but I have seen unbelievable things.' She gestured behind her.

'Apart from Percy.' Rosemary finished her hair and wound the tie back on. 'Percy doesn't count.'

'He'd be upset to hear that.'

Rosemary put her hands on her hips. 'Just because you have a dog no one else can see doesn't mean you believe in curses.'

'No, but it proves that we don't understand everything about this world. And we shouldn't underestimate the impact of belief on people. If Jasper thinks he has a curse, then we need to believe him.'

'I just... can't.'

'Surely you can. It's a way of showing support.'

Rosemary ran her hand across her head, pulling at the braid so that it was dangerously close to becoming unkempt again. 'I'm finding that very hard.'

'And yet you believe me.'

'Yes.' Rosemary stopped fiddling with her hair. 'Of course, I believe you. You are a very logical woman. Usually.'

'Your trouble is that Jasper is not a logical man. Usually.'

'I think that's the heart of it.' Rosemary picked up the bottle again.

'That's what you like about him, dear.'

'What bit of that do I like?'

'His gentle heart.'

Rosemary regarded her with a familiar look, a mix of exasperation and pensiveness. Mrs Lionel waited until Rosemary plonked the bottle down with a sigh. 'What do you think I should do?'

'Oh, it's not up to me.'

'Maybe not. You have an opinion, I'm sure.'

'Well, if it *was* up to me...'

'Go on.'

'Right.' Mrs Lionel adjusted herself on the stool. 'First of all, if it were me, I'd arrange a walk. You walk regularly, so this shouldn't be an issue.'

'What if he doesn't want to?'

'It's a health issue for him, so I'm sure you can convince him. His rehabilitation after his illness depends on regular walking and your encouragement to do so.'

Rosemary said nothing.

'Second, after a little time in silence, I would apologise for any hurt you caused him.'

'Apologise.'

'Yes, apologise. It won't kill you.'

'Right. Then what would you do?'

'Offer to help him.'

'With what?'

'Well, you've said in the past that you will help find his real father, so just extend that to helping him understand what this curse is to him.'

'I'm not a psychologist.'

'I'm not asking you to be, dear. Just a friend. He possibly needs counselling as well, but that will work better if he feels well supported at home.'

'Supported.'

'You've turned into a parrot.'

'Parrot.' Rosemary lifted her hand. 'Sorry. I understand what you're saying and I can do all that you suggest, but his support seems to come from another direction.'

'Do you mean Silkie?'

Rosemary grunted.

'And there's someone else. It worries you that you don't know who that blonde woman is.'

Rosemary tilted her head at her friend. 'Are you sure you aren't a counsellor yourself?'

'You know that I'm not. I'm simply someone who sees the situation clearly. Now.' She tapped Rosemary's hand. 'How about it?'

It was unusual to see sadness bring out the shadows under Rosemary's eyes. Mrs Lionel suddenly wondered whether she'd been too harsh on her, even while accusing Rosemary of being too harsh on Jasper. She was relieved when Rosemary blinked, straightened her shoulders, and picked up the laundry wash for the second time. 'Right,' she said. 'I'll give it a go. There's nothing to lose that's not already lost.'

'Good,' said Mrs Lionel. 'Now we've got that out of the way, there's something else I want to speak to you about.'

'Haven't you told me off enough for one day?'

'I'm not scolding you, as you well know.'

'Sorry. What is it, then?'

'It's the assistant job for Patti and Gerry.'

'What about it?'

'The Hubbard sisters are applying.'

'Which one?'

'All three.'

'Even Holly?'

'Correct.'

'How do you know?'

'Because each one has crept up to me individually to tell me.' Mrs Lionel counted on her fingers. 'Holly says she wants to test out a different way of life. Hannah tells me she thinks she might have a latent creative streak if only she could study Patti's work. And Heather...'

'What did Heather say?'

'Well, nothing, really. She had the printout of the job ad and she showed it to me before twirling.'

'Twirling.'

'You're parroting again. Yes, *twirling*. As Heather does.'

'You think she wants the job?'

'She didn't answer when I asked, but I thought the twirling was significant.' Mrs Lionel held Rosemary's gaze. 'She said she got the printout from you.'

'Yes.'

'Why did you specifically give it to her?'

'In case she hadn't seen it.'

'Rosemary Exeter. What are you up to?'

'Absolutely nothing.'

'Hmmm...' Mrs Lionel gave her a dark look.

Rosemary held up the bottle as she made her way to the door. 'Thanks for this.'

'Any time, as you know. Ah, Rosemary?'

Rosemary paused in the doorway, making the electronic frog croak go berserk. 'Yes?'

'I agree with you. Heather would be perfect.'

'Did I say that?'

'You didn't have to.'

Rosemary grinned and shut the door, leaving her friend shaking her head.

NINETEEN

Rosemary didn't immediately do as Mrs Lionel suggested. She saw how sensible it was, but something made her hesitate. It had been two days since she'd seen Jasper, and then the conversation about the box took all of ten seconds. He wouldn't look her in the eye, and that was most hurtful of all. 'I could have made him,' she said to a recumbent Sunny. 'I could have asked him to look at me.'

The cat rolled over and stretched. *You humans are so concerned about contact.*

Rosemary bent to run her hand over Sunny's ginger stripes just as her phone rang. 'Honey.'

'Hi, Mum. Wait: are you alright?'

'Yes.'

'You sound... sad?'

'No.'

'Mum...'

'Honey, I'm fine. What about you?'

In the background of Honey's call, came the shrill warble of a magpie family. 'Oh, I'm good. Just, you know, can't keep still. I've gone for a walk to escape Ronnie's sighing and the perpetual smell of butter and eggs.'

'Why is Ronnie sighing?'

'He's getting nowhere with Mrs King's dilemma. Everything he gives to her, she's not happy.'

'What's he given her?'

'The list of volunteers. Copies of the photos that were on the board. Names of every stall owner and shop owner, and even as many of the residents of Mulbury we could remember were there that day. Nothing has hit the mark.'

'What is she looking for, exactly?'

'Well, that's the trick. She won't say. Whatever it was that nearly killed her, she's keeping it close to her chest.'

'He needs to meet with her.'

'That's what I said!' The magpies warbled again, almost drowning out Honey. 'He needs to insist on seeing her or he won't go on with the case.'

'Sounds like he's got nothing to go on unless he sees her. Will he ask?'

'He spoke to Janet. Mum, he thinks Mrs King is hiding something.'

'No doubt. We all do.'

'Well, maybe. But Ronnie thinks this links to her heart condition. He's stuck, because she won't talk to him.'

'Does he know where Mrs King is at present?'

'She's convalescing on her property near Mulbury.'

'He should visit. She might find it harder to turn him away once he's there.'

'Yeah, okay, I'll tell him that.'

'And the butter and eggs?'

'What about them?'

'You said the smell was getting to you.'

Honey laughed, her deep, rich chuckle that made Rosemary smile. 'Everything is getting to me at the moment. I haven't made a cake for a whole day, but I feel like the whole house reeks of Madeira.'

'You're getting impatient.'

'Too right, I am! When are you coming out, Tallulah?'

In the pause that followed, Rosemary imagined Honey rubbing her abdomen. 'She'll arrive when she's ready.'

'You sound like my midwife. She's so calm.'

'That's a useful attribute for a midwife.'

That chuckle again, joined by the magpies who seemed to find Rosemary as amusing as Honey did.

'Thanks, Mum. You make me feel better just by talking to me.'

The door of The Preserved Mulbury jangled, and Rosemary glimpsed an older woman as she went to the pickle shelf. 'I have a customer, so I'll go.'

'Okay, Mum. Oh, wait!'

'What is it?'

'What are you making right now?'

Rosemary looked around her clean kitchen. 'Nothing. Although I have a bag of rhubarb in the fridge.'

'Rhubarb! You can cook them up with apples.'

'Yes.'

'I can smell it now. The apples tinge the air with sweetness but the rhubarb is more earthy.'

'Honey, I'm not even cooking them.'

'Oh, but the rhubarb is bubbling, and it's got a green, zingy fragrance.'

'Honey...'

'A bit like pine, but not really. A bit like strawberries, but not really.'

'Honey!'

She laughed. 'I'll let you go, Mum. Love you!'

'Love you, too.'

When Rosemary turned to go into the shop, the customer was watching her with the ghost of a wistful smile. Rosemary recognised her at once. 'Miss O'Shannessy. May I help you?'

'Was that your daughter on the phone?'

'Yes.'

'How lovely.'

'It is.' Rosemary waited, but the woman stayed silent. 'Do you need pickles?'

'Pickles?' Miss O'Shannessy glanced around as if surprised she was surrounded by jars. 'No pickles today.'

'Something else, then.'

Miss O'Shannessy frowned. 'I'm not really sure why I keep coming back.' She gestured with her free hand. 'I like an outing and I keep directing whoever my driver is to come to Mulbury. Today I've paid my neighbour to drive me, but she's as happy as Larry in that little bookshop.'

Rosemary's thoughts went straight to Jasper pottering around his shop with a half-read novel in his hand. It was a silly image, as Jasper was probably stocking shelves or hunting for more bargains on the internet and he was too busy to potter. She rubbed her forehead to dispel it. 'It's a good bookshop.'

Miss O'Shannessy stepped forward until she stood in the middle of the room, directly under the skylight. In the warm light, the lines on her face were acute. Although she was probably around Mrs Lionel's age, she looked older, with sharp creases in her dry skin. Her hair was short and wispy and caught in the collar of her brown woollen coat. Although her lips were painted pale pink, they looked dry. 'All your shops are good,' she said. 'You have thriving businesses in this town, unlike other places.'

'Mulbury has the history of the gold rush to thank.'

'Still.' Miss O'Shannessy squared her shoulders. 'History is not always kind.'

Rosemary leaned on her shop counter. 'No, it isn't. Do you know something about Mulbury's history?'

Miss O'Shannessy stared at Rosemary and seemed just about to speak, but the door burst open and Hannah Hubbard jangled in, dragging a smiling Heather by the hand. 'Rosemary!' she said. 'Do us a favour, can you, because Mrs Lionel is inundated with people? Entertain Heather for a moment?' She stopped when she saw Miss O'Shannessy, and Heather seized the opportunity to snatch her hand away.

Rosemary shook her head. 'Why do you need Heather entertained? She can look after herself.'

'That's the problem.' Hannah smiled briefly at Miss O'Shannessy, then hurried over to Rosemary to hiss in her ear. 'I'm trying to show Patti how good I am with customers and Heather keeps... well, doing better.'

'You've applied for the assistant job.'

'Yep.'

'What about Mulbury Feeds?'

'I can do both. It's only a part-time job. It's called *upskilling*.'

'You already have many skills.'

'Thanks, Rosemary, but knowing the protein content of wheat is a pretty limited skill. I just thought, you know, I'd try something different. Not many jobs come up in Mulbury.'

'True. But I can't help you. If Heather wants to go to Patti's with you, then you can't stop her. She's a free woman.'

Hannah turned to her sister, who stood in front of Miss

O'Shannessy, tracing the edge of her brown coat. Miss O'Shannessy stood like a statue and made no attempt to stop the young woman. Hannah went back to Rosemary. 'Please?'

Rosemary shook her head slightly but called Heather to her. 'Hannah wants to spend time with Patti by herself,' she said as Heather skipped over. 'How about you and I and Miss O'Shannessy have a cup of tea until you need to go back to work?'

'Hannah keeps knocking the dresses off Patti's racks,' said Heather, her finger out to trace Rosemary's collar.

Rosemary took Heather's hand and lowered it gently. 'She has to try, though.'

Heather nodded and whirled away, waving goodbye to her sister before disappearing into Rosemary's living area.

'Thanks, Rosemary,' said Hannah. 'I might have a chance now.'

'Sorry about that,' Rosemary said to Miss O'Shannessy as Hannah left for Patricia's. 'Those sisters work and live together, and I imagine it gets difficult sometimes.'

'Two sisters?'

'Three. Holly will be hard at work in their animal produce store.'

Miss O'Shannessy nodded and pushed a strand of hair away from her face. Her hand shook slightly.

'Would you like some tea?' asked Rosemary. 'That wasn't a ploy to get Heather to stay. I believe you were about to say something before Hannah came in.'

'No tea, but thank you. I'll have one with my driver once she's bought enough books to fill the back seat of the car. You are correct, though. I had something I wanted to ask you.' She waved in the Square's direction. 'There was a home here somewhere. I've forgotten where it was.'

'There are a lot of houses in Mulbury.'

'I can't be very specific about its location because my memory of it is vague.' Miss O'Shannessy shook her head. 'It was a residence that housed several people.'

'A lodging house?'

'Of sorts. It was called Sunshine House.'

'I don't recall that name.'

'No?' Miss O'Shannessy pursed her lips.

'I'm not the person to ask, though. There are many long-term residents who still live in Mulbury.'

'I have asked around. The old woman in the green cleaning shop said she only shifted to the district after she married.'

Rosemary bristled at Mrs Lionel being called old, especially by someone who was the same age. 'If Mrs Lionel doesn't know, your chances are slim.'

'She also said that they lost many houses in the Scarlet Tuesday bushfires.'

'True. That was before my time, but some say the destruction changed the look of the town. Even if the buildings were untouched, some big trees were lost. Not The Exceptional Tree.' Rosemary pointed out the window.

'The Exceptional Tree, yes.' Miss O'Shannessy grimaced. 'I think I remember that Tree. It wasn't as big, but there was something about it even then. It's quite magnificent.'

'You were here a long time ago.'

'Decades ago. Over sixty years.'

'A lot can change in that time.'

Miss O'Shannessy's shoulders dropped and her handbag slid off onto the floor. As she stooped to retrieve it, a tear fell to the warmly lit floorboards, darkening a spot for a moment before it was gone. She straightened and pulled the bag onto her shoulder again, looking Rosemary steadily in the eye. 'Thank you. I'll take my leave.'

'Tea's ready.'

Heather stood in the doorway to Rosemary's living quarters, her long, wavy hair framing her bright features. She held Rosemary's best teapot, a cerulean round-bellied pot given to Rosemary by Mrs Lionel. She smiled at Miss O'Shannessy, who faltered slightly under the spell of Heather's angelic-ness. Rosemary hid a grin. 'If you could stay for a quick cuppa, it will appease Heather.'

Miss O'Shannessy followed Rosemary to the dining room and sat awkwardly at the table until Heather poured her a strong brew and emptied two teaspoons of sugar into it. 'And how did you know that is how I like my tea, young lady?' she said.

'I know,' said Heather, pouring Rosemary her usual number.

'How *did* she know?' Miss O'Shannessy asked as Heather went to top the pot up with hot water.

'I don't know. Heather is a remarkable woman.'

That thought seemed to occupy Miss O'Shannessy's mind as she said nothing while Heather chatted amiably about dead birds and feathers. 'I gave Bruce to Robert,' Heather said eventually.

Rosemary had lost the thread of the conversation several minutes earlier and had been thinking of her newly planted corn patch. 'Bruce?'

'Bruce.' Heather pulled a long, dark feather from her pocket.

'Bruce was a raven, I take it?'

'Yeah.' Heather twirled the feather in her hands. 'So many Bruces at Robert's. Bruce hit the window, and I stuffed him for Robert.'

'You're a taxidermist?' Miss O'Shannessy stared at Heather as the young woman nodded before turning to Rosemary. 'She doesn't, you know...' Miss O'Shannessy widened her eyes at Rosemary.

'Heather only uses already dead birds for her taxidermy.'

'Robert's new windows,' said Heather. 'Very clean.'

'The birds will have to get used to them.'

'This Robert is renovating?' asked Miss O'Shannessy, finishing her tea.

'Yes. He bought the old mayoral residence that has been neglected for a long time.'

'Good to hear he's doing something about it.' Miss O'Shannessy stood. 'I must find my driver.' She reached out to touch Heather's shoulder. 'Thank you for the tea.'

'Pleasure,' said Heather, absorbed in the feather.

Rosemary walked her to the door and pulled it open with a lively jangle. Miss O'Shannessy hesitated on the pavement. 'It is a different town to what I remember. Beautiful in its way, even if the fires came through. I hope your Robert's renovations go well and his house reflects the altered state of the town.'

Rosemary watched as the older woman joined her companion to walk back to their car. Mulbury had been through many transitions in its time, but she had the feeling that Miss O'Shannessy knew of one that Rosemary didn't.

TWENTY

Ronnie stood at the start of a long, gravelly driveway that wound its way through an avenue of bottlebrushes. The house at its end peeped through the shrubbery, its pale lemon sandstone featured a bright splash of light at the end of the vista. He'd parked the station wagon at the side of the gatepost, unsure whether he would be more quickly turned away from Mrs King's home if he was on wheels or on foot. It would certainly be a slower exit if he had to use shanks's pony. He squared his shoulders and started the long walk to the house.

Unlike other properties owned by rich people that he'd read about, this one had no obvious security. It was no wonder that the townsfolk nearby had been cagey when he'd asked where it was. It wasn't until he went to the post office that he had any luck. 'Oh, Mrs King's house?' the post mistress had said, lowering her reading glasses to study Ronnie better. 'Now, what would you want with an old lady like Mrs King?'

'I work for her,' said Ronnie, truthfully. 'We usually contact via the phone, but I really need to see her.'

The post office lady kept her gaze on him and Ronnie felt his face do that annoying motley look that happened when he was embarrassed or unsure. He was a bit of both. Eventually, he must have scored low on the 'dangerous villain' scale and she'd directed him to the sandstone house with the long driveway.

The house came into proper view. It was a long, low building with rectangular windows underscored with white stone ledges. A neat rose garden ran along its front and up the sides of a paved pathway that led from the driveway to the front door. A brass knocker in the shape of a cow's head sat in its middle. Ronnie raised it carefully, then let it drop. It sounded with a deep thunk that he could hear resonating inside. A dog barked, the noise coming closer until it stopped just behind the door. The door handle rattled, a voice scolded the dog, and a woman in a smart pants suit opened the door.

'Yes?' she said. 'What do you want?'

'Hello,' said Ronnie, trying to ignore the horse-sized canine the woman held by the collar. 'I'm Ronnie Edwards, the private investigator doing work for Mrs King. Are you Janet? We've talked on the phone several times. I'd really like to see Mrs King if I can.'

'Yes, I'm Janet Spinney. I was warned you were on your way.'

'From the lady at the post office?'

'Yes.' Janet eased the tension on the dog's collar and it stepped forward, muzzle lifting to Ronnie's waist. He shifted his satchel across to protect his stomach. 'Why do you want to see Mrs King?'

Ronnie tried a smile, but felt it come out without mirth. Janet looked him up and down, and he shifted uncomfortably. 'Well, to explain, really, that I'm not getting anywhere and maybe she could give me a new direction to look? I'm missing something, I'm sure.'

'You're missing something?' Janet pursed her lips. She let the dog go and it immediately rested its chin on top of Ronnie's satchel. 'Wait here. I'll ask.'

'Thank you, I appreciate it,' said Ronnie, although she was already walking away.

It was probably five minutes before she returned, enough time for the dog to decide Ronnie was harmless but that he owned a dog himself. It had sniffed Ronnie all over in chase of Cuddles, its great nose huffing warm, wet air now and then on Ronnie's trousers. He was about to shoo it carefully away when Janet said, 'Come in. She wants to talk to you.' She clicked her fingers at the dog as she turned away. 'Beast, stop that.'

Beast backed away, knocking an umbrella stand over as he went and spilling its contents onto the floor. He grabbed a long piece of wood that had been amongst the brollies and started up the corridor, wagging his tail happily. It looked so comical that Ronnie whipped his phone out and took a secret shot.

Janet took the wood from the dog and repacked the stand. 'Naughty Beast,' she said, but fondly. She beckoned to Ronnie again. 'Come on, Ronnie.'

Ronnie shut the massive door and trailed after the woman and Beast. The corridor into the house was wide and inviting, lined with proud photographs of dark red cattle and tan and white kelpie dogs. A coat rack extended down one side, heavy with waterproof coats and wide-brimmed rabbit skin hats. The corridor opened into a light, open-plan area that included a welcoming kitchen at one end and a range of comfortable sofas at the other. Mrs King sat in one, a mauve mohair rug over her knees. Beast plonked himself at his mistress's feet.

Ronnie had only seen Mrs King in the flesh once before, and that was a brief look at the Mulbury Gala. Nonetheless, he could see that her sudden bout of cardiomyopathy had taken a severe hit. Mrs King was gaunt and frail, the hands resting on the rug large-knuckled and aged-spotted. Still, she held his look with intense, blue-washed eyes. 'Hello, Mrs King,' he said quietly. 'I hope I'm not bothering you.'

'Yes, you are, young man.' Mrs King shifted uncomfortably on the soft sofa, as if it hurt to sit. 'But I suppose you have your reasons. You're my private investigator, hmm? Not what I expected.'

'Oh,' said Ronnie, feeling the flush of heat in his cheeks again. 'I'm sorry to disappoint you.'

'You haven't disappointed me. I think your work up to date has been quick and thorough.' Mrs King lifted a hand to her carer. 'Tea, if you wouldn't mind, Janet. I suspect Mr Edwards would like refreshment after travelling so far.'

'Thank you,' said Ronnie, 'although it wasn't far, only half an hour or so-'

'Yes.' Mrs King waved her hand to make Janet go and then at Ronnie to make him sit. 'Now, what is it you want?'

Ronnie slid his satchel to the floor and took a moment to retrieve a notebook. He wasn't quite sure what to say next, but decided in the end that Mrs King would prefer he was direct. 'I haven't been able to talk to you. Your family stopped me.'

'Rubbish,' said Mrs King, tucking her hands under the blanket on her legs. 'My family wouldn't dare do anything without consulting me. I didn't want to talk to you and Janet knows this, which is why she told you it was my family's fault. You're doing a fine job on your own without talking to me.'

'But...'

'But what, young man?'

'You're not telling me something,' Ronnie blurted. 'I can't find something if you won't tell me what I'm looking for.'

Behind him, in the kitchen, Janet crashed crockery onto the bench, making Mrs King flinch. 'What makes you think I'm not telling you something, Mr Edwards?'

'I've given you everything you've asked for, but it's not what you want.'

Mrs King smoothed a strand of loose hair across her head and refastened a pin to hold it there. She kept her eyes on Ronnie, though, as if weighing something up. Finally, her hands dropped back onto her lap. 'You are correct, Mr Edwards. I am not telling you everything.'

Ronnie nodded, but said nothing.

'I *can't* tell you everything.'

'Then I probably won't be able to help you further.'

'You don't get out of it that easily, Mr Edwards.'

'I'm not trying to get out of anything, Mrs King. I'm just a little, well, stumped.'

Janet brought the tea to a table in between them and settled the tray down. Mrs King waited until her carer had served tea, then beckoned her to sit as well. 'It's difficult, Mr Edwards.'

'What is, Mrs King?'

'The reason I'm holding something back from you.'

Ronnie took a sip of the scalding tea and put the cup back on its saucer. 'Are you scared, Mrs King?'

For a millisecond, something that looked like disdain flashed across Mrs King's thin face, then it resumed its usual stern look. 'What do you think I could fear, Mr Edwards?'

'I'm not sure.' Ronnie turned his notebook over nervously. 'I wondered whether the shock you had was because someone did something on purpose. You know...' he waved the notebook, '... perhaps they had something to gain if you were, well, dead?'

Mrs King's face hardened. 'You think someone was trying to give me a heart attack?'

'It's possible.'

There was quiet for a while as Mrs King thought this through. Ronnie took another ill-fated sip of his tea, burning his throat as he swallowed hastily.

'I imagine,' he said carefully, 'that there would be people who would gain financially once you have...'

'Dropped dead?' finished Mrs King. 'Do you know the contents of my will?'

Ronnie shook his head, making the cup rock in its saucer. 'Of course not. I have no idea.'

For a second, he thought Mrs King might reveal those contents, but she only shrugged. 'I am an exceedingly wealthy woman, Mr Edwards, but my children have created their own lives and money, in case you were thinking they had something to do with anything. However, there is no doubt that many will benefit from my eventual demise.'

Ronnie swallowed. 'And perhaps some who wouldn't?'

'What on earth do you mean by that?'

'I have read about wills that those who think they should get something and don't have contested.'

Mrs King turned to look out the large windows. The view through them was of unending paddocks, all smartly fenced with wooden posts. Groups of horses and cows stood in the distance, and it was the animals that Mrs King seemed to focus on. 'And are they successful, Mr Edwards? Those contenders?'

'I don't know,' said Ronnie, his face betraying him again. 'I haven't been involved in any actual cases.'

'I see.' Mrs King turned back to him. 'Is there anything else you've been thinking about? I'd like to know all your theories about my incident.'

'Oh, right. Well, maybe someone has been diddling your books and is trying to cover it up?'

Mrs King grunted. 'I have always done my own books and I can assure you my finances have not been *diddled* with.'

Ronnie swallowed. 'That's... great. What about disgruntled employees wanting to harm you?'

Mrs King gave a tight-lipped, abrupt laugh. 'I'd like to see them try. Anything else?'

'Well, I guess my other thought is that you saw something that unintentionally gave you a shock so badly that your heart, well, you know, got very shocked.'

'That's your last theory, Mr Edwards? I inflicted my condition on myself?'

'Not intentionally, Mrs King. I only meant that on reading about Takotsubo cardiomyopathy it said that a great shock will cause it.'

'What would be an example of such a shock?'

'Well, the article said things like the death of a spouse. Or the death of a pet. Or even a surprise party.'

'A surprise party?'

Ronnie felt the almost permanent stain on his cheeks glow hotly again and wished he hadn't mentioned parties. It was clear that Mrs King, although she might not like a party, wouldn't be so emotionally upset that it would cause her heart condition. Then he felt bad that he had shoe-horned

Mrs King into the 'I hate parties' box when he really couldn't tell whether she did or didn't. His face burned severely.

Mrs King watched him closely, as if she could read his every thought. 'Get him water, Janet,' she said suddenly. 'The poor lad is about to buckle.'

Swifter than he imagined, a glass of cold water appeared in his hand and he drank it noisily. Once he had set the empty glass on the table, he found Mrs King looking at him with amusement. 'I'm sorry,' he said, voice raspy despite the water. 'I didn't mean to offend.'

'You didn't. It was kind of you to think you could. I am well used to people's opinions of me, founded or not, and I decided long ago that I wouldn't care.' She leaned back and tugged the soft rug a little higher. 'It isn't easy, Mr Edwards, being rich and being an old woman. People expect you to become loopy as you age and they're somewhat disappointed that I'm not.'

'I certainly don't think you're loopy.' Ronnie took a deep breath in and a short one out. 'Although you are still hiding something from me.'

Mrs King gave that guarded smile again. 'Well done, Mr Edwards. You are correct. I do apologise, but I cannot tell you what it is. All that you can do to remain in my service is to continue to do what I ask, even if it doesn't bring me, or you, joy.'

Ronnie looked down at his notebook for a moment. It bulged with names of people at the Mulbury Gala, information about hearts, and screeds about the cattle Kings. 'What would be the next thing you'd ask me to do, Mrs King?'

'Well now, that is a hard question.' Mrs King curled a finger at Janet, who immediately came to her side. 'I'm not sure.' She pushed the rug aside and used the other woman's hand to help her stand. Beast clambered to his feet and stared at Ronnie. 'I am tired, Mr Edwards, and I don't think well when I'm tired. I'm going to leave the next part of the investigation to you. Report back here when you have something. Maybe it will prompt me to tell you more.'

Ronnie stood as well as the two older women made their way slowly across the room, Beast like a sentry by their side.

'Be in touch, Mr Edwards.'

'I will, Mrs King.'

'Can you let yourself out, Ronnie?' asked Janet over her shoulder.

'Yes, sure.' Ronnie repacked his satchel and watched the two women and the dog as they disappeared into a side room. Mrs King was tiny compared to the more solid Janet, although both weren't what he would call large. He felt sad suddenly, and it took him the walk down the corridor to the front door to work out why. The house was large for two people and a pet, even if the pet was the size of a horse. Although light and comfortable, the house had a loneliness about it, as if it should have been filled with children and laughter.

It was as he closed the door behind him he saw what Beast had so delightedly hauled up the corridor. It was part of an old sign, peeling paint juxtaposed against the handsomely styled handles of the umbrellas, a capital letter S the only visible text. *What a strange thing to have in an umbrella stand,* Ronnie thought briefly, until the dilemma of finding out what Mrs King wouldn't tell him filled his head once more.

TWENTY-ONE

The shop had been empty for half an hour, and Rosemary tidied all that needed tidying. Sunny watched her mistress roam around the shelves, swishing her thick ginger tail gently from side to side. When at last Rosemary stopped in the middle of the floor, the cat meowed once. 'Yes, I know,' said Rosemary impatiently. 'I'm going now.' She flicked her sign over to read "Back in 5 pickly minutes" and went out the door.

Outside, the air was still, holding its breath. The ten steps to The Read Mulbury took only a few seconds. Rosemary stood at its door for another one or two, then pushed it open to reveal a gaggle of readers crowded around Jasper as he explained the order of books in a series about urban vampires. He saw her over their heads, hesitated in his speech, but she waved him to continue and went back outside. The door closed again, shutting out his familiar, warm voice.

The last thing she wanted to do was to go back inside her lonely shop and straighten her jellies in their already straight lines. Instead, Rosemary took a deep breath, let it out hard and fast, and marched towards Robert Sparkling's mansion. She passed The Sweet Potato, where faint chanting floated down from the open upstairs window. The café itself was empty, as was the Square. Perhaps the entirety of tourists were in the bookshop listening to Jasper. She arrived at the old mayoral residence sight unseen.

Scaffolded and stripped, the old home looked somewhat indecent. Nothing, though, could obscure the fact that it was a mighty property, built with arrogance, but used appropriately when it counted. It was easy to imagine its vastness as a haven for bushfire refugees. There was a solidness around it that must have been comforting when the world around it was on fire. Rosemary stepped inside the front gate to see the façade more closely. If it had been used as something else, a lodging house, for example, there might have been signage painted on its front. She went closer, then jumped as the front door opened unexpectedly.

A paint-spattered Robert looked out. 'Rosemary. Come to help me?'

'No.'

'Thanks for considering it, anyway.'

She glared at him. 'Why aren't you at work?'

Robert looked toward his garage. 'No work.'

'That's hard to believe. I had heard you were quite a talented mechanic.'

'I am.' He grinned. 'Haven't had your car in there yet.'

Rosemary thought of her metallic blue sedan. *Alasdair's* blue sedan. 'I had it serviced recently.'

'Well, it must almost be due again.'

'When I need you, I'll let you know.'

The smile faded from his face. 'Anyway, why aren't you at work?'

'No customers. I was taking a walk.'

'In the middle of the day?'

'It happens.'

'Just like my garage.'

They stood for a moment staring at each other, then Robert stepped back.

'We're eating lunch. Come and join us.'

Rosemary glanced back at her shop, but the day's inertia was still apparent and the area under the veranda remained empty. 'I only have a moment.'

'A moment will do. You can explain why you were staring at the front of my house so intently.'

Rosemary followed him down the hall, noting the advances he'd made on repairing plaster cracks and floor-boards. It was admirable the way he worked on by himself when he had the means to hire whoever he wanted. As they entered the huge centre room, however, she heard a young woman's laugh coming from the kitchen, and almost changed her mind. Maybe he wasn't the one-man show she'd thought he was?

'We're in here.' Robert strode ahead of her, unbuckling his overalls and rolling them down to his waist. Rosemary only had a moment to consider his slim-fitting T-shirt before she arrived at the kitchen to see Heather Hubbard sitting cross-legged on the table, facing the end wall and chuckling.

'You've got Heather helping you.'

Robert went to the bench and heaped a salad roll onto a plate. '*Helping* is probably too strong a word,' he said as he handed lunch over. 'She likes to come in here every few days. She seems to know when I'm getting bogged down.'

'What do you mean?' Rosemary leaned back onto the bench and took a bite of the roll. Her own zucchini pickle taste flooded her mouth.

'Good, isn't it?' Robert grinned as he joined her in

eating. 'Heather didn't want anything, so it was lucky you came along.'

'You said that she comes here every few days.'

'Ah, yes. She tells me she's talking to her friends.'

Rosemary watched Heather lean forward intently, the laughter gone, as if listening to a story. 'She's seeing something.'

'I guess she is.' Robert munched on another mouthful.

'That doesn't concern you?'

'Should it?'

'I don't know.'

He balanced the roll on its plate and pulled a handkerchief out of his pocket to wipe his mouth. 'Heather doesn't worry me. She's mainly happy, although she has these moments of what I'm calling *melancholy.*'

Rosemary studied Heather. The young woman had her head bowed and her hands grasped in her lap. It was impossible not to interpret her posture as deep sadness. 'What's wrong, Heather?' Rosemary asked quietly.

Heather didn't answer. After a moment, she lifted her head and smiled into the corner of the room. The sadness fell away.

'Curious, isn't it?' Robert finished his lunch and put the plate down. 'My haunted house.'

'You never see or hear anything?'

He shook his head. 'Nothing. If Silkie was around, she'd say I was an *insensitive.*'

'Have you seen her?'

'Silkie? No.'

'If there really are lost souls here, I thought she'd be hanging around this house like a persistently foul odour.'

'That's what I thought, too, especially after the last time she was here and the song and dance she made about the place.' He took Rosemary's empty plate from her. 'What's going on there, do you think?'

'I don't know. Both sisters have become uncharacteristically quiet.'

'You still haven't said.'

'Said what?'

'What you were doing standing in front of my house, gazing at my windows.' Robert smiled mischievously. 'Were you hoping for a glimpse of me through the glass?'

She regarded him sternly. 'If I wanted a glimpse of you, Robert Sparkling, I'd knock at the door and bellow for you to open it.'

'Subtle.'

'But effective.' She shrugged. 'I was looking for a hint of what this place may have been after the mayor vacated and before the fires came through.'

'What do you mean? Wasn't it empty for a long time?'

'You tell me. You have the title.'

'I know who owned it, but I didn't think they lived in it. Am I wrong?'

'Hard to say. Do you have those photos Mrs Lionel gave you?'

'They're in my study. Do you want a look?'

'Yes.'

They left Heather humming on the table and walked up the stairs to the next level. Although the renovations had stalled up there, it was still a lovely area. Robert led her to one of the side bedrooms where he'd set up a desk and computer. The photos were stacked neatly to one side. He picked them up. 'They've helped me work on the outside repairs but were no use for the inside.'

'Do you have the time period they were taken?'

'Mrs Lionel gave me a rough idea.'

'Which ones were taken about sixty years ago?'

He looked at her. 'That's specific. Why?'

'Just show me.'

He shuffled through the photos as she continued to hold them until he arrived at a batch that was quite faded. 'These.'

Rosemary put the others down and took her time gazing at the three left. The pictures were similar: the front of the house from slightly different angles. One had a woman strolling past looking crossly at the camera as if she'd tried to hurry to get out of the shot. One had a cat that stared up from the doorstep. The other was void of living things and showed nothing more interesting than windows draped in heavy curtains. Rosemary brought it closer and pointed to something to the right of the door. 'What's that?'

Robert peered over her shoulder. 'What's what?'

She tapped the photo impatiently.

'That long mark? I don't know. A tree branch?'

'There were trees in the front yard? There's not much room.'

'Maybe they were further out on what's now the nature strip.'

Rosemary shook her head. The mark was too straight to be a tree branch. It looked like a pointer protruding from the wall. She looked at it for so long, it blurred. Robert still leaned over her shoulder, studying it just as intently, and she suddenly noticed how warm his close presence was. She looked at him and he smiled at her, his eyes even darker than usual in the dim room.

'Right,' she said, straightening so that he had to step back. 'Mind if I keep this one for a while?'

He shrugged. 'Why?'

'There's something about it, but don't ask me what.'

'Okay, you take it and tell me what you're up to once you work it out.'

The irritation in his voice was slight, but Rosemary still caught it. 'I would like to know what they used this house for in that lost time.'

'Well, so would I, seeing as it's my house.'

'I'll find out and we'll both know.'

'I could help.'

'How?'

He tucked his hands into his overall pockets. 'If I uncover anything interesting, I'll let you know.'

'Deal.' She lifted the photo in thanks and walked out of the room, down the stairs and outside without seeing if he followed.

As the door closed, she spun around to study the bricks where the mark on the photo was, reaching up to touch the wall. Under her fingertips, she discovered two round holes about the size of a ten-cent piece and masked by cobwebs and dust. She frowned and stood back. They were positioned next to the door, as if they had once held a swinging sign heralding a shop or a pub, but there was no evidence in any records that the mayoral residence had been either. What, then, had it been?

TWENTY-TWO

Rosemary crossed the Square, detouring to the shade of The Exceptional Tree. Its thick branches wound up into its canopy and ended in frills of pointed leaves that waved gently in the breeze. She stared up into them for a moment, glimpses of sunshine they let in dazzling her eyes, then looked across from where she'd come from. The mayoral residence tucked in behind The Sweet Potato, but she could see it from where she stood, scaffolding caging it in.

'Heavenly, isn't it, darling?'

Rakisha swept up behind her, carrying a large paper tray. The smell of Cornish pasties filtered into the air.

'You've been to Franco's.'

'Oh, yes.' Rakisha lifted her package and sniffed. 'I needed something, well, *substantial* today.'

'Right.'

Rakisha came closer, her long frizzles playing around her head with the breeze. 'Silkie is leaving, darling.'

From the gleam in Rakisha's eye, the pending absence of her sister wasn't worrying her too much. 'Did she have a pleasant holiday with you?'

Rakisha blinked. 'Was it a holiday, darling? I suppose it was, in a sort of scheming, family way. We don't *holiday*, never have. How do you holiday from Mother Nature and the catastrophes we humans have bestowed upon her?' She shook her head, then gazed up into the Tree. 'And besides, having this gorgeous reminder of the pure domination of earthly things is like having a holiday every day, don't you think, darling?'

Rosemary said nothing. While having the ancient Tree at the centre of Mulbury was a beautiful and majestic piece of luck, she'd never associated it with a vacation. From the way Rakisha sniffed her pasty, she hadn't noticed Rosemary's lack of an answer. 'Did you decide anything about your mother's possessions?'

Rakisha stopped mid-sniff, holding her breath for so long Rosemary almost grabbed her in alarm. Rakisha breathed out. 'We have distributed Mama's things between us.'

'I imagine the journal was a sought-after piece.'

'Oh no, darling. Silkie was only too happy to leave it with me.'

'It didn't reveal the correct things for her.'

Rakisha smiled, a broad wide curve of her lips that transformed her always slightly worried features into pure happiness. 'Poor Silkie. She knows now.'

'She knows what?'

Rakisha patted Rosemary's arm. 'The truth, darling. It's a good thing, isn't it, to know the truth?'

Rosemary blocked the image of Alasdair that immediately rose into her head. 'I don't know. It can be very painful.'

Rakisha nodded solemnly; the smile gone. 'Yes, darling. Painful. But a *good* pain. A *healing* pain.' She waved the pasties around. 'A pain that infiltrates the lies and lurches them out, sending them forth to be squashed and flattened.' The pasties did another circle, sliding noisily in their cardboard tray. 'The truth is painful, but cleansing. *Cleansing*, darling.'

Rosemary watched as the pasties settled. 'Perhaps.'

Rakisha smiled again, a little less feverishly than before. 'I must go, Rosemary darling. Silkie must almost be ready. Enjoy your meditation with the Tree.'

Rosemary leaned on the entangled barricade around the Tree as Rakisha flowed back to The Sweet Potato, her layers of tie-dyed cloth floating around her. Through the café window, Rosemary could see Silkie sitting at the rattan table inside. A pasty must have appeared in front of her as she picked up a knife and fork and ate. A second later, Rakisha sat beside her. The yellow light of the cafe interior juxtaposed the two heads of the sisters: one dark, one light. Yet they picked up forks in the same way, index fingers stretched across the silver to the edge of the tines.

A babble of voices caught her attention as the group of book lovers emerged from The Read Mulbury, chatting excitedly and holding stamped paper bags of books. Rosemary began the walk back to The Preserved Mulbury, but the small crowd veered the other way to peruse Patti's clothes of many colours.

Rosemary crossed the road and tried to go back to her shop, but her feet took her the other way. Before she could think, she'd pushed the door of the bookshop open.

Jasper looked up from his counter. 'Oh,' he said.

'Oh? Is that all you can say?' She hadn't meant to sound so cross, but the sight of his placid features turning to stone when he saw her made her heart hurt.

'No,' he said, 'I could say more.' He closed the top of his computer.

'You sound like a petulant child.'

'And you sound like a bossy teacher.'

They locked eyes. 'Right,' said Rosemary. 'I suppose I do.'

'Yes. Then that's settled.'

Jasper was the first to drop his eyes. He fiddled with a pen and paper in front of him, writing himself a note that Rosemary saw, on coming closer, was indecipherable. 'Jasper,' she said quietly, 'I'm sorry.'

'Are you now.' He still didn't look up. 'Are you really?'

'I said I was, so I am.'

'Yes, but what are you sorry about?'

She waited until he lifted his head. He didn't quite look her in the eye, but it was an improvement. 'I'm sorry I hurt your feelings.'

Now he looked directly at her. 'Anything else?'

Rosemary blinked. She cast her thoughts back, rolling through the last time they'd spoken and the unfortunate reaction he'd had to mention of that ridiculous curse. 'No. Is there something else?'

Jasper picked up a book on the counter. It was the urban vampire story, something that involved a total invasion of the world by the look of the cover. He pounded the counter with it. 'Yes, Rosemary, there is something else. It's called being a friend. It's called being supportive of your friend.'

'I am supportive of you.'

'But you don't believe me.'

'What about?'

He gave the counter another whack. 'You see, that's it!'

Rosemary folded her arms. 'Jasper, I don't know what you're talking about.'

'I know you don't! I know.' He let the book drop, smoothing its hideous cover as if apologising to it. 'I know.'

'Right.' Rosemary glanced around the room. Through the doorway, she could see Snowy's tail waving gently from the couch, as if to show he was aware of the noise. Of the discord. 'Let me start again, Jasper. I'm sorry that I hurt your feelings. I am supportive of you. You are my friend. Of course, I support you.'

'But you don't believe in my family curse.'

She was about to agree with him, but held back. 'I believe *you* believe in this curse. I'm sorry that I can't as well.'

He considered that, rocking slightly on his heels. With all the counter pounding, his long hair had fallen over his shoulders and caught at his sweater. She resisted the urge to brush it back, to smooth it down. It was, she realised, a maternal gesture. Is that how she felt about Jasper? *Maternal?*

'Why are you shuddering?' he asked.

'I wasn't.'

'You were. I saw it.'

'Listen,' she said, putting both her hands on the counter so they mirrored his. 'We need to compromise. I can't believe that you have a family curse that chases you around and gives you bad luck, and you can't believe that I can't believe you have a family curse that chases you around and gives you bad luck. We're at a crossroads here.'

He stood up, his hands leaving the book to flick his hair back. 'We are.'

'We can be friends still. Friends always disagree about something.'

'You and Mrs Lionel don't.'

'We do. She tells me off all the time.'

Jasper smiled. It was brief and weak, but it was a start.

'Come on, Jasper...'

He was quiet for a long time. Outside, tourists went up and down the pavement. Rosemary tried to block thoughts of them taking jars from her shop without paying or stealing Sunny. The latter wasn't a genuine concern: Sunny would fight like a cat possessed if a stranger picked her up. She kept still, not taking her eyes off the man in front of her.

'Okay.'

She let her breath out. 'Right. Good.'

'I'll prove it to you?'

'What?'

The door of The Read Mulbury sighed open, letting in two older women and the sounds of a suddenly busy Mulbury. Jasper leaned forward. 'I'll prove to you that curses exist. That I am not making it up or being paranoid or any of those other things that stop you-' He pulled back.

'Stop me what?'

He shook his head, then smiled past her as the women approached the counter.

'Jasper,' whispered Rosemary furiously. 'Stop me what?'

He leaned further over, so she did as well. Their heads met over the middle of the counter. 'Stop you from loving me.' He whipped upright. 'Hello there. Can I help you with a selection?'

Rosemary stepped away as the women made it to the counter and turned sharply to leave as fast as she could. She didn't dare look back, instead wrenching the door open and almost leaping over the step to land on Gerry's foot as he stood surveying his wife's products.

'Oh, Rosemary, there you are.' Gerry didn't look at her, but nodded briefly toward the racks. 'You started that.'

Rosemary could hardly work out what he was saying. She felt cold but hot, a shivering feeling, but with sweat forming on her forehead. 'What did I start?' She knew exactly what she'd just started, or perhaps continued, with Jasper.

'That.' Gerry smiled. 'We're hosting trial days for those who applied for the assistant position.'

'I know. Gerry, the ad hasn't closed yet.'

'Does that matter?'

'Technically, yes.'

'Oh, well, maybe we shouldn't then...'

He said that with such little enthusiasm, that Rosemary turned to see what he was watching.

Patti's products had, once again, spilled over onto the pavement, racks lining up against the imaginary barrier that was the start of Jasper's shop. A couple of heads stuck out over the top of them: Hannah Hubbard's spiky blonde one, the top of Patti's apricot coif, and another that Rosemary didn't immediately recognise until the person stood up straight. The smooth, black hair was the same, but she had done it up in a high beehive ponytail. 'That's Silkie.'

'Yes,' said Gerry, grinning. 'Turns out she really likes Mulbury and wants a job here.'

'What does Rakisha think of that?'

'I imagine she's quite pleased.'

'I imagine she isn't. Silkie was meant to leave today.'

'Oh, was she? She said nothing about that. She turned up a few minutes ago and made a genuine effort. Do you see what she's wearing?'

'No.'

Gerry took Rosemary's elbow and steered her over to the edge of the pavement. 'Now look.'

Rosemary had a complete view of Silkie as she carried a frock to the end rack. Gone were the flowing layers that had made up her signature statement. Instead, she wore three-quarter-length trousers with a slim-fitting striped top, and her eyes were made up into cat eyes. She was the picture of a 1960s woman, a far cry from the mysterious seer she'd tried to be. 'I see.'

'Amazing, isn't it? She looks just right for the role.'

Rosemary saw Hannah notice their scrutiny of Silkie. Hannah cast her eyes down to her own outfit, a practical blend of comfortable jeans and a slightly sagging T-shirt. There was nothing wrong with what she was wearing for a touristy town shop assistant, but it was more animal food than upcycled seamstress-ing. 'This isn't about how your assistant looks, Gerry,' said Rosemary, watching the determined way Hannah spaced the garments on the rack. 'It's how they operate.'

'Yes, Rosemary, I hear you. But I think it's important to Patti to have a certain look as well. After all, people are flocking to Mulbury because of her style.'

There was no disagreeing with that. Even as they watched, another car pulled up and a pile of visitors rushed over to Patricia's, squealing enthusiastically. The noise was so loud that Jasper came out of his shop to see what was going on. He smiled at the crowd, but then saw Rosemary. His eyes lingered for only a split second, then his gaze slid past before he went back inside.

Great, thought Rosemary. *We're back to square one.*

TWENTY-THREE

Hannah Hubbard finished the trial day at Patricia's in a foul mood. The squealing tourists had set her teeth on edge, and she thought more than once of the peace and quiet of the produce shed at Mulbury Feeds. There, nothing was louder than the reverse beeping of the new forklift, and even that had a rhythm to it that was more hypnotic than annoying. The shrill cries of 'Daphne, you look gorgeous!' and 'Tanya, your waist is beautifully slim in that' were so deafening that she took up one of Patti's famous beanies and shoved it on her head.

'Um, Hannah,' said Gerry in her ear at some stage. 'You aren't meant to wear the products.'

'Take it out of my wages, Gerry,' Hannah had growled at him.

'Er, Hannah, we aren't paying you any wages. It's a trial.'

It was the last straw. Hannah fished out a ten-dollar note from her pocket and handed it to Gerry. 'Thanks, but no thanks to the job. I can comfortably say that it didn't work out.'

Back in the hay shed, Hannah sat on a chaff bag with the beanie twirling in her hand. There was no sound but the scratching of mice somewhere, but she didn't even move to find a trap. Holly was talking to someone in the enclosed area they called the shop, and Heather was nowhere to be seen. Hannah breathed in the summery smells of the large shed, and contentedly pulled out a strand of lucerne from a nearby bale to chew.

Holly laughed.

Hannah stopped chewing. Holly was known to laugh, but it was rare. Her serious older sister was more into frowning and worrying than hilarity. Hannah sat up as Holly did it again. It was a lovely laugh, full of real joy, and Hannah was more suspicious than ever. She slid from the bag and sidled over to the shop door.

Holly stood with a young man that Hannah took a moment to recognise. Without his uniform, or at least a shirt and tie, Toffee was much more ordinary. Still, he stood with ease in front of Holly, one hand extended to touch her elbow, and was leaning in when Hannah wrenched the door open, making it creak wildly and Toffee to jump back. 'Hiya,' said Hannah as if she'd just marched into the shed. 'Sorry, am I interrupting?'

There was no sign of laughter on Holly's face any more. She glared at her sister and tapped her watch. 'I thought you were working all day.'

'I did, didn't I?' Hannah twisted her sister's arm so she could see the watch as well. 'Well, nearly. I couldn't stand it, Holly. Too much...' she waved her hand around in circles.

'You don't want the job?'

'It wasn't the job so much as the chance to do something different. You know what I mean.'

Holly's glance at Toffee didn't go unnoticed. 'Yes, I do know what you mean.'

Hannah's stomach lurched a little. She stared at the man, but his gaze hadn't left Holly's. 'Aren't you going to try out at Patricia's as well?'

'I've changed my mind.'

Hannah frowned. 'Wait a minute...'

'What?' said Holly crossly.

'What's going on here?'

'Hannah...'

'What are you two up to?'

'Hannah!' Holly turned a reddened face to Toffee. 'I'm sorry. She was born in a cowshed and has no manners.'

'I was born in the same place as you, Holly Hubbard, and it wasn't a cowshed, as you well know.'

'Then how about you act like you *weren't* born in a cowshed?'

Hannah grinned. 'I beg your pardon, my lady. I'll just fetch your wrap so that you can take a turn around the garden.'

'I'll give you a turn.' Holly fished in her pocket and pulled out a set of keys. 'Here. You lock up when it's time. We're going to get Heather.'

The grin faded from Hannah's face. 'Why? Where is she? Is she okay?'

'Yes, she's fine. She's at Robert's. She's been spending a lot of time there, so I want to know what's going on.'

'Should I come along?'

'No, you shouldn't. There's a box of guinea pig pellets to unpack before we shut, so you go for it.'

'Thanks a lot, sis.'

'No problems, *sis*.'

Hannah watched as Holly and the young man went to

the door. He held it open for her, but Holly ushered him through first, turning as she followed to give Hannah a last-minute stare. Hannah wriggled her fingers at her.

It was only once Holly and her companion had disappeared that Hannah felt another lurch in her stomach. Holly was a hard worker and had put her everything into making Mulbury Feeds a great business, but it was no longer in the family. Even though Robert Sparkling had said the sisters could buy it back from him, Hannah sensed that Holly's heart wasn't quite in it. She worked just as hard, but Hannah had caught her casting longing glances out through the vast tin shed doors as if there was something there that had caught her eye. And that was before the mysterious Toffee had come along.

Hannah rubbed at her head and surveyed the box of guinea pig food. *Good luck that I'm better at animal produce than upcycled denim,* she thought. *Looks like I'm needed here.*

THE FRONT DOOR of the old mayoral residence was propped open, but Holly paused on the doorstep to knock. 'Hello? Anyone there?'

The hall echoed her words, but no one answered.

Holly shrugged and headed down towards the big centre room, Toffee behind her. The beautiful ballroom was empty, and sunlight through the vast windows along the side lit the floor and showed up a gentle tumble of dust motes. She stood for a moment, listening, but there was nothing to hear.

Toffee caught her arm. 'Dance?' he said.

'What?'

He spun her around and grasped her hand, leading her into a vigorous waltz around the floorboards.

'Stop, Toffee, stop.'

He stopped immediately, letting her hand go, and she tugged at her shirt so that it fitted better over her hips. 'Okay, I'm right now.' She grabbed his hand. 'One, two, three.'

A grin spread across his face, and Holly smiled back. Who would have thought that dancing around a derelict building could be such fun? She urged him faster, and they sped around, her ponytail working free, so hair flew out behind her as they went.

On their third turn, Holly saw Heather standing at the door to Robert Sparkling's kitchen. Holly spun out of Toffee's arms and swept Heather up instead, whirling the startled young woman around the room.

After half a turn, Holly looked up at her sister's face and slowed. They came to a swirling stop, and Holly gripped Heather's arms. 'What is it, Heather?'

Instead of being exhilarated by the dance around the place, Heather looked terrified. Long strands of hair striped her face, and Holly brushed them back to get a better look. Always wide, Heather's eyes were almost bulging. Holly gasped. 'What is it, Heather? What's happened?'

Heather blinked slowly, two fat tears rolling rapidly down her cheeks. 'They took them away, Holly.'

'Who did? Took what?'

Heather waved her arm out to take in the enormous room. 'Took them from here.'

'Robert's been robbed?' Holly looked around the space. 'But there's nothing much to take. Did they steal the paint?'

Heather shook her head slowly. 'Took them.'

Toffee walked slowly over. 'Is she okay?'

'No, not really.' Holly rubbed her sister's arms, trying to warm Heather's vibrancy back into her. 'Can you look around? She thinks someone's stolen something.'

Toffee's footsteps were firm and fast on the bare boards. He disappeared into the kitchen, then came out shaking his head. Holly gestured at the stairs and he leapt up them two at a time. After a few minutes, he came back down and shrugged. 'I don't know the place,' he said, 'but there's nothing obvious missing. Robert's computer is still there, so they weren't after that.'

'Hello?'

Holly turned quickly, pulling Heather behind her, but it was only Robert standing in his house, looking a little startled at his visitors.

'Is everything alright?'

'Yes. No.' Holly let Heather go as her sister moved back to the kitchen. 'Sorry, we knocked, and no one answered. Your door was open.'

'Oh, yeah. I had to go to the garage for a bit. Is Heather okay?'

'She thinks you've been robbed.'

'Really?' Robert glanced around the room, then ran up the stairs to retrace Toffee's steps. He came back slowly, shaking his head. 'I can't see anything missing. What did Heather say?'

'She said something was taken. And she was crying.'

Robert's face creased as he frowned. 'I can't see anything gone that would be worth crying about. Does she cry often?'

'Only if there's a reason.' Holly put her hands on her hips. 'Would there be a reason?'

'I don't think so. She came in earlier and went into the kitchen where she's been spending a bit of time.'

'In the kitchen? Why? She doesn't cook much.'

'Oh, it's nothing to do with cooking. She sits on the table and chats away.'

'To you?'

Robert shook his head. 'Not always.'

'Oh, crumbs.' Holly felt for her ponytail, but the band was gone and the curls fell messily to her shoulders. She scooped her hair up and tucked it into the collar of her shirt. 'She's found another imaginary friend.'

'*Another* imaginary friend?'

'Yeah, she's had a collection of them over the years. We used to think it was because we didn't pay her enough attention, but it's more than that. She has a vivid imagination.'

'So,' said Toffee, 'nothing has been stolen?'

Robert regarded him. 'I know you, don't I?'

Toffee offered his hand. 'I'm Christopher Gillespie.'

'You work with Geoffrey?'

'That's right.' Toffee blushed. 'Only I don't call him Geoffrey.'

Robert laughed. 'No, I suppose not.'

'So, what's Heather talking about?'

'I have no idea.'

Holly shook her head, then headed to the kitchen, hearing the men follow her. Heather was indeed sitting on a broad wooden kitchen table with her legs crossed. The tears had gone. Instead, she leaned forward earnestly toward the corner of the room. Holly crossed over to her and put a hand on the worn surface of the table. 'Heather? What's going on?'

Heather took her time to look at her sister, but when she did, her eyes were clear. 'Holly, terrible things.'

'What terrible things?'

Heather shook her head impatiently. 'They were taken.'

'Robert says nothing's been taken. Everything's fine.'

Heather frowned. 'Not now. Then.'

'Heather, I don't have any idea what you're talking about.'

Heather's face twisted, and Holly thought she was going to cry again. Instead, though, Heather sat up and shook her finger at the corner of the room. 'Then *listen*, Holly!'

Holly blinked in surprise. Although it wasn't unusual to see Heather emotional about things her other sisters couldn't feel, she rarely got angry. 'What was taken?'

'Not what. *Who*.'

Holly turned to glance at Toffee and Robert, who stood with equally puzzled faces. She turned back to her sister. 'Heather, who was taken?'

Heather shook her finger at the room again, then stared fiercely at Holly. 'The little ones, Holly. They took all the little ones!'

TWENTY-FOUR

Rosemary heard Mrs Lionel jangle into The Preserved Mulbury, but kept her eyes on the computer screen. Even so, she could see out of the corner of her eye that her friend was approaching. When Mrs Lionel reached the shop counter, she put her clasped hands on it with a thud that made Rosemary type something strange. She closed the lid of the laptop and turned to face Mrs Lionel's music. 'What can I say? He still isn't talking to me.'

'I suppose you told him you still didn't believe in his curse?'

'Of course.'

'Why on earth, Rosemary Exeter?'

'What do you mean?'

Mrs Lionel sighed and undid her hands to pat a soft curl away from her face. 'There are times, as you well know, that you have to do a little shoe shuffle.'

'A shoe shuffle?'

'Yes! A little dance around the truth for the sake of friendship.'

Rosemary frowned. 'No, I still don't know what you

mean.'

'I mean, you should have lied.'

'And told him I believed in his curse?'

'Yes! It's not a lie, it's a white...'

'Lie. A white lie is a lie, isn't it?'

'No. Well, yes. But at times you have to.' Mrs Lionel stretched an arm out and tapped her finger on Rosemary's stock book. 'It wouldn't hurt you to stretch yourself.'

'I told him that I understood he thought he had a curse.'

'Then what did he say?'

'That he was going to prove it to me.'

'Oh, no.'

'What?'

'Well, don't you see? Now he's going to go out of his way to make sure that his curse is on display with his every move.'

They fell silent. Outside, Goldmarket Road was empty, despite the mild day. Rosemary could just hear Patti Yale humming as she rearranged garments on the pavement racks, and vaguely wondered who else was with her.

Sunny came out of the house and made her way to her mistress, winding herself around Rosemary's legs and purring loudly. Rosemary bent over and swept her up. 'What you're implying,' she said slowly, 'is that I've just made Jasper worse?'

'It's not entirely your fault.'

'Only eighty percent my fault.'

Mrs Lionel smiled. 'It's not really anyone's fault, it just is. That's what you have to tackle.'

'I still have to tackle it?'

'Do you want Jasper talking to you again?'

Rosemary's shoulders slumped involuntarily, and she hid the movement by shifting Sunny up in her arms. The cat responded by butting her under the chin and purring even more loudly. 'I'd like that very much.'

'Sorry, I didn't hear that?'

Rosemary glared at her friend. 'I'm sure you heard me.'

'Of course I did, dear. I'm just checking that you're going to do what it takes to make amends.'

Rosemary set Sunny on the floor, and the cat went back inside. 'I'll try.'

'Very good.' Mrs Lionel clapped her hands to her side. 'I'll leave you with some news.'

'News.'

'Yes.' Mrs Lionel started for the door. 'Jasper's shop has that mysterious woman in it. Not mysterious to me. I know who she is.'

'Who is she?'

'Ah.' Mrs Lionel tapped the size of her nose. 'There's something for you to talk to Jasper about. See you later, dear.'

The thud of the door closing seemed to echo around the shop. Rosemary stayed where she was, listening intently for any noise through the dividing wall, but she couldn't hear anything useful. Patti was still humming outside, and the low rumble of Gerry's voice joined in. They laughed and then even that sound was gone. Rosemary felt the emptiness stretch around her.

The upbeat song that heralded a phone call from her daughter was a welcome relief. 'Honey.'

'Hi, Mum.'

'Everything alright?'

'Yes. Yes, yes, yes.'

'I see. So, everything is *not* alright?'

'I'm fine.'

There was a shuffling noise, and then Honey's voice

came louder. 'Do you want to know what I did today?'

'Of course.'

'I got up at four o'clock, wandered around the house, went back to bed at five o'clock, got up at six o'clock, washed the kitchen floor, cooked breakfast, did a load of washing, made a cake in the shape of an elephant, ate its trunk, washed the dishes, called you.'

'I see.'

'Somewhere in that time, I also helped Ronnie type up his notes from an insurance case, took Cuddles for a walk to the corner of the block and back, and pruned back a dead branch from the plum tree out the front.'

'You sound busy.'

'I can't seem to stop. I feel really...'

'Restless?'

'Yeah. Restless.'

'And Tallulah?'

'She's just as restless, although in a different way. She's bunkered down, but sometimes I can feel her stretching.'

'And otherwise you're fine?'

'Yes. So' Honey let out a sigh that filled the phone with the sound of a tornado. 'What are you doing?'

'Minding shop.'

'Busy day?'

'Not particularly.'

'Anything else going on?'

'Patti and Gerry are trialling some people interested in their assistant position.'

'Really? Who?'

'Hannah Hubbard.'

'Hannah? Why is she interested in being a shop assistant? A clothes shop assistant at that?'

'You'd have to ask her.'

'I will. Who else is trying out?'

'Silkie.'

'Rakisha's sister? I thought she was only in Mulbury for a short time.'

'So did Rakisha.'

'Anyone else?'

'Heather.'

'Oh, perfect. And how did all these applicants go?'

'You'd have to ask Patti.'

The phone went quiet. Rosemary heard the squeak of Honey and Ronnie's sliding door as it opened and then the happy panting of Cuddles as he came inside. 'I think I will. In fact, I think I'll do that now.'

'You're going to ring her?'

'No, I'm coming for a visit. Put the kettle on.'

'Honey...'

But Honey was probably already in the car.

Rosemary slipped the phone back in her pocket. The thought of Honey coming for a visit washed away the uneasiness she'd felt ever since Mrs Lionel had left. It would be at least thirty minutes before Honey arrived. Time enough to go into The Read Mulbury, introduce herself to the other woman, and get it over and done with, whatever 'it' was. She flicked her "Back in 5 pickly minutes" sign over, went outside, and marched to the book-shop. She had her hand on the warm wood panelling of the heavy door when Rakisha ran across the road towards her, tripped on the gutter and crashed into a rack of Patti's skirts. The resulting cloud of garments and noisy shrieks made Rosemary stop. She sighed, let her hand fall, and went to help Rakisha.

'Oh, Rosemary, darling,' said Rakisha from underneath a denim miniskirt trimmed with fake fur. 'I've fallen over.'

'Yes.' Rosemary held out her hand. 'Can I help you?'

'No, I don't think so, darling. Not just yet. I think I'll just stay here for a tick.'

Rosemary looked down at the woman, who folded her hands across her stomach as if she was settling in for a sleep.

'Oh,' said a voice behind her. 'Is Rakisha alright?'

Rosemary caught the scent of flowers, spring rain, and sunshine and guessed it was Patti. 'She says she is.'

'Goodness,' said a deeper voice that could only be Gerry. 'I don't think she can stay there. She's flattening your minis.'

'Rakisha, sweetie. Let's get you up.'

Rakisha shook her head. 'No, darling, but thank you. I'm very content here.'

'What on earth is she doing?'

This third voice didn't have the sweetness of Patti or the concern in Gerry's. It was more like a thundering menace. Rosemary guessed immediately that it was Silkie.

'She tripped,' said Rosemary.

'Rakisha, get up!'

'No, Silkie, darling, not yet.'

'You're disturbing the customers.'

'Oh,' said Patti. 'We don't have any customers at the minute.'

'You're squashing Patti's clothes.'

'She is,' said Gerry, squatting awkwardly down to Rakisha. 'You are.'

'I'm so sorry, Gerry, darling,' said Rakisha, not moving.

'Is there a reason,' said Rosemary, 'that you're lying there?'

Rakisha strained to see her sister. 'She'll tell you.'

Silkie stood back as the others turned to her. 'I don't know what she's talking about.'

Rosemary studied the woman. She wore a hip-hugging skirt and a Peter Pan collared shirt, and her long hair hung in a high ponytail. It was about as far from floaty tie-dye as she could get, and it suited her. 'You were leaving.'

Silkie glanced at Rosemary. 'Who told you?'

Rosemary shrugged, and Silkie nudged her sister with the toe of her shoe.

'Now, Silkie darling, tell them everything,' said Rakisha from the ground.

'Do you have a story to tell us, Silkie?' Gerry eased himself up, gripping his thighs and groaning softly.

'Ask her about her attire, Gerry darling.'

Gerry's round face reddened. 'I don't think I...'

'You *have* changed your style,' said Rosemary.

'Is that a crime?' Silkie tossed her ponytail over her shoulder.

'You look lovely,' said Patti, plucking a small lint from Silkie's shoulder. 'It quite surprised me when you came to see us.'

'I didn't recognise you,' said Gerry. 'You look so...' He waved his hand around.

'Different,' said Rosemary.

'Ask her why,' said the voice from the ground.

'Why?' said Rosemary.

'None of your business,' said Silkie quickly.

'Right.'

'Ask her what she was wearing when she came to first see me.'

'Quiet, Rakisha.' Silkie stooped to right the rack that had tumbled when Rakisha fell into it. 'I can wear what I like.'

'She wears what she thinks she is,' said Rakisha, struggling to sit up. Gerry knelt back down to help her.

'Well,' said Patti, frowning. 'Don't we all?'

'No,' said Rosemary.

'But you do, Rosemary darling.' Rakisha heaved herself into a sitting position, her legs stretched out in front of her. 'You wear those.' She waved her hands at Rosemary's jeans and navy-blue jacket.

'Yes.'

'But they're *you*, darling! If you suddenly wore...' Rakisha pointed at Patti, '... a swing dress. Why, we'd think you'd gone bananas!'

Rosemary tucked that fact away.

'Anyway,' said Rakisha, pulling at Gerry so she could stand, 'Silkie has a lot of different costumes.'

'I do not.'

'You do.'

'But,' said Gerry, rubbing his head where Rakisha had put her hand to steady herself in the final centimetres of her ascent, 'you came along to try the job out in vastly more suitable clothes than those you normally wear. Those, you know, *layers*.'

'You see, darling,' said Rakisha, 'there's no need for Silkie to wear them anymore.'

'Quiet, Rakisha.' Silkie took her sister's arm. 'That's enough. How about I take you back to the café in case you need a lie down.'

'I don't need a lie down, darling.'

'I think you do.' She tugged at Rakisha.

'Wait,' said Rosemary. 'Why were you running across the road, Rakisha? You looked like you needed to tell someone something.'

'Yes,' said Rakisha, 'I was hurrying...' She frowned. 'The little tumble has momentarily taken it away. Wait, darlings...' The frown deepened, then her eyes widened.

'Ah yes, got it.' She twisted out of Silkie's grip to face Rosemary. 'There's a woman in The Sweet Potato who won't move.'

'Won't or can't?'

'Won't, darling. She just keeps ordering another earth-friendly legume coffee but she doesn't actually drink them.'

'Won't or can't?' said Gerry softly behind Rosemary, and Patti nudged him sharply in the ribs.

'What is she doing, then?'

'Crying, mainly. And a bit of this.' Rakisha rocked backwards and forwards, hugging herself.

'How long has she been doing that?'

'Most of the morning.'

'And you didn't think to help her?'

Rakisha stopped rocking and blinked. 'But I am, darling. I'm getting you.'

'Why me?'

'She's talked to you before, she says. Something about a house?'

Rosemary nodded. 'Did this woman tell you her name?'

'No, darling. She's far too upset to name herself.'

'Can you describe her?'

'Oh, yes, darling. She's...' Rakisha waved her hands up and down to show a thin woman about her own height.

'Very useful.'

'She said you would know her. She's been here before. Maybe I know her, too, darling? Let me think...' Rakisha tapped a fingertip on her lip.

Honey Blossom saved Rosemary by arriving in the bee station wagon. She heaved herself out as Rosemary swooped on her. 'Mum, what the...?'

'Come on,' said Rosemary. 'I want you to meet Miss O'Shannessy.'

TWENTY-FIVE

Jasper watched through the window of his shop as Rosemary linked her arm with her daughter's and they made their way across the road. He stood until they disappeared into The Sweet Potato, and even then, he lingered on, the books in his arms ready for display getting heavier.

'Jas,' said a woman behind him. 'What are you doing?'

'Oh, nothing. Just looking.'

The woman came to stand beside him, the top of her blonde head level with his shoulder. 'Don't tell me something exciting is happening in Mulbury?'

'I know you won't believe me,' Jasper said, squatting to lower the books onto the broad window ledge, 'but Mulbury is a hive of excitement.'

'Really?'

'Yeah. In a domestic, heartfelt way.'

'That's not really the type of excitement I'm used to.'

'It's the sort of excitement that does me these days.'

The woman took his arm. 'Are you sure, Jas? You don't want to come back to the city and live a little?'

'What makes you think I'm not living a little here?'

'These.' The woman pointed at the books he was now lovingly stacking onto a piece of pink fabric.

'What's wrong with these?'

'Regency romance? Is that what floats your boat these days?'

Jasper felt his face flush. 'It's what always floated my boat. I just couldn't let you, or anyone else, know it.'

'By anyone else, do you mean Isabella?'

Isabella. Jasper hadn't consciously thought of his ex-wife for a long time. *Isabella Salvia Cockington-Brown.* Now her name scrolled through his brain, bringing with it an image of her long, auburn hair and the piercing green of her stare. He shivered. 'Don't, Iris.'

'What is wrong with you, Jas? She's been out of your life a long time.'

'She made it worse.'

'Made what worse?'

'Nothing.'

'Rubbish nothing. Tell me.'

Jasper looked at Iris, her fierce gaze reminding him of someone else. 'Isabella made my curse worse.'

Instead of rolling her eyes, which is what the person he'd just been reminded of probably would have done, Iris nodded earnestly. 'I'd believe that. Isabella is a nasty character.'

He settled a few more books in place. 'Do you ever see her?'

'Only accidentally. Once at a café and once in a bookshop. That was ironic.'

'Why do you say that?'

'I didn't know she could read.'

Despite the tension now resident in his gut, Jasper smiled. 'You know she read a lot.'

'Social media, hairdresser's magazines, wine bottle labels. Do you think they count?'

'Now you're getting catty.'

'Yep. And you love me for it.'

Jasper put a book on an angle so that the cover shot of Miss Middleton showed in all her regal glory. 'Yes, I do.'

'Shucks, thanks.' Iris used his shoulder to kneel beside him. 'Anyway, what's with all this public display of emotion?'

'What do you mean?'

'These books. Why are you sticking romance books out here for everyone to see?'

'Why wouldn't I? People love romance books.'

'So you tell me, which is why I don't get why you're putting them on display.'

'You aren't making any sense.'

'I'm telling you something you once told me. Don't market things that are going to sell, anyway. Market the extraordinary or the mundane to pull new customers in.'

'I told you that?'

'A version of it.' She fluffed up the pink fabric so that it gathered at the base of the books. 'Romance sells anyway. Shouldn't you be using this area for some other genre?'

'I've had Mum's books in here a lot.'

Iris smiled. 'That's lovely.'

He sat back on his heels. 'It's the least I can do.'

'Are you sure it wasn't for another reason?'

'Now what are you talking about?'

Iris finished her arrangement and stood up. 'Well, you know. I thought you might have used Mum's books in a display to attract your father.'

'Oh.' Jasper stood quickly. 'I have done that.'

'Well, who knows? Maybe your dad, unlike mine, will

be into Regency romances, just like his son?' She spun away, laughing.

Jasper followed her, glancing back once to see whether Rosemary and Honey had emerged from The Sweet Potato, and nearly walking into a shelf as he did. There was no sign of either woman. There had been a moment early that afternoon when he thought Rosemary was headed his way, but she'd stopped to manage some kerfuffle at Patricia's, and now she was off for afternoon tea at the best earth-friendly café in town. It gave him an idea.

'Iris,' he called. 'Do you want a brownie?'

'A brownie? You got some?'

'No, but I could duck out and grab a couple if you wouldn't mind keeping shop for me.'

'Mind? I'd love to! You know that I'd move here to help you in a heartbeat if you'd let me.'

'You just told me to come to the city and live a little!'

'Yeah, well, but it's so cute here.'

'Iris, you know you can't move here. Your kids are in the city and Doug would hate the country life.'

Iris leaned back on the shop counter and pouted. 'Stop pointing out the obvious things in my life that are holding me back.'

Jasper thought of Iris's job as the manager of a chain of posh furniture stores. 'You really think they have held you back?'

'Yes. Well, no. Who knows? I might have been a rock star in another life.'

'You can't sing.'

'Doesn't seem to have held some rock stars back.'

'Anyway. I'll be back in a moment.' He turned to go, but swivelled almost immediately. 'Iris?'

'Yeah?'

'Thanks for staying with me. It's... nice.'

She smiled at him, that familiar sisterly grin that always warmed him. 'I get a holiday out of it, too, you know.'

'Yeah, well, I appreciate it.' He pulled the door open and waved as he left.

Outside, Mulbury was at peace. Patti's garments swung gently, sending him a whiff of wool wash and tenderness. Rakisha and her sister stood in the sunlight, staring at each other like they were in some sort of contest. They ignored him as he crossed the road, as did Robert Sparkling, who was crouched down over a car bonnet with its owner. The Square was empty apart from the generous spread of The Exceptional Tree. He reached The Sweet Potato and peered through the front window.

An older woman sat at Rakisha's little rattan table, both hands over her face, sobbing helplessly. Honey was next to her, as close as someone could get with a full-term pregnancy. Rosemary stood a little way apart, a grim look on her face. She noticed Jasper through the glass, and for a moment she smiled. Then she seemed to remember the scene in front of her and she grew serious again. Jasper hesitated, then pushed his way inside.

Honey looked up at him but didn't stop the gentle circling of her hand on the sobbing woman's back. Rosemary shook her head once at Jasper, although he hadn't been about to say anything. He came to stand near her.

After a few more minutes, the woman dropped her hands. 'I'm so sorry. I feel so happy for you.' She wept a little more.

'It's okay,' said Honey. 'I'm sorry to have upset you.'

'Oh, it's not you. It could be anyone. I used to handle it, but now I can't. Isn't that ridiculous? Here I am, a woman in her eighties, getting upset at the beautiful sight of a pregnant woman.'

'I don't think it's ridiculous,' said Honey. 'It doesn't matter how old you are in years; your thoughts stay the same.'

'No, they don't.' The older woman unclipped a handbag that sat on her lap and pulled out a delicate hanky. 'My thoughts have finally caught up with the fact that I have missed out on so many things that I thought were still possible. I am at the end of my life, dear girl, and I feel *bereft*.'

'Oh.' Tears ran down Honey's cheeks. 'That's so awful.'

'In what way,' said Rosemary softly, 'do you feel bereft, Miss O'Shannessy?'

'Mum, perhaps Miss O'Shannessy doesn't want to talk about it.'

'It's okay.' Miss O'Shannessy smiled wanly at Honey. 'I would like to explain.' She dabbed at her cheeks with the hanky. 'It's been obvious for many decades now that I would not get my own children, but I thought I would have a chance to be a great aunt or be something to someone. But, no, I'm a nobody to everybody.'

Honey gave Rosemary and Jasper a startled look.

'I'm sure that's not true,' he said.

'It is. Sad, but true, as they say. I have no one young in my life, only a bunch of other sad women, all in the twilight of their very full lives.'

'They can't be all sad if they've had full lives,' said Rosemary.

'Perhaps not sad all the time. But everyone is getting older and very few have families that care for them. Care *about* them, that is.'

'You're including Mrs King in this conversation.'

Miss O'Shannessy looked sharply at Rosemary. 'How would you know that?'

'Mrs King has family, but I don't see any signs of them caring for her.'

'They care.'

'I'm sure they do. But *care* and *caring* are two different concepts. I imagine Mrs King's closest companion is Janet.'

'Well, that I wouldn't know.'

Rosemary went to the little table and pulled out the second chair there. 'But you're friends. So you said.'

'We were best of friends at a time when friends were in short supply. But we haven't spoken for sixty years.'

'Is there a reason for that?'

Miss O'Shannessy shrugged. 'Circumstances.'

'And all this time later, you're suddenly interested in Mrs King again.'

'I've followed her life through the newspapers. Then I read about her being in Mulbury. I never thought she'd come back...'

'She's been here before?'

Miss O'Shannessy coughed and patted a strand of hair back into place. 'I've said too much.'

The café was quiet for a long minute, in which Rosemary looked at Honey, who looked very puzzled. 'Is there anything we can help you with?'

'No. Thank you.'

Rosemary sat back a little in her chair. 'I can't help but notice that there is something that connects Mrs King and you. Something that makes you intently concerned for her. Perhaps you even care about her more than her family does because of this connection.'

Now the silence filled the shop. Jasper felt like he was in some awkward soap opera, but he'd stepped inside and couldn't now step out as if he didn't care. *Care* seemed to be needed at the table right now, and although Rosemary spoke softly, he knew from experience that her gaze was sometimes too confrontational even though, to those who knew, it only signalled a genuine interest in the situation. He unstacked two more chairs from a pile in the café's corner and set them down, signalling to Honey, who sat gratefully, her hand on her belly. 'Miss O'Shannessy, my name's Jasper Lu,' he said quietly. 'I own the bookshop. I'm sorry to have stepped in on such a private matter, but it would feel wrong for me to leave now. Unless, of course, you would like me gone.'

Miss O'Shannessy stared at him. 'You have lovely eyes, Jasper Lu. I'm very sorry that you've seen me like this.' She turned her look to Rosemary. 'Is he your husband?'

'No.'

'I'm sorry, did I use the wrong word? You say partner these days, don't you? I didn't mean to cast aspersions. It's just that you had that look that passed between you both as if you know each other well.'

Jasper shook his head faintly, but Miss O'Shannessy was tearing up again. 'Can I ask,' he said, 'what has upset you so much?'

'This,' said Honey, pointing at her bulge. 'Tallulah.'

Miss O'Shannessy gave a choking gasp. 'Is that what you're calling your baby?'

Honey looked alarmed. 'Yes. Why? Is something wrong?'

Miss O'Shannessy's tears had started again, this time a stream of water that poured out with no accompanying sobs. 'No. It's very nearly perfect.'

Honey's alarm turned to bewilderment. 'Is it?'

'Oh yes, yes!' Now Miss O'Shannessy was smiling, tears

gathering in the creases around her mouth. 'My baby's name was Matilda. Tilly, I would have called her, just like you might shorten Tallulah.'

'Miss O'Shannessy, I don't understand.' Honey glanced at her mother before turning to the older woman. 'What did you mean by *your* baby?'

'My baby.' Miss O'Shannessy turned an anguished face to Honey. 'The one they *stole* from me!'

TWENTY-SIX

Rosemary frowned. 'Who stole your baby?'

'Who? Authorities, my parents, the people who adopted her.' Miss O'Shannessy shook her head sadly. 'I was a disgraced girl who had no choice in the matter.'

'Right.' Rosemary felt the wave of grief flow from the woman in front of her to the group gathered around the table. Having your baby taken from you was unimaginable.

Honey Blossom was looking as upset as Miss O'Shannessy. Rosemary saw her clutch at her stomach, as if protecting her baby from being snatched, and put a hand out to grasp her daughter's arm. 'Honey, careful now.'

'I'm alright,' said Honey, her voice shaky. She held her tummy tighter. 'Oooof, another Braxton Hicks.'

'What's happening?' asked Jasper, his eyes wide.

'Practice contractions,' said Honey, breathing more easily. 'They're very annoying.'

'Are you sure they're only practice ones? I mean, you looked in pain.'

Honey gave a short laugh. 'They aren't comfortable, that's for sure.' She glanced at Miss O'Shannessy, but the older woman was busy dabbing her cheeks again. 'What do we do, Mum?' she whispered.

Rosemary squeezed Honey's arm and let go. 'Let's keep sitting here for a while.'

'I can sit here. I don't have anything else to do.' Honey nodded to the outside world. 'Looks like you've got visitors.'

A touring coach was parked alongside the Square, spilling forth a gaggle of people who hit the gravel and dispersed in all directions. Some went immediately across the road and disappeared into the four shops under the veranda.

'I can stay as well,' said Jasper. 'My shop's covered.'

'Who by?' asked Rosemary, but before Jasper could answer, Rakisha burst into the café, her long hair catching on the door frame.

She yanked it free. 'Oh, darlings, excuse me. Here comes the crowd! Bus passengers are always ready for some of my lovely organic produce.'

Rosemary nearly disputed this as bus passengers almost always didn't know what they were getting when they ordered Rakisha's produce, but there was no time. She stood up, exchanging a look with Jasper, who quickly averted his eyes. 'I'll go. Will you be alright, Miss O'Shannessy?'

'Yes, yes. My friend will be here soon. She went to buy something from that lovely farmer just out of town. He has a little farm store.'

Honey nodded to Rosemary and turned back to Miss O'Shannessy. 'You mean Justin?' Rosemary heard her say as she left. 'Yes, he's a real sweetie...'

Rosemary smiled as she went over the road. The real sweetie, she could state categorically, was Honey. It's as if her name had branded her from the moment she was born. *I wish I had some of her sweetness,* she thought suddenly. *It might help with the Jasper situation.*

She tucked the Jasper situation into the back of her mind and thought instead of Miss O'Shannessy's stolen baby. She served the many happy customers in her shop while her brain brewed ideas. Wave after wave of people came in and out of the shop until she was certain that the entire busload had bought at least one jar of something from The Preserved Mulbury. They stripped the winter citrus conserves shelf, and the one containing the tangy tomato chutney that people paired with a sharp cheese and water crackers. There was no time to restock until the bus sucked its passengers inside and they left.

Rosemary went down to her cellar to bring up more product, but found herself staring mindlessly at a box of beetroot. If Miss O'Shannessy had indeed had her baby taken, it must have been sixty years ago or thereabouts. Even so, after all that time, it had certainly upset Miss O'Shannessy to see Honey. *I wonder whether she would have been as upset if she'd seen Honey in Big Town and not Mulbury?*

'Rosemary?'

The voice above was Mrs Lionel, who peered into the cellar. 'Hang on, I'm coming out.' Rosemary balanced the box of beets on her hip and climbed the creaky wooden ladder to emerge into her kitchen, where Mrs Lionel was fussing about with the kettle. 'Need a cuppa?'

'Oh, goodness me, yes. What a lot of business I've done in the last hour.' She waved a hand at the box. 'You too?'

'Yes. Hardly anything else left.'

Mrs Lionel nodded. 'My soaps are gone. I'll have to ask Ronnie to come and help me again. Do you think he would mind? I mean, Honey's so very close.'

'Honey's in The Sweet Potato.'

'I meant close to having that little baby. What is it, dear? You look disturbed. Is Honey alright?'

Rosemary set the box on the kitchen bench and shut the trapdoor into the cellar. 'I left Honey with Miss O'Shannessy. She's very upset.'

'Honey?'

'No, Miss O'Shannessy. She became very emotional at the sight of Honey.'

'Sometimes people are like that with pregnancies. Reminds them of their own time, perhaps.'

'Miss O'Shannessy said she had her own baby taken from her a long time ago. She said she was a disgraced girl.'

'Oh.' Mrs Lionel rubbed her hand wearily across her face. 'It happened more than you think.'

'Really?'

'The reasons were usually complicated family ones. Stigma, disgrace, shame. She would not have had a say in it. It happened to thousands of women across the country in the early part of the last century.'

Rosemary put her head down. 'Thousands? That's terrible.'

'Yes. Long-lasting psychological effects.' Mrs Lionel filled the kettle. 'Did she say whether she'd been reunited with her baby? Some people were.'

'She didn't say, but I doubt it. She was so upset.'

Afternoon tea with Mrs Lionel, usually a chatty, warm affair, was unusually sombre. The horror associated with Miss O'Shannessy's situation hung over them as they sipped Darjeeling tea. Mrs Lionel seemed exhausted from the deluge of tourists and kept rubbing her gnarled fingers as if they were aching. On the pretence of getting more hot water, Rosemary texted Ronnie to come as soon as he could to help with the making of more soap so that Mrs Lionel wasn't tempted to start by herself. *On my way,* Ronnie texted back, and Rosemary smiled. 'Looks like Ronnie has some spare time this afternoon for you.'

Mrs Lionel sighed. 'Today? Goodness, I thought I could have a little rest.'

'He's getting good at making the soap, you said. Just point him in the right direction.'

'Yes, he's pretty handy. He talks to me about the business as he works, did you know that? I think he and Honey have a hankering to run a little shop of their own.'

'Not a great time to start a new venture.'

'Probably not.' Mrs Lionel sipped at her refreshed cup. 'But often there isn't a right time. You have to go with the flow. Isn't that what the young ones say?'

'Which is how you started your own shop.'

A smile relaxed Mrs Lionel's face. 'Yes. Mr Lionel had died, I'd sold the farm, and suddenly there was a void in my life that I couldn't think how to fill. But then I bought the shop, and that was that. It fell into place. I'm not saying it wasn't hard work, but it was worth it.'

The door jangled and Rosemary put her cup down, waving at Mrs Lionel to keep sitting while she went to the shop. A woman stood in the middle of the room, looking lost. 'Can I help you?' said Rosemary automatically, looking beyond the woman to the empty Square. There was no sign of Honey or anyone else.

'I'm not a customer,' said the woman, sounding amused. 'I'm wondering where Jas is?'

Rosemary shifted her attention to the woman, seeing at once the blonde hair, the wide smile and the T-shirt that read *I heart reading.* 'Jas?'

'Jasper. You know? He lives next door?'

'Jasper. Jasper is in The Sweet Potato.'

'Yeah, he was getting me a brownie, but he must have forgotten about it.' The woman stepped forward and held out her hand. 'I don't think we've met, although I feel like I know you. I'm Iris.'

Rosemary took it. 'Iris. Jasper's sister.'

'That's me.' Iris tipped her head. 'You sound surprised.'

'Have you ever been here before?'

'In Mulbury?' Iris shook her head. 'Once or twice. Passing through to somewhere else usually. Too busy to visit, you know.'

'You're here now.'

'I'm helping Jas with...' She stopped, tucking a strand of hair behind her ear in a way that reminded Rosemary of Jasper. 'Well, some family things.'

'What things?'

'Oh.' Iris looked astonished. 'Jas will tell you, I'm sure. He's always spoken so highly of you.'

It was Rosemary's turn to be astonished. Mrs Lionel saved her by leaving. 'Hello, Iris,' she said, on her way to the door. 'I must get going. Ronnie will be here soon.'

'Let him do everything,' called Rosemary.

Mrs Lionel wiggled her fingers in farewell and the door jangled shut.

Rosemary stared at Iris, who was staring right back at her, head still tipped as if waiting for more. Rosemary felt a little like she was being dissected and shifted uncomfortably. 'Cup of tea?' she said loudly.

'Don't drink tea. I'll have a coffee if you have one. Or I could whip over to where Jas is and get us both one.'

'The Sweet Potato doesn't serve coffee.'

'Really?'

'Not the type you can drink, anyway.'

Iris laughed, a strong sound in the quiet shop. 'Well, I'll just have to go with what you've got.'

Rosemary led the way through the connecting doorway and left Iris crooning to Sunny while she re-boiled the kettle. Although she had her back to them, she could tell Iris was a winner with the ginger cat. A loud purr sounded after a few seconds.

'She's truly gorgeous,' said Iris, sinking into a dining room chair with Sunny in her arms as Rosemary put a coffee plunger on the table. 'Where did you get her?'

'She was a present from my husband.'

Iris nodded, scratching Sunny firmly under the chin. 'You got at least one good thing from him, then.'

Rosemary said nothing, choosing to pour the coffee instead.

'Sorry, but Jas tells me everything.'

'Does he, now.'

'I shouldn't have said anything.' Iris leaned down and lowered Sunny to the floor. 'Sorry.'

Rosemary took a large sip of coffee, burning her mouth and wishing she'd gone for a relaxing lemon and camomile tea instead. Iris's candidness was both disturbing and honest. 'Jasper talks to you a lot.'

'Yep, he does. We've always been close. Not like him and Helena. Hey, this is great coffee. Thank you.'

Rosemary pushed a plate of date biscuits towards her. 'Are you staying long?'

'No. I'm going soon.' Iris took a large bite, but kept talking. 'I've stayed to make sure Jas is okay.'

Rosemary put her cup down so heavily, coffee dribbled down its side. 'What's wrong with him?'

'Jas? Nothing's wrong with him at the moment. But, you

know, something's bound to happen after...' She pointed a finger behind her, stabbing the air a few times.

'Meaning?'

'Meaning his curse. Surely you know about that? Well, after that meeting we had with Helena, something bad will happen to him.'

'I don't get it.'

'Don't you?' Iris looked genuinely surprised. 'When something good happens to Jas, his curse makes something bad happen. It's how it's always been.'

'That doesn't make any sense.'

'Yes, it does.' Iris put her cup down and counted on her fingers. 'He wins a scholarship to university; Mum dies and he can't go. He gets a new job; Isabella divorces him. He inherits money to start his bookshop from Uncle Cormac; Jas gets sick. It's Jas's bad luck. JBL, we call it.'

'That's ridiculous.'

Iris went still. 'No, it isn't. How would you know? I've known him all my life and I've seen it.'

Rosemary didn't feel like arguing. She leaned back to diffuse the tension. 'Something good has happened now that makes you think bad will follow?'

'Oh yes.' Iris grinned. 'Helena says she's found Jasper's father.'

And that was all Iris would say about it. 'Jas will tell you when he's ready,' she said as she went back out the door. 'It's sad that he hasn't already.'

Sad wasn't quite the word Rosemary had in her head as she watched Jasper emerge from The Sweet Potato with Miss O'Shannessy on his arm. He steered the older woman toward a car driven by her friendly neighbour and headed back to The Read Mulbury. *Strange,* was how Rosemary would describe the situation. Unlikely, even. But there it was. Jasper hadn't told her and since he was barely talking to her, it was quite likely he wouldn't.

She was saved from further dark thoughts by Honey walking back across the Square at the same time as Ronnie pulled up in the old bomb and parked behind the bee car. The couple stood by the station wagon for a time, talking. Honey kept a hand on her belly, and Ronnie a hand on his wife's shoulder as Honey talked, no doubt telling him about the morning. Rosemary turned away. They didn't need her spying on them, although it was evident from Honey's blotched face that the event was still upsetting her.

Sunny sat on the floor directly under the skylight, her tail neatly wrapped around her body with its tip resting on her front paws. She lifted her head slightly as Rosemary went back and was rewarded with a firm pat along the marmalade-coloured stripes flowing down her neck. 'It'll work out,' said Rosemary. 'Jasper will tell me the story of his father and Miss O'Shannessy will reconcile her grief.'

Sunny flicked her tail once and stalked to the windowsill, curling up on a pile of Patti's tablecloths. She looked back at her mistress. *Don't count on it,* she seemed to say.

Rosemary ignored the cat and spent a few minutes earnestly straightening jars. She thought of Miss O'Shannessy and the tragedy of losing her baby. The birth of Honey Blossom was the most extraordinary moment of Rosemary's life, and she couldn't imagine the pain of having her taken away. Her hand shook as she spun some pickles to show their label more clearly. It was absolutely possible, despite what she'd said to Sunny, that grief reconciliation would never happen for Miss O'Shannessy, but it was odd that she'd come to Mulbury to sit in The Sweet Potato to display her raw agony. Why now? Why here?

The bell jangled as Ronnie and Honey entered. Ronnie looked sombre, but Honey was brightening again. 'Everything alright?' asked Rosemary.

'Not really, as you know.' Honey sighed. 'But I'm trying not to feel too sad in case it affects Tallulah. She's been kicking hard all that time in the café. Mind if I have a rest, Mum?'

'Of course not. The couch is free.'

'Ronnie's going next door to help Mrs Lionel.'

'Yes, I will,' said Ronnie. 'Can I tell you about my visit to Mrs King first?'

'Yeah, I almost forgot about that.' Honey waved her arm in the direction of the living quarters. 'Come in here, though. I want to hear what Mum thinks.'

Rosemary ushered Ronnie in front of her and went for the kettle, setting cups and saucers up on a tea tray while Ronnie settled Honey on the couch. She smiled to herself as Honey said, 'Stop fussing, Ronnie. I can plump my own pillows.' By the time the tea was drawing, Honey was on her side on the couch and Ronnie sat clutching a cushion in the armchair next to his wife.

'You went to see Mrs King.'

'Yes.' Ronnie gently tucked the cushion behind Honey, who rolled her eyes at her mother. 'I'm not sure I gained a lot of direct information, but at least I got to meet her.'

'Tell Mum what she was like.'

'Let me guess,' said Rosemary, pouring the tea. 'After a health scare like that, on top of how she looked at the Gala, I imagine she looked frail but sounded strong.'

'I hadn't thought of it that way, but yes.' Ronnie took the proffered cup. 'She was more ill than I imagined, but she still wouldn't give up any more clues about what I was looking for.' He took a noisy sip. 'Janet was there, and this gigantic dog called Beast.'

Honey chuckled. 'Not that I know her at all, but I can imagine someone as formidable as Mrs King calling a dog Beast.'

Rosemary nodded. 'What did Mrs King have to say?'

'She admitted she wasn't telling me everything, but she said she hadn't been threatened, despite knowing that everyone did not love her. I don't know what to do.'

'How was the house?'

'What do you mean?'

Rosemary pushed a plate of biscuits Ronnie's way. 'I

mean, she has Janet to care for her, but in reality, they are two older women alone.'

'Yeah, you're right. I thought the house was too big and empty for them.'

'I bet Beast took up a bit of room,' said Honey from the depths of the couch.

'I've never seen a dog so big! He got hold of a piece of wood that was in the umbrella stand and dragged it up the hall.' Ronnie pulled his phone from his jeans pocket. 'See?' He offered the phone to Rosemary.

The dog was enormous, but the piece of wood was no bit of kindling. Rosemary zoomed the photo out and studied it more closely. It was flat and long, covered in peeling green paint. Beast had drooled on it, leaving a dark patch that showed up a different coloured paint. Faint yellow showed through. Rosemary tipped the phone towards the light and zoomed out for more. 'There's writing on the wood.'

'What does it say, Mum?'

'I'm not sure. I can see an S. The rest is blurry.'

Rosemary magnified the picture, getting closer and closer glimpses of Beast's muzzle as the dog slobbered over the wood. The last frame was of a dog's nostril and a closeup of the paintwork. '*Sun*,' Rosemary read. '*Sun* something, something, *use*.'

'Sun use?' said Ronnie. 'Weird.'

Honey sat up. 'How's it written, Mum? What's the gap between letters?'

Rosemary took a pad and pen she had on the coffee table and wrote the letters as she saw them.

'*Sun use*,' said Rosemary. 'Ah.'

Honey reached for the paper. 'What do you mean, "ah"?'

Rosemary took another coloured pen and filled in the gap. 'I mean, now I see. It should read: *Sunshine House.*'

'Which means nothing to me.'

'No, it wouldn't. Miss O'Shannessy mentioned it to me during a visit. She asked whether I knew of a place in Mulbury called Sunshine House.'

'Why?'

'She didn't say why.'

'Why do you think, Rosemary?' asked Ronnie.

'I think she was asking about a place where she once stayed.'

'From the way you said that, Mum, you don't think it was a holiday.'

'No. Not from what she said then and not from what happened today.'

Ronnie frowned. 'I don't get it. Why would Mrs King have a piece of wood with "Sunshine House" on it and what's it got to do with Miss O'Shannessy?'

Honey took Ronnie's phone and did a quick internet search. 'There are a lot of Sunshine Houses on the web, but mostly they're talking about houses in the city of Sunshine. There's nothing about a Sunshine House in Mulbury.'

'It's possible they didn't want this sort of house advertised. I imagine they went to great lengths to keep it from the public.'

Honey stared at Rosemary. 'You think this is the place where they took Miss O'Shannessy's baby?'

'Yes.'

'Hardly a sunny Sunshine House then.'

'No. I imagine it was a place of much pain.'

Ronnie leaned forward to put his elbows on his thighs. 'Yeah, but what's the connection to Mrs King?'

Honey shook her head. 'Pretty obvious, sadly. Miss

O'Shannessy agreed she had a connection with Mrs King but that she hadn't seen her in sixty years. I reckon Mrs King had a baby stolen from her as well.'

Ronnie sat back with a thump. 'Oh. That's terrible.'

'Yes.'

'It might be different for Mrs King,' said Ronnie. 'Miss O'Shannessy said she didn't have any children. Mrs King does.'

'I don't think so, Ronnie,' said Honey. 'It wouldn't matter how many other children you had; you're still missing one.'

A deep silence followed, one which was finally disturbed by Sunny jumping onto the couch to settle against Honey.

'So,' said Ronnie slowly, 'what is Mrs King doing with the sign?'

Honey took a biscuit from the plate. 'And what has this all got to do with her stress cardiomyopathy?'

'Maybe nothing,' said Ronnie. 'I guess it was really stressful back when it happened, but it's not a recent stress. Takotsubo cardiomyopathy is from a *sudden* stressful situation.'

'What do you think, Mum?'

Rosemary stared out her back window to the trees waving in the wind. The day was ending, with the spring light fading from cornflower blue to a pale wash. The colour of the sky was like a metaphor for time passing, she thought. All those events and memories fading in intensity, no matter how sharp they'd appeared at the moment of their happening. Ronnie was correct. Mrs King's cardiomyopathy was caused by something acute, but he may not have been right about it not being connected to past events. 'I can't say what I think right now,' Rosemary said, patting Honey's hand.

Honey sat straighter. 'That means you have an idea.'

'I have lots of ideas. First, though, I'm curious about Sunshine House. It was a big house in this town sixty years ago.'

'Well, there are a few big houses left around Mulbury.' Honey shifted Sunny closer to her. 'Jules and Roman's house, for starters. That has, what, six bedrooms?'

'Yes. They built those houses at the height of the gold rush for various rich people.'

'Not the poor miners who were stuck in tents.' Honey grimaced. 'Or their families.'

'Of course, there's one house that is most notably large and has been used for various purposes.' Rosemary raised one eyebrow at her daughter.

Honey nodded. 'Of course.' She heaved herself up, making Sunny tip over onto the cushions. 'Let's go.'

'Go where?' said Ronnie.

'You're going to Mrs Lionel's.'

'Yeah, but where are *you* going?'

Honey slipped her jacket on. 'The mayoral residence.' She smiled at Ronnie. 'Once known as Sunshine House.'

Rosemary closed the shop five minutes early to walk with Honey to Robert Sparkling's. The Square was empty except for two women standing under The Exceptional Tree looking up into its branches. As Ronnie disappeared into The Green Mulbury, kissing Honey goodbye as he did, Rosemary studied the women more closely. One wore a long, pastel, crocheted shawl while the other had a rocka-billy dress covered in red hearts. They couldn't have dressed more differently, although the arch of their necks as they gazed upward was eerily similar.

Honey closed the door on the croaking frog and stood next to her mother. 'What are Rakisha and Silkie doing?'

'Watching for purple spotted lyrebirds?'

'You're terrible, Mum.'

'I am. But they look intense. Should we find out on our way?'

'Why not?'

They went across Goldmarket Road and onto the Square, Honey puffing slightly up the curb. They arrived at the Entanglement next to the sisters, who glanced briefly at them. 'Thank the earth mother,' said Rakisha with a wave of her fingers at Rosemary. 'You'll be able to get him down. He might damage the Tree.'

'Who?' said Honey, looking up as well. 'No one's allowed to climb... Jasper!'

'What?' Rosemary leaned over the barricade to peer into the Tree. About two metres up, Jasper Lu sat on a branch, gripping it with both hands. He was also looking up and, as Rosemary stretched further, she saw what he had his eye on. 'Heather.'

'Heather's up there as well?' Honey tried to see, but her belly blocked her getting any closer. 'What's going on?'

'He will fall,' said Silkie suddenly. 'He will fall and then...' She let her voice trail away and blinked at Rosemary with heavy eyelashes.

'He won't fall if he's careful.' Rosemary cupped her hand and yelled up at Jasper. 'What are you doing?'

Jasper's face, framed by his black hair, was pale in the low light. 'Helping Heather.'

'Really? What does she need help to do?'

'She's putting a baby raven back into its nest.'

'Why does she need help to do that?'

Jasper shifted his hands, swaying a little as he did, making him lock his feet together. 'Why wouldn't she need help? I saw her go up and thought I should follow.'

'He will fall,' repeated Silkie solemnly. 'He will fall and...'

'Heather's quite capable of climbing a tree and getting back down in one piece,' said Rosemary to Jasper over Silkie's proclamation. 'Not sure about you.'

'Well, that'd be right. You're not sure about me for lots of things.'

'Jasper, don't be silly. I'm just wondering when the last time it was that you climbed a tree.'

'He will fall...'

'Silkie, darling,' said Rakisha, a hand on her sister's arm. 'I don't think saying that helps anything, does it? I mean, Jasper *might* fall, but he doesn't have to hear that you think he *will* fall.'

'He will fall.'

Rosemary took both hands from the barricade and folded her arms across her chest. 'And what makes you say that, Silkie?'

'You know. You know all too well.'

'I know much less than you think.'

Silkie held up a red-tipped finger. 'The curse. Of course, he will fall.'

'Curses don't make people fall. Clumsiness might.'

'And where, she-who-knows-nothing, might that clumsiness come from?'

'Lack of exercise? Genetics? Poor eye-hand co-ordination?'

'Are you talking about me down there?' Jasper tried to sit back and rocked on the branch. 'Don't you talk about me.'

'I am defending you, Jasper Lu,' said Silkie. 'Defending your curse.'

'Jasper,' said Rosemary. 'Even if you think you have a curse, you can get out of the Tree safely.'

'Oh,' said Jasper, lying down on the branch. 'You think the curse will make me fall.'

'I do not.'

'I do,' said Silkie. 'I know these things.'

'You don't, darling.' Rakisha twirled a grey ringlet around her finger. 'Mama said.'

Silkie pursed her lips and said tightly, 'You shush, Rakisha.'

'Jasper,' said Honey, 'you won't fall. Come down the same way as you went up.'

'But Heather...'

'Jas Jas Jasper.' Heather's legs came into view as she sidled down to stand on a branch level with Jasper. 'I saved the chick.'

'That's great, Heather.' Jasper sat up again, the branch dipping and swaying as he did.

'Are you scared, Jas Jas?'

'No. Well, not much.'

'I'll help you.'

'No, Heather, I don't think you can.'

Heather's light laugh floated down to the small crowd underneath. 'Of course I can.'

'He will fall,' said Silkie, but softly.

'Shush, darling.' Rakisha put her hand up. 'I can see the nest, glorious nest that it is, being held by the Tree in a loving fork.'

'The Tree has loving forks?' whispered Honey to Rosemary, but Rosemary was watching Jasper as Heather showed him the way down, putting her hand where he should put his. He followed her every move and was on the ground within seconds.

'He didn't fall,' Rosemary couldn't help but point out to Silkie, but the woman wouldn't look her way.

'No, darling. The Tree protects the good people of the town. I've always known that.' Rakisha stepped closer to Rosemary, so the scent of vanilla and nutmeg was strong in the air. 'Mama said,' she whispered.

'Your mother said that the Tree protects people?'

'No, Rosemary, darling. Mama said I know things.'

Rosemary eyed the beaming woman. 'That's what she wrote in the diary.'

'Yes, darling.' Rakisha tugged her shawl a little closer. 'Silkie was ever so upset but Mama said Silkie had no skills of a sensitive at all.'

'But you do.'

'Oh, darling!' Rakisha shook her arms so that her bangles clashed. 'Not as much as dear Mama but...' she dropped her voice '... more than Silkie. That's why she's dressed up.'

'She's trying to change her image.'

'Silkie is a chameleon. That's her special skill.' Rakisha stroked the shawl lovingly. 'She's no longer interested in Mama's things. I can keep them.'

'But she still has to mention Jasper's curse.'

'That,' said Rakisha, 'is the only thing of her Akita she has left.'

'Scaring others?'

'No, darling. Remember.' Rakisha tapped her nose. 'Silkie is a thief.'

Rosemary watched as Heather brushed bits of bark and leaf from Jasper's clothing. His face had warmed again, and he laughed as Heather produced a tiny down feather from the debris that clung to his sleeve. Rosemary stepped forward as Silkie did the same.

'You nearly fell,' said Silkie, so close to Jasper that her skirt brushed his legs.

'You didn't fall,' said Rosemary. 'We have things to do.'

'We do?' asked Jasper, eyes on Silkie.

'*We* do.' Rosemary indicated Heather. 'You, me, Heather, Honey. We're going to see Robert.'

'Robert Sparkling?'

'Do you know of another Robert in Mulbury?'

Jasper frowned, but at least his attention had moved from Silkie. 'Why do you need me?'

'Jasper.' Rosemary took a deep breath in but couldn't quite say what she thought she should. 'We need to talk to him about something, and you'll be interested in what he has to say.'

'I will?'

'Yes, you will. Heather, we need you as well.'

Rakisha leaned on the Entanglement. 'I will keep an eye on the chick, Heather darling. All is good.'

Silkie opened her mouth as if to talk, but Rosemary held her hand up. 'I think you should stay and chick-watch, too.'

'Don't tell me what to do, Rosemary Exeter.' Silkie tossed her ponytail back over her shoulder and stalked back to The Sweet Potato.

'We're going to see the sparkle?' said Heather, twirling the little feather between her fingers.

'Yes.' Rosemary started forward, Honey and Heather following.

Jasper fell in step beside her. 'Can I ask why?'

'I want to know what he found when he cleaned the rooms of his house.'

'Boxes of junk. He showed me.'

'Right.'

'What are we looking for?'

'I'm not entirely sure.'

They rounded the corner and saw a powerful light in the mayoral residence. By its position, Robert was working in the ballroom. Heather arrived first and pushed open the front door without knocking. The others gathered on the front step until Robert appeared. 'Okay, this is not normal. What's going on?'

'We think we've found something out about your house,' said Honey.

'Old plans? They would be useful.'

'No, more like what it was used for a long time ago.'

'Filling in its history? Great.' Robert stood back so that they could enter. 'I look forward to having some gaps filled.'

Rosemary was the last to step in. The old door was heavy and swung slowly. It was almost closed when she grabbed the edge and pushed it open again. 'Wait. Robert, do you have a torch on you?'

Robert felt in the tool bag around his waist until he pulled out a head torch. He gave it to Rosemary, who pointed the beam at the front wall of the house. 'What is it?' asked Robert as she steadied the light onto something.

'See?'

'No.'

'The round things. Bolts, perhaps. Something that fastened things to the wall.'

'Like what?'

She let the beam drop. 'Like a sign.'

'A sign? Like an old-fashioned shop sign?'

'Yes, but not a shop. A lodging house.'

'How would you know that?'

'We don't for sure. But was there anything that you found that might have resembled a sign? Or something that would hold a wooden board?'

'Maybe. I didn't take much notice. Come and see.'

Rosemary walked behind Robert as he went through the large expanse of the ballroom and up the stairs to the next level. Below them, Rosemary heard Heather in the kitchen, laughing as she said something to Honey. Faintly, she heard Jasper say, 'No, really? You know that?'

Robert went into one room to the left of the corridor. 'I

put everything I found in boxes I made from Hannah's pallets so that I could sort it at night.'

'And have you?'

'Not at all.'

Rosemary studied the array of boxes in front of her. Everything in them was dusty and cobwebby, but she could dismiss the couple of boxes that housed kitchen equipment. She pulled another toward her and started dismantling it. Robert did the same.

They worked in silence for a while, diligently handling each strange object as it came out. There were random bits of old cornice, broken crockery, rags, half-bricks and wooden pieces. None seemed to fit the bill for a hanging sign. Rosemary went to the next box and then a third. There, among a tangle of hinges and iron pokers, was a wrought iron L-shaped rod with a curl at its end. She turned it over and held it up. 'Robert.'

Robert stopped his rummaging and sat back on his heels. 'Yep, that's it.'

Rosemary peered back in the box and found two large coach bolts that slid easily into holes in the rod. 'Definitely.'

'You haven't said what the sign read.'

'I believe it was "Sunshine House".'

Robert frowned. 'Sunshine House?'

Rosemary lowered the metal frame. 'What is it?'

'You're sure it's Sunshine *House*?'

'I'm not sure, but it adds up.'

Robert stood up. 'Come and look at these documents.'

Rosemary put the sign holder down, dusted herself off, and followed Robert into the living area of the floor. It was difficult not to stare at the sophisticated setting, so starkly smart against the patina of the rest of the house. Robert noticed her staring and grinned. 'Good, isn't it?'

'You've made a proper home here. Tiny, but real.'

He shrugged as he collected a notebook from a slim-legged desk against the wall. 'The reality is I don't need this whole house. I'm happy taking up just this area.'

'You'll have to do something with downstairs or the spiders will take over again.'

He nodded as he walked to her. 'I know.'

'You have an idea?'

'I'm told that Mulbury often comes up with its own solution.'

'Who said that?'

'I can feel it in my bones.' He grinned and handed her the book. 'Look at this.'

'What is it?'

'The only record I can find that helps me with how this house was used over the years.' He opened it for her.

'It's a delivery register.'

'Yes. I've kept it going. See? I've entered that order of silicon and Jasper's fantasies in here.'

Rosemary traced the neat entries upwards, turning back through the pages until she arrived at a thick blue line separating the bushfire time from something else. 'Bed Linen, 20 lbs.'

'Yes, a big order, but can you see what name it's under?'

Rosemary flicked back a page to where the business name sat alone on the line. 'Not Sunshine House, then. That was just a cover.'

Robert nodded. 'Correct. The business name was Sunshine Deliveries.'

'How ironic.'

A noise on the stairs made them both turn. Jasper stood with one hand on the banister, looking at them with narrowed eyes. 'Whatever it is you're doing,' he said, 'you'd better come down and see Heather.'

Rosemary put the book down and hurried along the corridor. 'Is she okay?'

'She's fine. I think we've discovered the source of her ghosts.'

'Really?'

Jasper turned, and they went together down the stairs. 'Not ghosts at all. *Ravens*.'

TWENTY-NINE

Secretly, Ronnie thought that making Mrs Lionel's batch of banana smoothie fragranced soap was the best of all. There was something about it that reminded him of his mother, probably associated with holidaying in Queensland and eating as many bananas and papaya and custard apples as he could get his hands on. He held out a cake for Mrs Lionel to sniff. 'Isn't that amazing?'

Mrs Lionel leaned on the workbench in the laundry beside him and took in the fragrance. 'You are getting very good at making soap, dear.'

'I meant the smell of it. It's...'

'Like being on holidays?'

Ronnie didn't have time to reflect that maybe his favourite fragrance was not a tremendous secret. Someone pushed on the shop door and, when it didn't open, rapped sharply on the glass. 'I'll get it, Mrs Lionel,' Ronnie said. 'You look tired.'

'Thank you, dear. I am. I'm going to sit down for a moment.'

'Have a lie down on your bed. I'll manage things.'

'You are a dear, dear. I'll do that.' Mrs Lionel patted Ronnie's arm as she left the room.

Ronnie put the soap away and walked into The Green Mulbury, flicking the light on as he went so that the products on their shelves sparkled beneath their wrappings. It was difficult to see who it was at the door because darkness had fallen outside, but Ronnie expected a stranger. A Mulburian wouldn't have stood so awkwardly on the doorstep. He tackled the lock, making the frog croak excitedly, and got the door open. 'Can I help you?' he said to the woman outside.

'Sorry to disturb you,' she said. 'I've come to collect the boxes I left here from the Gala. I should have rung, I know, but I was passing through the town on my way home. Is that okay?'

'I don't know about any boxes, and Mrs Lionel is having a rest. Did she say where she'd left them?'

'No, just that they were at her shop.'

Ronnie stood back. 'Come in, anyhow. We'll have a look.'

The woman stepped inside. Under the light, Ronnie saw she had a tanned, outdoor face with fine laugh lines filtering out from her eyes. Her jeans were worn, and her jacket patched in brown stains. She must have seen him looking and tucked a large necklace down her jacket before zipping it up neatly. 'Sorry about the state I'm in. I've been at a lost trade show.'

'Right.' Ronnie closed the door and stepped away to shut the frog up. 'A lost trade...?'

'Oh, that's what they call them. Lost trades, as if they've been deliberately misplaced. What they mean are those old-fashioned wares people used to make as a matter of course.' She waved her hand around at Mrs Lionel's products.

'Homemade soaps, for example. Dried herbs. Pot-pourri. Hardly lost. There's always been someone keeping the old ways alive.'

'Okay. I didn't know they were lost, either.'

She laughed, an almost silent, tight-lipped sound. 'I'm Leila,' the woman said, extending her hand.

'Ronnie.'

'Well, Ronnie, can we have a look for my things now?'

'If you don't mind staying here, I could go into Mrs Lionel's cellar and have a look. What exactly did you leave here?'

'Boxes of leather offcuts.' Leila shrugged. 'I'm a saddler.'

'You make saddles?'

'Yes, although there are more requests to make handbags than saddles these days. Such a shame.'

'Wow,' said Ronnie. 'That must take quite some skill.'

'And what do you do for a living, Ronnie?'

'Oh.' Ronnie felt his face mottle and tried to quell it. 'I'm a private investigator.'

'That must take a lot of skill as well.' Leila waved her hand at Mrs Lionel's products. 'As does this. We are all skilled in some way.'

'I've never thought of it like that.' Ronnie ran a hand over his face. 'I sort of fell into my line of work.'

'Are you succeeding?'

'I'm getting new cases, if that's what you mean.'

'Then you must be doing something right. You have skills other people want.'

'Thanks.'

Leila tipped her head at him. 'Are you allowed to say what you're working on at the moment?'

'Not really.'

'Broadly speaking?'

Ronnie grimaced. 'Broadly speaking, I'm trying to find out why an old lady nearly died.'

Leila nodded. 'Someone tried to murder her?'

'We don't know. Something gave her such a fright she developed a problem with her heart. We don't know if it was deliberate or not.'

'How awful.' Leila turned her head slightly to gaze outside. 'What a shocking thing.'

'Yep.'

'Are you getting anywhere?'

'It's been tricky.'

'You'll need all your skills.'

'Plus, some from other people.'

'You employ other investigators?'

'No. I just have some clever family members.'

Leila smiled, a quiet, closed-lip, guarded smile. Ronnie frowned.

'So, Ronnie. Could you please look for my boxes now?' Leila glanced at a large watch on a firm, tan leather band. 'Sorry to seem pushy, but I've got to get going. I really need the one with the leather scraps in it.'

'Right, right, sorry.' Ronnie nodded vigorously. 'I'll go have a look.' He left Leila and went to Mrs Lionel's laundry, where the trapdoor to the cellar sat.

It took a little while to rummage through the boxes of ingredients and empty bottles and recycled containers, but Ronnie could definitely say there was no leather down there. He was halfway up the steep cellar steps when Mrs Lionel's head appeared over the entrance. 'I don't need any more products made just yet, Ronnie.'

'Oh no, I wasn't. I'm looking for boxes left by one of the Gala people. A saddler? She said they were here.'

'They were,' said Mrs Lionel, as Ronnie climbed the

rest of the way out. 'But Rosemary took them when she saw they were blocking my way.'

'You don't really get up and down these steps, do you?' said Ronnie, as he heaved himself out and closed the trapdoor.

'I have to. It's where I keep my spare ingredients.'

Ronnie shook his head and filed that information away for another day. 'Leila's in your shop.'

'Leila?'

'The saddler. Do you want me to tell her to go next door?'

'That would be good, dear. I'll text Rosemary to let her know.'

Ronnie nodded. 'After that, I'll get going, then. Honey is probably wanting to go home.'

'Thanks again, Ronnie.'

'Any time, Mrs Lionel.'

Mrs Lionel walked behind Ronnie as he went into the shop. Leila stood at the dried herbs, crushing a few leaves in her hands from the display of oregano. Ronnie heard Mrs Lionel stumble, and turned to see if she was alright, but she waved him to go, giving the saddler a long, hard look before turning back to the house.

'I'm sorry to take so long,' said Ronnie. 'I'm afraid it's not there. Mrs Lionel had it taken next door to my mother-in-law's. We can get it from there.'

'From the jam shop?'

'Rosemary would probably prefer it called the preserves shop.'

Leila smiled. 'Prickly, is she?'

Ronnie thought before he answered. 'No. She just likes to call things as they are.'

'Okay.' Leila smiled. 'Thanks for your help.'

'I'll come with you. We're on our way home.'

'You don't live here?'

'No, we live in Big Town.' Ronnie cast a look back into The Green Mulbury as he held the door for Leila. 'For now.'

The frog cut out mid-croak as the door closed behind them. The jangling bell on the door of The Preserved Mulbury was sweet in contrast. 'We're here,' called Ronnie as Leila went to stand in the middle of the shop.

'In here, Ronnie,' called Honey from the living quarters. 'Mum's getting the box from the cellar.'

'Do all the houses along here have cellars?' said Leila as Ronnie showed the way into the lounge room.

'These along Goldmarket Road do. Probably others. Wasn't it a way to store food back then? There's a rumour that the mayoral residence has one where the mayor kept gold nuggets.'

'Where's the mayoral residence?'

'On the road beside the Square. A huge house, covered in scaffolding for now. You can't miss it.'

'I think I saw it on the way in.' Leila stopped as Honey heaved herself from an armchair. 'Oh, don't get up.'

'Too late.' Honey grimaced and put a hand on her back. 'It's okay. I can't sit for long, anyway.' She held her other hand out to shake Leila's. 'I'm Honey.'

Leila smiled broadly. 'That you are. You look so wonderful. I'm Leila.'

'Thanks, Leila, but I don't feel wonderful. I feel enormous.'

'When are you due?'

'Technically, today. I just don't feel that babies care about being technical.'

'Mine never did, that's for sure.'

'You have kids?'

'Big kids now.'

A crash from the laundry made Ronnie jump.

'Are you okay, Mum?' called Honey.

There was a moment's silence. 'The bottom fell out of a box,' said Rosemary, her voice strangely muffled.

Ronnie went to help and found Rosemary on the floor with bits of leather on her lap. 'Are you alright, Rosemary?'

She held up a section of tan leather and Ronnie was astonished to see the glint of a tear in Rosemary's eye. She blinked, and it went away, making Ronnie wonder whether he'd imagined it. 'Picking up the pieces,' she said.

Ronnie hesitated, suddenly remembering that Honey's father had been a shoemaker. He watched Rosemary closely, but she'd gone back to gathering up the fallen bits and putting them in a washing basket. 'I'll help.'

Rosemary stood. 'You pick up the rest and I'll mend the box.'

By the time they returned to the lounge room, Honey was sitting down again, having her back rubbed by Leila, who looked up as Ronnie came close. 'I'm still a registered midwife,' she said. 'This always seems to help my ante-natal patients.'

Honey sighed heavily. 'It's great, thanks.' She waved her hand toward her mother. 'This is Mum. I mean, Rosemary.'

'Hello,' said Leila. 'Thank you for minding my things.'

'Not a problem,' said Rosemary, coming closer. 'Have we met before?'

Leila shook her head. 'Not formally. I had a stall at the Gala so I think we corresponded. Am I right? You were on the committee?'

'Yes.'

'It was a good day. Except for the old lady collapsing in

front of us.' Leila paused. 'Do you know whether she's okay?'

'She is,' said Ronnie. 'Well, it took a lot out of her, but I saw her recently and she was very bright.' He shrugged, thinking of Mrs King's composure from the throne of her sofa. 'Intimidating, actually.'

Leila did that closed-lipped smile again, and Ronnie blinked. For a moment, Leila could have been Mrs King, only much younger and fitter. Mrs King's smile had also been quiet and contained, and she'd kept her lips firmly closed as Leila did. *Perhaps lots of people laughed like that?*

'Are you alright, Ronnie?' asked Honey. 'You've gone pale.'

Ronnie put his hand on his cheek. 'Aren't I usually?'

'Well, yeah. But you're practically chalky.'

'Yeah, thanks, Honey.' He turned to take the box from Rosemary. 'I'll put this in your car if you like. There's another one down there.'

'Thanks. Do you mind if I pick up the second box another time? My car's pretty full.' Leila gave Honey's back a last circle and stood straight. 'I hope that feels better.'

'Yes, thank you.' Honey stretched. 'Not long to go, then I'll have my normal pain free back return. I hope.'

Ronnie led the way to Leila's car, letting Rosemary hold the door. He put the box down at the back of the boot to wait for Leila, but she was talking earnestly to Rosemary as they stood in the doorway. It seemed like something best not interrupted, so Ronnie waited, hearing snatches of conversation. '...just before she collapsed,' said Leila, and Rosemary answered with a low sentence Ronnie couldn't hear until '... thank you for that', and Leila was on the move again. Her face, which had been relaxed, was now frowning, and she opened the boot for Ronnie without a word. As she closed it, she glanced his way.

'Okay, then?' he said.

'Thanks.' She opened the door to the driver's side and slid in, but didn't close it. 'You're investigating a lady's near-death, you said.'

Ronnie nodded.

'Would it be that woman at the Gala?'

'What made you say that?'

'Oh. Nothing.' Leila pulled the door shut, holding her hand in farewell as she did, but Ronnie saw her look at The Preserved Mulbury before she drove away.

Ronnie stepped back onto the footpath, looking towards the shop as he did. Rosemary stood silhouetted in the doorway, arms folded across her chest. He would have liked to run a thought past her, but there was no time. Honey came out the door and they drove back to Big Town, Honey shifting uncomfortably in the seat the entire way. As they arrived home, and Ronnie helped her out of the car, he had the distinct feeling that things were ramping up in all aspects of his life.

THIRTY

Saturday dawned brightly. Rosemary threw back the curtains in her bedroom, and sunshine swamped the room, lighting up Sunny as she curled in a delicate curve on the bed. She put a paw over her eyes. *Really?* she seemed to say. *You had to do that?*

'Come on, Sunny,' said Rosemary, pulling on her day clothes. 'Let's enjoy the sunshine while it isn't too hot. It'll be summer before we know it.'

The early-morning light lit The Preserved Mulbury when Rosemary pulled the blinds up as she waited for the kettle to boil. Outside, the Square was empty, apart from Mrs Lionel sweeping the gravel under The Exceptional Tree. From the way her friend paused now and then and spoke to something near the ground, Percy was with her, as he probably would be every day of her life.

Percy's perceived presence made Rosemary think of Heather and her connection with the ravens of the mayoral residence. And then, as if conjured out of Rosemary's head, Heather walked past the window dressed in a mid-shin-length plaid skirt and a long-sleeved cardigan. Her hair hung around her shoulders in its usual beautiful wild abandon, but a broad ruby ribbon held it back from her face tied in a bow on top of her head. She skipped as she went.

Rosemary couldn't resist the temptation. She unlocked the door and called out. 'Morning, Heather. Where are you off to so early?'

Heather paused and twirled around to face Rosemary. 'I'm working, Rosemary Rosie Rose.'

'Right. Clearly not with animal feed.'

'I'm working at Patricia's.' Heather whirled again, her hair fanning out around her.

'Are you Patti's new assistant?'

Heather stopped and smiled. 'Of course. Who else?'

Rosemary smiled. 'Who else indeed? What did your sisters say?'

'Holly hugged me for a long time. Hannah told me what I already knew.'

'Which was?'

'I'm perfect for the job.'

'Ah. But aren't you too early?'

'Patti said to come for breakfast.' Heather shook her head. 'But I've had breakfast. I'll start early.'

'You might find Patti and Gerry are still in bed.'

Heather's eyes widened. 'Bed? But the sun's up.' She shrugged. 'So should they be.'

'Good luck with that.'

Heather smiled. 'Thank you, but I don't need any luck.' She spun once again and headed toward Patricia's.

'Heather,' said Rosemary after her. 'I agree with Hannah.'

Heather didn't look back but lifted a hand in acknowledgement. She arrived at Patti and Gerry's and rapped loudly on the door.

Rosemary left her to the task of getting Patti and Gerry up and went back to her kitchen. Sunny was on the windowsill, gazing to the balcony. Rosemary made tea and went to see what she was looking at. It was Jasper, leaning out over his backyard, a steaming mug in his hand. Rosemary hesitated, then opened the door. He turned at the noise and raised his mug.

'Hello, Jasper.'

'It's going to be a great day. Sunny, cloudless, warm. The weather bureau-'

'Jasper. Don't.'

'Don't what?'

'Talk about the weather when we never talk about the weather.'

'Country people talk about the weather all the time.'

'Yes, but *we* don't.'

Jasper looked at her steadily. 'We never used to.'

'Then let's not start.'

He left the back rail and came to stand against the one that divided his balcony from hers. 'We have to start somewhere.'

'We don't.'

'Rosemary...' He sipped his tea, looking sad. 'We do. I feel like we have to start again.'

Rosemary felt an ache start in her throat. 'Right.'

'You still don't get it, do you?'

'That's where you're wrong, Jasper.' Rosemary took a deep breath in and let it out slowly. 'I get that I've hurt you by not believing you have a curse. I'm really sorry about that.'

'You still don't believe in curses.'

'No, I don't.' She put a hand out to catch his arm. 'I never will. But I know you believe it and that should be enough for me. Can we agree to disagree?'

Jasper looked at her for so long, she felt swallowed by his gaze. His kind eyes seemed frosted, much more piercing that she'd ever known them. She dared not move, even when her arm ached from being held out in front of her. He opened his mouth to say something when a movement in his doorway distracted them both.

'Is Iris here?' asked Rosemary, trying to pull him back to a decision.

Jasper sighed and dropped his eyes, pulling his arm from her grip. 'Not Iris. Someone else you know.'

'Rosemary,' said a familiar voice. 'Come to say goodbye?'

Silkie stood just inside the step, dressed in a deep purple coat that buttoned to the neck. Her hair was pulled back neatly in a French braid, and the lightest of makeup blushed her cheeks. 'You're leaving?' Rosemary asked.

'I am.' Silkie shrugged a leather tote higher onto her shoulder. '*We're* leaving.'

'Sorry?' Rosemary went back to Jasper, resisting the urge to claw his arm again. 'You're leaving, as well?'

He wouldn't look at her. 'Yes.'

'Forever?'

His sigh was heavy and made his shoulders sag. 'I need time away to think.'

Rosemary dropped her voice. 'With her? You're leaving with *her*?'

Now he looked at her. 'What if I am?'

Rakisha's voice echoed in Rosemary's head. 'She's stealing you away?'

Jasper blinked. 'I wouldn't put it like that. I'm going to stay with Iris for a few weeks. There are things to work out.

'About your curse?'

'It's real, Rosemary. And I'm about to test it out. I'm on the brink of something good happening, and that's when my curse comes out in force.' He stared at her. 'Helena says she's found my father.'

They stood quietly for a moment.

'I said I would help you find him,' said Rosemary eventually.

'Yes, you did.' Jasper's shoulders softened. 'But I know now that this is something I need to do by myself.'

'It's scaring you.'

'Yes.' Jasper grimaced. 'But it excites me, too.'

Rosemary clutched the railing. 'Silkie is staying with Iris as well?'

He frowned. 'Why is that so important to you, Rosemary? Silkie is my friend.'

The ache in Rosemary hardened to a knot. 'Your friend.'

'Yes, like it or not.' Jasper stepped closer. 'Friend. You know? Just a friend.'

'She stayed with you overnight.'

'Friends do that sometimes.'

'Jasper,' said Silkie, shifting her bag again. 'It's time.'

'What about your shop? Do you want me to open it for you? I could work mine half-time, and yours at the other times.'

'No. Thanks. I'm closing the shop for now.'

'What about your online orders? I could do those. I set the system up in the first place.'

Something flickered over Jasper's face, some sort of softness that quickly reverted to neutrality. 'Thanks. That would be good. I'd appreciate that.'

'And Snowy?'

'I was going to take him with me.'

'I can look after him.'

'Jasper,' said Silkie impatiently. 'Come on.'

'Actually, Rosemary,' Jasper said, 'that would be great. He's too old to adapt to the city.'

'Yes, he is. He's a country dog.'

'He's a couch dog.'

Rosemary tried a smile. 'He can have my couch until you come back.'

He didn't answer. Rosemary felt her eyes prickle, and she swallowed. Then he leaned forward, brushed her cheek with his lips, and turned away.

Rosemary didn't stay to watch him lock the glass door, nor did she strain to listen for the sound of his car as he loaded the boot before driving away. She played loud rock music to cover any noise and fiddled with an old blanket to cover the couch. When she'd given him, and Silkie, enough time to have gone, she used her key to unlock The Read Mulbury and entered without looking left and right. With Jasper's laptop under her arm, she coaxed the old dog from his couch and walked him out onto the pavement, securely locking the bookshop behind her, not daring to think how long it may be before it opened again.

Mrs Lionel stood on the pavement outside The Preserved Mulbury, tugging her cardigan tighter. 'Goodness,' she said, looking at Snowy. 'What on earth... oh.' She shifted her gaze to Rosemary. 'I see.'

'Jasper's gone away,' said Rosemary, as lightly as she could manage.

Mrs Lionel hurried forward and gave Rosemary a hug. 'It'll be okay. You'll see.'

But Rosemary could hardly see anything for the

annoying mist in her eyes. She was glad when the door to Patricia's squealed open and a rack of clothes appeared, Heather pushing it from behind. 'Hello, Mrs Lionel,' the young woman said.

'Hard at work, Heather?'

'Not hard. Easy.' Heather lowered the end of the rack down the step and pushed it to the edge of the veranda just as Gerry appeared with another.

'You've got a good worker there, Gerry.'

The little man grinned as he steered his rack to run alongside the other. 'Yes, indeed. We've left Patti to sew her ingenious creations while we do all the setting up.' He nodded at Rosemary. 'Your good idea. Thank you.'

Rosemary blinked her eyes clear. 'I didn't think that you'd thank me after your early-morning start.'

'Well, that was different, for sure.' Gerry chuckled. 'But it's got us going early, which is lucky. Look.'

The first visitor of the day had pulled up in Goldmarket Road, even though most shops didn't open for ages. It was a big car, catching the sun with an expensive glint to its paint-work. The driver got out and hurried around to the other side to assist the passenger. 'Oh, goodness,' said Mrs Lionel. 'It's Mrs Caroline King.'

Mrs King leaned heavily on a walking stick but stepped up the gutter to the relative safely of the pavement outside The Preserved Mulbury. Janet stood close to her side, but Mrs King caught sight of the group watching and shooed her away. She took a wobbly step forward and stopped, looking down to where Heather crouched, stroking Snowy's ears. 'A splendid old dog you've got there,' she said.

Snowy wagged his tail, taking a few wobbly steps of his own to approach the older woman. She crouched slightly in order to rub his grey-flecked head. 'He's Snowy,' said Heather.

'Aren't we all?' Mrs King chuckled briefly.

'How are you, Mrs King?' asked Mrs Lionel.

Mrs King straightened slightly. 'You know who I am.'

'Oh, yes,' said Gerry, leaving his rack where it was. 'You are quite famous. Particularly in Mulbury.'

'Hmph,' said Mrs King, both hands now resting on top of her cane. 'Infamous, I suspect, after what occurred at your recent Gala.' She gave a curt nod to Mrs Lionel. 'Thank you for asking. I am quite well.'

Rosemary took in the thin woman with her carefully rouged cheeks and begged to differ, but she felt Mrs Lionel's arm on hers.

'It is good to see you...' Mrs Lionel waved her hand.

'Upright, you mean? Alive, even?' Mrs King grunted again. 'Yes, I am glad to say that I am both upright and alive, because for a time, I didn't think I would be.'

'Neither did I,' murmured Janet.

Mrs King tapped her cane on the ground. 'Perhaps I wouldn't be, Janet, without you looking after me so well.'

Janet Spinney's face warmed. 'Well, it's my job to do that.'

'You do more than your job. You are a good friend as well.' Mrs King spoke firmly, as if to quell any doubt, and Rosemary couldn't help but feel chastened. 'You are also the one to suggest this little trip back to this town...'

'Mulbury,' said Janet.

'Mulbury,' said Mrs King. 'It's a trick of an ageing brain to think that I would ever forget this place.'

'You know it well?' Mrs Lionel glanced at Rosemary. 'Forgive my surprise, but I haven't seen you here except for the day of the Gala.'

'There would be a reason for that.' Mrs King tapped her cane again. 'I haven't been back here for many decades.'

'But you're back today.' Rosemary tipped her head. 'Why would that be?'

Mrs King studied her and must have found something agreeable, for she nodded. 'It's time to face my past.'

THIRTY-ONE

Just how Mrs King was about to face her past was answered in part by the movement of another car into Goldmarket Road. It parked behind the first, and two older women got out. The first said something to the second, jabbing her finger excitedly at Franco's patisserie in the Square. The second woman nodded, turning away from her companion as she hurried across the road towards the pastry delicacies, and clamped her eyes on the group still on the footpath. 'Miss O'Shannessy,' said Rosemary.

Miss O'Shannessy acknowledged her name with a bob of her head. She stepped up onto the pavement under the veranda and approached slowly. 'Hello,' she said to one person in particular. 'Hello, Caro.'

Mrs King pushed down on the handle of her cane to stand straighter. 'No one has called me that for a very long time.' She studied Miss O'Shannessy, her face tight. 'Lizzie.'

Miss O'Shannessy smiled faintly. 'And no one calls me that anymore.'

'Caro and Lizzie.' Mrs King lifted a hand to smooth

away a strand of steel grey hair from her face. 'Names from a different life.' She let her hand drop back. 'I haven't seen you for an age, Lizzie O'Shannessy.'

The two women stared at each other for a long time. Gerry twisted his fingers together and Rosemary put a reassuring hand on his arm. Snowy lay down with a heavy sigh, and Mrs Lionel stooped to pat him. Still, the women stared. Finally, Miss O'Shannessy took a few steps forward and wrapped her arms around Mrs King. Janet started but stopped as Mrs King put a hand carefully around Miss O'Shannessy's back. 'There, Lizzie. There, there. Here we are, together again.'

'I didn't think you would return,' said Miss O'Shannessy, pulling back. 'I haven't, not since I saw that you'd been here. And you'd nearly died.'

'That's an exaggeration, Lizzie.' Mrs King shifted her feet so they settled more firmly on the ground. 'It'll take more than that to get me to kick the bucket.'

Miss O'Shannessy frowned. 'More than what, Caro?'

Mrs King dropped her head and fiddled with the buttons on her cardigan. 'More than what happened that day.'

Rosemary was suddenly aware of how the small crowd had fanned around the old friends, as if they were watching a play. She crouched down to Snowy and put a hand under his chin. 'Time to go inside, old man.'

Snowy heaved himself up on wobbly legs, wagging his tail happily as he achieved standing. Heather hooked her hand under his collar.

Another car came around the corner, a blue and black bee emblazoned on its side. 'Here's Honey and Ronnie,' said Gerry. 'Right on time.'

Rosemary turned to him. 'You were expecting them?'

He had the grace to go bright red. 'Yes. Patti said she was going to return the favour you did for us, Rosemary. But maybe you don't know…?'

'Know what?'

'Is that the young woman who's expecting soon?' said Miss O'Shannessy, her hand at her throat. 'Her name escapes me: Syrup?'

'Honey,' said Rosemary. 'My daughter.'

Miss O'Shannessy put her hand on Mrs King's. 'A daughter.'

'Caro,' said Mrs King. 'You didn't have any other children?'

'No.' Miss O'Shannessy's voice was barely audible. 'Unlike you.'

'I have three independent children who ring regularly but hardly ever visit.' Mrs King smiled grimly. 'I often wonder whether she would have been like them.'

'She?' said Mrs Lionel kindly. 'You had another daughter?'

When Mrs King hesitated, Rosemary stepped forward to help Honey up the gutter. 'Talking of daughters.'

'Were you talking about me?' Honey groaned and rubbed her back. 'Or Tallulah?'

'Honey, shouldn't you be at home?' said Mrs Lionel. 'You are overdue.'

'Only by one day.' Honey stared at the old dog wagging his tail at her. 'Is that Snowy? I've never seen him off the couch.'

'He's staying with me for a few days.' Rosemary bent to stroke the dog's head so she wouldn't have to look at Honey. 'Jasper is away.'

'Sunny's not going to like that,' said Ronnie, arriving at his wife's side.

'Oh.' Honey groaned, putting her hand heavily on Ronnie's shoulder. 'I'm so sorry to be whinging, but my back is killing me. Is that lovely woman who rubbed it yesterday around?'

Rosemary shook her head. 'No.'

'She was great, a real professional.' Honey shifted awkwardly. 'I don't suppose you saw her necklace?'

'No. Should I have?'

Honey moved toward The Read Mulbury's door and leaned against it with a sigh. 'Only that it was unusual. Costume jewellery, probably, but gorgeous. Really heavy chain. A simple design, looked like a leaf but she said it was a four-leafed clover.'

Rosemary saw the two older friends stiffen. 'Pardon?' said Miss O'Shannessy. 'Are you sure it was a four-leafed clover?'

'Oh, yes.' Honey traced an imaginary pendant on her chest. 'Leila said it was a family heirloom from her grandmother. She wears it all the time. It's sad, because she said she doesn't know who her grandmother is.'

Miss O'Shannessy looked at Mrs King. 'Do you think...?'

Mrs King nodded curtly. 'I do.'

Rosemary waited, but neither woman elaborated. 'Your business logo is a four-leafed clover, isn't it, Mrs King?'

'Yes.' Mrs King looked at Rosemary steadily. 'My maiden name was Clover. When my husband died, I made the cattle my own business.'

'And you once had a four-leafed clover necklace, one with a heavy chain. It's in the photograph Miss O'Shannessy keeps in her bag. You left the necklace with your newborn daughter.'

Mrs King's eyes shone, but she blinked the moisture away. 'I did.'

Honey shook her head. 'Are we talking about Leila's necklace?'

Mrs King said nothing.

Rosemary put a hand out to her daughter as she went to step forward. 'Leila, the leather artisan, is your granddaughter, Mrs King?'

Mrs King held Rosemary's gaze with a steely look. 'I believe so.'

'Oh,' said Ronnie. 'I get it now. Do you mean you've never seen her before?'

'I've seen her once before.'

'At the Gala?' asked Rosemary.

'At the Gala,' said Mrs King.

Ronnie clapped his hand over his mouth, then let it drop. 'That was the sudden shock, wasn't it? You recognised her. But how?'

Mrs King shuffled uncomfortably. 'She looks uncannily like my other granddaughters, who look immensely like their own mother.' She shrugged. 'It goes to reason the first time I return to Mulbury I am met with my past.'

Rosemary nodded. 'They took away your daughter from you as well at Sunshine House.'

'You knew?'

'I'm piecing bits together.'

'Well, that's the crux of the story.' Mrs King turned to Miss O'Shannessy and gave a rare, warm smile. 'What you haven't heard is how we fought it. We tore down the sign and ran away.' The smile faded. 'They brought us back. We were young and powerless.' She rapped her cane on the pavement. 'I've let no one take over my life like that again.'

'You were the strong one, Caro,' said Miss O'Shannessy. 'I wasn't. I'm still not.'

'Nonsense,' said Mrs King, taking her friend's arm. 'You survived, Lizzie. We survived. You are much stronger than you think.'

'Do you think we have a chance to find them?'

Mrs King nodded. 'We'll find them both. We'll start with the one I found, wherever she is now.' She shuffled again and gave Janet a quick look as her carer leapt forward. 'You said returning to Mulbury might help.'

Janet took Mrs King's arm. 'I hope it does.'

'Leila will be back,' said Ronnie. 'She needs to pick up another box of her things left from the Gala.'

Mrs King nodded slowly. 'We'll wait for her to return. In the meantime, we should face our demons. Where is that wretched Sunshine House?'

'We believe it's the old mayoral residence,' said Rosemary.

'Would you like me to take you there?' asked Ronnie.

'I'll take you,' said Heather. 'I'll take you to Ravenshome.'

Mrs King raised an eyebrow at Heather. 'Ravenshome?'

'Heather seems to have renamed Robert Sparkling's house,' said Mrs Lionel.

Mrs King glared at Heather. 'And what has this to do with you, young lady?'

Heather smiled and brushed her curls back over her shoulder. 'The ravens told me everything. They have familial memories.'

'What does that mean, dear?' asked Mrs Lionel.

Heather shrugged. 'They pass memories on. They told me about the babies.'

Miss O'Shannessy shook her head, but Mrs King frowned. 'Ravens?' She turned to her friend. 'You remember the ravens?'

Miss O'Shannessy nodded. 'Oh, yes. They were watching when we stole the sign and ran.'

'The sign that read Sunshine House,' said Rosemary. 'The one you still have, Mrs King.'

Mrs King thumped her cane on the pavement. 'Why is it that people in this town know our deepest secrets? I have kept this from every journalist in the country!'

'But then you hired Ronnie,' said Rosemary. 'He investigated your case, as you wanted him to.'

Ronnie shrugged. 'I got some help with bits of it.' He indicated the small crowd.

'I see,' said Mrs King. She glanced at Miss O'Shannessy. 'I find myself at a crossroad, however, bravery comes from facing your fears.'

Rosemary immediately thought of Jasper heading out to find his father.

Mrs King straightened. 'It is probably for the best the whole ugly incident comes out now. Before it's too late.'

'Yes,' said Miss O'Shannessy. 'Before we have no chance of finding our daughters.'

'Or grandchildren.'

'Or great-grandchildren,' said Ronnie. 'Or great-great-grandchildren.' Mrs King gave him a sharp look and his face mottled.

'Come on, then.' Mrs King started forward. 'Where is this horrid place?'

'Not so horrid now,' said Heather, offering Mrs King her arm. 'It's sparkled.'

Mrs King looped her thin arm through and Heather steered her around. 'What on earth does that mean? You are a strange child. First ravens, then sparkles...'

'Shall we?' Ronnie said to Miss O'Shannessy and Janet. 'It's a short walk.'

'I'm remembering,' said Miss O'Shannessy. 'The night we ran, we went under this veranda and down the road...'

Her voice disappeared as the older women and their entourage continued down the pavement towards the infamous Sunshine House, leaving Mrs Lionel shaking her head at the historical mess of it all, and Honey looking crestfallen. 'Do you think Miss O'Shannessy will find her lost daughter, Mum?'

'She might.' Rosemary leaned down to Snowy again and encouraged him to walk. 'A long time has passed, though. She may not find her in the flesh, but at least she may discover her life.'

'That's gre- oooooo...'

Gerry started forward. 'What is it, Honey? You look in pain.'

'I am...'

'Goodness. Mrs Lionel? Rosemary?'

Mrs Lionel was already at Honey's side. 'Braxton Hicks, Honey?'

Honey breathed out, shaking her head. 'I don't think so, Mrs Lionel. This feels different.'

Mrs Lionel turned to Rosemary. 'It's started.'

Rosemary nodded and indicated her shop. 'Inside, then. I'll call Ronnie.'

'Oh, heavens.' Gerry jiggled on the spot, wringing his hands.

Rosemary frowned. 'Get Ronnie, Gerry. It'll be quicker than me calling.'

'Righto.' He scuttled off.

Rosemary looked over Honey's bent shoulders to eyeball Mrs Lionel. 'It's been a while since either of us have done this.'

Mrs Lionel smiled. 'It has indeed.'

Honey stopped, bent over further, and groaned. 'Neither of you told me it would be like this.'

'Would it have made any difference?'

'No. Noooooooooooooo.'

Rosemary gathered her daughter in one arm and kept hold of the old dog in the other. 'Come on, then. Inside.'

They crept slowly down the pavement, stopping every few steps for Honey to breathe deeply. Mrs Lionel's frown deepened as they went. They reached the door of The Preserved Mulbury and stopped for an increased length of time. 'Honey,' said the older woman, 'just how long have you been feeling contractions today?'

Honey let her breath out. 'Contractions? I don't know, but I was pretty uncomfortable all morning, and it got worse as soon as I got in the car today. I thought it was just my back, but maybe...' She shook her head. 'I don't know. This feels like the real thing.'

Rosemary guided her daughter up the step and into the shop. 'I suspect you were experiencing the real thing for quite a few hours. Honey, you might be further on than you think.'

'What do you mean, Mum?'

Mrs Lionel closed the door behind them. 'It means that maybe we call the ambulance rather than have Ronnie drive you to the Big Town hospital.'

'Really?' Honey stopped again, leant heavily against her mother and groaned. 'Oh, no.' She leaned down, feeling her leg. 'Sorry, Mum. I'm wet. It's really happening now.'

Mrs Lionel studied the amount of liquid on the floor. 'Yes, Honey, your waters have broken.'

Honey panted for a moment, then grinned. 'Action stations?'

Rosemary whipped her phone out and called the emergency number as Mrs Lionel said, 'Let's get ready for Tallulah.'

THIRTY-TWO

Unsurprisingly, the ambulance from Big Town was going to be at least thirty minutes, so it was an interesting development when a lights and sirens police car pulled up in Gold-market Road a few minutes after the call. Rosemary heard it, but kept her attention on Honey, who was pacing the lounge room. Sunny watched the action from her windowsill, her tail swishing. *Getting noisy in here,* she seemed to say. 'Going to get noisier,' said Rosemary.

'What's that, dear?' said Mrs Lionel, busy sorting towels in the lounge room. She didn't pause for an answer. 'What's Geoffrey up to?'

Rosemary glanced out through her shop. 'Not sure it is Geoffrey. It looks more like Holly's friend.'

'Holly has a friend?' asked Honey, before clutching the top of the couch and breathing deeply. 'I mean, what kind of friendddddddooooooooo.'

'Breathe through it, dear. You're doing well.'

'The sort of friend that may end up more than a friend,' said Rosemary.

Honey smiled through the bits of hair that had pulled from her ponytail. 'That's great.'

The door of The Preserved Mulbury crashed open, making the bell jingle almost as loudly as the police siren, and Ronnie burst in, looking scared. 'Honey? Why are the police here?'

'I'm here,' said Honey crossly, 'and I have no idea.'

'Right, right.' Ronnie rounded on Honey and tried to hug her, but she swatted him away. 'Sorry, sorry.'

'No, I'm sorry.' Honey walked on again, her hands on her back. 'I should have known what was happening. I don't mean to push you away, Ronnie.'

'That's fine, Honey. Tell me what to do.'

Honey parked herself at the couch again. 'Rub my back. Hard.'

The door jangled again, and Mrs Lionel nodded to Rosemary.

'I'll shut shop after this one,' said Rosemary, leaving the lounge labour ward.

The door was just closing, and a woman stood by it, looking hesitant. 'I'm sorry,' she said. 'I've probably come at the wrong time.'

Rosemary studied the woman. She wore a long-sleeved flannel shirt and had her hair tied back in a tidy bun. She looked every inch like her grandmother. 'No, Leila, you're just in time.'

Leila tipped her head toward the noisy house quarters. 'Labour started?'

'Well on its way. Ambulance is coming.'

'But it'll take a while. Always does when it comes out to country towns.' Leila looked at Rosemary. 'Need a hand?'

'All hands are welcome.' Rosemary put her arm out to

show the door to the lounge area. 'You already know my daughter, Honey.'

Leila nodded and made her way forward, Rosemary following. She got to the door and remembered that she was going to shut the shop and turned back. Too late. Spilling in the doorway were Mrs King, Janet and Miss O'Shannessy. Following them was Holly and the young constable, Toffee. Heather, Gerry and Robert tagged behind.

'Excuse us,' said Miss O'Shannessy, 'but we thought we saw a woman...?'

'Yes.' Rosemary held her hand up to stop the crowd. 'But Honey has gone into labour.'

'I see,' said Mrs King. 'I suspect it's too late for your daughter to be driven to the hospital?'

'The ambulance is on its way. I do not know why the police are here.' Rosemary moved so that she could see Toffee.

The young man fiddled with the buttons on his uniform shirt. 'I was out and about and heard the ambulance call. I thought I could help.'

'You can deliver babies?'

Toffee blushed. 'Not specifically...'

Rosemary watched Holly, who slid her hand into Toffee's. There may be a baby on the way, but the reason Toffee made any excuse to come to Mulbury was right next to him. 'Thanks,' said Rosemary. 'It seems under control so far. But you may be of use for another reason. Do you have access to any databases?'

'Databases? Only a few from the car. If I need to know any more, I can call in or wait until I get back to the station.'

'There's no particular hurry, but I wonder if you can find records for a Sunshine House in Mulbury? It was where young women went to give birth decades ago.'

'Sunshine House? I can try. Do we know where it was?'

'It was my place,' said Robert. 'Another incarnation of the mayoral residence.' He shrugged. 'I might eventually find they used it for more than several unsavoury old practices, like taking babies from young mothers.'

Rosemary studied his sad face. 'It's not your fault.'

'Not directly.'

A yell from the lounge room caught Rosemary's attention, and she left Robert with an apologetic touch of her hand on his arm. Back at the couch, Snowy was upside down sleeping contentedly while Honey stood with her elbows on the couch's back, groaning heartily.

'New phase,' said Mrs Lionel. 'We might take over your bed, Rosemary.'

'Where's that ambulance?' asked Ronnie, peering past Rosemary as if the paramedics were hiding behind her.

'It'll get here when it gets here,' said Leila, rolling up her sleeves. 'Now, this is where you get to be very important, Ronnie.' She looked up as Mrs King and Miss O'Shannessy came into the room. 'More spectators?'

Mrs King stared at Leila and Leila smiled. But Mrs Lionel led Honey to Rosemary's bedroom, and Leila shook her head slightly and followed. Mrs King switched her look to Rosemary, a hint of sadness in her eyes. 'Later?'

'Yes, unfortunately.' Rosemary indicated the kitchen. 'Help yourself to tea and nutmeg biscuits, everyone. Heather knows where everything is.'

'You've got Jasper's dog,' said Robert, coming into the room. 'Sorry. I know you've got other things going on. I'm just curious.'

'Jasper will be back,' Rosemary said, though Robert had not mentioned it. She felt certainty rise. 'He would never leave Snowy for long.'

Robert seemed to get it. 'No,' he smiled. 'That he would never do.'

Rosemary nodded and went to Honey.

'Mum,' Honey said when she appeared in the doorway. 'Don't leave me.'

Rosemary hurried to Honey's side. 'Never, Honey. I'm here.'

Honey grasped her mother's hand and groaned, her face flushed and sweaty.

The next twenty minutes were condensed to a flash of time. Rosemary remembered bits clearly, especially the moment when Tallulah emerged slippery and dark-haired, but others were a fog of action and noise. The ambulance arrived just after Tallulah and the officers gave the mother and baby ticks of good health. Leila joined them to help their note taking before they prepared the stretcher, leaving Honey, Ronnie, Rosemary and Mrs Lionel in the room staring in wonder at the new arrival.

The baby nestled quietly into Honey's arms.

'Patricia,' said Ronnie.

'You aren't calling the baby Tallulah anymore?' said Rosemary.

'What? Oh, no, I mean, yes. She's baby Tallulah.'

'Who's Patricia then?'

'He's not talking about the baby, Mum,' said Honey, running a finger softly over Tallulah's cheek. 'He's talking about Patricia's. Or, as it's going to be known, *Honey B's Teas*.'

'I'm not sure I understand, dear,' said Mrs Lionel.

Honey grinned, the last few draining hours falling from her face. 'That's why we were here today to talk to Gerry and Patti. We're shifting to Mulbury to lease Patricia's.'

'You're taking over the dress shop, dear?' asked Mrs Lionel.

'No.' Honey held Tallulah closer. 'Patti and Gerry are moving the shop and their home to Ravenshome. Robert is leasing them the downstairs rooms. He said it was too big for one person to live.' Honey sighed. 'We're going to have our own tea rooms here, in Mulbury. Tea and cake, anyone?' She laughed, making Tallulah open her eyes briefly. 'Can't you smell the sugar icing on my cupcakes, Mum? It's sweet, like a baby's breath.'

Rosemary lifted a sweat-drenched strand of hair from her daughter's face. 'I'll be your very first customer, Honey Blossom.'

ACKNOWLEDGMENTS

A Tricky Treat was inspired by the heroic older women I've encountered during my lifetime, especially those who've done it alone.

Thanks also to my editorial team and ARC readers who help me see what I should be seeing but just can't.

All remaining errors are entirely my own.

ALSO BY JUNO HARVEY

Mulbury Mysteries

#1: A Sticky Situation

Mulbury is a quiet place where visitors wander happily around Goldmarket Square. When the body of an old man is found under The Exceptional Tree, everyone assumes that he died peacefully. Everyone, that is, except Rosemary Exeter.

A small-town mystery with quirky residents and an unimpressed cat.

#2: A Pretty Pickle

Winter in Mulbury, and frost hardens the ground. The tourists still flock to the little town, going about their happy business with no hint of what's been discovered in Jasper Lu's backyard. Who do these bones belong to? Rosemary Exeter is determined to find out.

Novella: One Christmas Pickle

Christmas time in Mulbury, Australia. Plum puddings, roast turkey and blistering hot days. Who overcooked the fire brigade's fund-raising Santa? With the team of fire-fighting volunteers stuck in Mulbury until their truck is fixed, and almost certainly one of them a murderer, Rosemary hides the one clue she has while searching for others.

A Mulbury Mystery novella with punch... and brandy sauce.

Other books by Juno Harvey

Because I Know it's True

Since the car accident that altered her family's lives, Grace Worthington has always been a loner. Now, with her father's death, she is truly alone. When she reads about Alexander Cameron's search for his missing sister, she sees an answer for both their problems. She has no family: he has no sister. Grace follows Alexander back to Scotland, and becomes involved in the biggest act of her life.

ABOUT THE AUTHOR

Juno Harvey lives in Victoria, Australia, with her family. She makes jam on the weekends and works in a university during the week.

Want to join Juno's Reader's Team?
Go to www.junoharvey.com and receive a free story!

https://www.junoharvey.com/

Books of light...and shade.